TELLING TIME

TELLING TIME

A NOVEL BY

Austin Wright

BASKERVILLE
PUBLISHERS, INC.

FALLING IN LOVE AGAIN (CAN'T HELP IT)
by Frederick Hollander & Sammy Lerner
© Copyright 1930 by Ufa Verlag (Renewed 1957)
© Copyright 1930 by Famous Music (Renewed 1957)
© U.S. Copyright 1991 Samuel M. Lerner Publications
International Copyright Secured All Rights Reserved
Used by Permission

Baskerville Publishers, Inc.
7616 LBJ Freeway, Suite 220, Dallas, TX 75251-1008

Library of Congress Cataloging-in-Publication Data

Wright, Austin McGiffert, 1922-
    Telling time : a novel / by Austin Wright
       p. cm.
    ISBN 1-880909-36-7
    I. Title.
    PS3573.R49T45   1995
    813'.54--dc20   95-32562
                           CIP

Manufactured in the United States of America
First Printing, 1995

For *Madeline* AND *Elizabeth*

PART ONE

THURSDAY

LUCY WESTERLY: To George Westerly

George? What is this thing, an answering machine? I hear your voice, don't you hear me? Should I pretend you do? I can't talk to someone who isn't there.

If I try, how much time do I have? You want me to think up a message before the machine cuts me off, a message? I have no message; what I have is news, George. It's bad news, but you'll cut me off before I can tell you.

What good is an answering machine that doesn't answer? It's a wonderful invention, so modern and efficient, I'm proud of you, but I can't speak to it. Call your brothers or sisters, they'll tell you my news. Or me. You could call me. Yes, it's so long since I've heard from you. I don't even know where you are, except you have an answering machine, and that was your sweet deaf voice not answering.

What do I say now? Stop? Roger? Over and out? Thank you and good night? Do you *read* me?

RUPERT NEWTON: *Item in the* Island News

A teller at the Island National Bank today took his own family hostage in his home, confined with a gun. Sam J. Truro, 28, well known to customers of the bank, where he has been employed for five years, retreated into his house at 25 Shoal Point Drive, and announced he was holding his wife, Georgette, 26, and children, Dinah, 7, and Roger, 5, prisoners. The nature of his demands was not known.

Thomas Westerly, 72, of Peach Street, was shot when he tried to intervene. According to witnesses, Westerly approached the house calling upon Truro to give himself up. He was shot on the front walk after ignoring several warnings from Truro, who was standing in the upper window with a rifle. Westerly was taken to Island Center Hospital, where he was described last night as resting comfortably. The nature of his injury was not disclosed.

Police have ringed the Truro house in a standoff. The siege began this morning when Truro called Edward Nelson, the Town Clerk, to state that he was holding his family hostage and would kill them if any attempt were made to rescue them. Asked if he intended to negotiate with Truro, Sheriff Jack Haines said, "We're waiting for him to make demands. Then we'll see." He called it "a ticklish situation."

Westerly, the man who was wounded, is former President of River City University, Ohio, and a controversial figure in the academic world. He moved to this Island in 1988.

Neighbors called Truro a quiet man, a loner, a good neighbor. His fellow employees at the bank said he was moody and variable. Several customers at the bank described him as helpful and friendly. Others did not remember him.

ANN REALM: *To George*

Mother asked me to find you since she can't talk to your answering machine. I got your machine too but since you don't return calls, here goes.

She wants you to know Dad's dying. He's been dying for six months but this is different. Now it's a stroke. He was in remission and seemed fine but he's back in the hospital. How bad I don't know, but when she asked the doctor if she should summon her children he said decide for yourselves. Everybody has visited him this last six months, Philip, Henry, Patty, everybody but you. I've been going every other weekend. Consider yourself informed.

I'll go back again tomorrow, one last quick visit. It has to be quick because Frank and I are moving to London next Tuesday. Career move for Frank, career move for me. You'd know this if you had talked to anyone these last months. Up we go in the world, write for details.

Mother thinks you're in the Canadian wilderness writing another of your so-called lovely nature articles, but I doubt it.

PHILIP WESTERLY: *To his wife Beatrice*

Left on the kitchen table, Ithaca.

Going to the Island again, tomorrow before you get back. Dad's had a stroke.

I tried to call you at the Holiday Inn. Student party tonight. If Dad dies, you should come to the Island too. Hope you enjoyed your trip.

I'll give the kids to Mrs. Hook.

PATRICIA KEY: *Fax to Philip*

Please tell me what happened to Dad. Mother called when I was out and told William he had a stroke. When I came back Mrs. Grummond called on Mother's behalf and told me someone shot him while he was taking a walk. A crazy man with a rifle out a window.

3

So which is it? Dad's in the hospital from a stroke or because he got shot? I presume he still has cancer either way. No answer from Mother when I called again. Can't stand the mixup, so I'm faxing you. If you should happen to know.

LUCY WESTERLY: What to tell her children

This morning he was his usual self though uncomfortable, reading the paper, eating his cereal. At lunch quieter than usual, thinking about his writing, I supposed, which makes him uncommunicative. After lunch he went for his walk. I was out front with the watering can, and he went by without speaking. That's unusual. He was like not knowing whether to go or trying to remember an errand. I watched him up the street in a shuffly way, making me think how old we're getting, thinking it for both of us, not just him. But something wasn't right.

When the policeman came, I was still on my knees with the spade by the garden bed, looking at the garden earth. I saw the policeman's feet first, then Thomas behind with a shabby lost look like a bum. Here you are, the policeman said. This where you live?

The kind policeman, who said to me, Your husband, ma'am, he seems a little disoriented.

Well, I never saw him look like that. His eyes empty like a bolt of grief. He bumped the door jamb going into the house, where I followed and found him on the bed. I thought I mustn't let him go to sleep or he'll die, so I talked to him, asking him, trying to make him speak while he stared at the ceiling with his mouth open. When I saw his eyes again I called 911.

What else is there? They took him on a stretcher. Neighbors peeking out their windows to see what's being shoveled into the ambulance from the Westerly house. I went with him. In the hospital room, he showed more life. No talk—he hasn't spoken since it happened—but he knew where he was and knew me. He looked scared.

I called Philip and Ann and tried to call George. I called Patty but got William. Mrs. Grummond called Henry for me and Patty again to make sure she got the message.

PHILIP WESTERLY: *Anticipating a memoir*

Entered on his computer in Ithaca, in a file c:\personal \memblue.515, from which a paper copy will be made in a day or so.

This episode began with the apologetic voice of my mother on the telephone. It was 7:30. I was alone in the house after a pizza and was in the bedroom taking off my clothes for a shower before the party. Her voice with soft anxiety: Philip? Thomas. Hospital. Stroke. I leap for the conclusion but she holds back having a narrative to tell. Her dramatizing impulse, negating the badness in the pleasure she gets from deferring the end. Telling the story in her good time while I sat on the bed with my pants off. Should I come, I said, ashamed not to know if this was a reasonable question.

Then what to do with quick calculations about the pages of appointments with patients filling up tomorrow, Saturday, next week, the awkwardness of canceling or changing, the discomfort of a distinct guilt about something, the calculations which Myra would have to handle with a bunch of phone calls, not "the flu" this time nor yet a "death in the family," but "a family emergency," with Dr. Friedman standing by expecting the same for him sometime.

Also had to decide between the morbidity of not going to the party and the callousness of going, unless the callousness could be called emotional strength, telling myself the young people would be disappointed. I went to the party then with doubled guilt doubly excused: without my wife because of her trip and without my father because the students would be disappointed. They drank wine out of transparent plastic cups, and the music played and they danced while I talked to a small group about glaucoma and cataracts and specializing in ophthalmology.

If I put this in the speckled notebook instead of the blue I can be a little freer telling about listening to the loud music and watching a future psychiatrist named Linda Wesson dance, watching without Beatrice yet without realizing what I was watching because of the flight of my father through the music while this was happening, the voices, the wine, the small room full of people, and the darker room beyond where people danced in a purple light. The sudden pain of my father's flight. Be more accurate. Six months ago it was sudden and this is the fruition. Yet six months ago it was not sudden either, my father at seventy-two having lived his biblical span, short though that may seem now after all the years when he seemed immortal in his good health and it looked as if what I had thought inevitable was in truth impossible, before the event put everything back in place and I could once again anticipate the great loss with everything unstringing and the world falling apart.

Meanwhile, excuse this party in honor of Steve because the medical students wanted and Steve was counting on it. Otherwise it's mope all evening thinking about time's losses, though I suppose I could have written a poem if I could get the right slant. When I got home the fax machine had Patty with a crazy rumor. Not a stroke but a rifle shot. Which to believe? What a distraction. Hope it's not the rifle shot, which would be an irrational intrusion on the natural development of events.

Meet my patients in the morning, then fly to Boston in time to catch the late ferry. Myra'll reschedule the week.

6

ANN REALM: *Diary*

Thursday, May 19, Boston. DAY. Pack, office, bank, box books. Dinner + FR, Flaming Stork.

NEWS: TW stroke. Revisit? London Tues, vacate house, tix, big. LW sigh, bye bye, TW die. Ask FR. Bedside w/o talk? Dying, know? Know, care? Jam conversation w/Infinite?

BUT: Momneed, daddeath, big. Thump heart. FR: OK, squeeze time, packself.

SO: Fly Isl Fri. Ret Bost Tues, London per plan. Betterfeel, less rue.

PLUS: Rushwrite GW Mombehalf. GW 0 X mos, ans mach. Selfish pig.

LUCY WESTERLY: *To her dead mother*

It was good of me not to scold George on his new answering machine. Let's hope he doesn't come.

I had the following thoughts when Thomas was lying on the bed looking dead.

• Horror lest he needed CPR or emergency first aid which I don't remember how to give or that he be already dead while I was figuring out what to do. It took me a while to think emergency loud enough to go to the phone and dial 9-1-1 with my heart jumping at what to tell the operator.

• Regret for the Cruise, remembering my head full of whales and fjords, as I realized we would have been in Oslo today. Thank God for cancellation insurance.

• Answer to the Question, Who Will Go First? Now I can think with a clear conscience how to get along after he's gone. I used to wonder how much time I'd have for widowhood. It looks like I'll have plenty now, more than I want.

• Predictable Regret. I saw all forty-seven years in Thomas's white head on the hospital pillow, with his open mouth and sleep rattling his throat. I saw him with the nurses' eyes, how old he looked to them. Not to me. I thought we were still the Younger Generation. You're the Middle Generation and Grandpa and Grandma are the Older one.

• Widow. I try to adapt to the words that fit. The word *girl* is obsolete. Widows grieve. It's part of the definition. Don't tell anyone, but I seem to be more exhilarated than grieved. Changes excite me, history in the making. I wonder what unpredictable feelings are sneaking across the map, and the danger of being ambushed by a revolutionary crowd.

• Worst Case. This would be if Thomas doesn't die but drags on in ambiguous illness in a wheelchair needing to be diapered, crotchety, helpless, etcetera.

• What to tell people. I teeter between recluse and gregarious. I want to chatter. On the other hand, I'm not ready. I need to prepare my speech. That's why I'm writing you. It gives me practice, for my speech isn't ready.

PART TWO

FRIDAY

LUCY WESTERLY: Composed in bed

Thanks for your message. I'll describe it for you. Someone's using a tractor, this early. A shovel clinking near the garage. Foghorn—though the air seems clear. It must be fog in the harbor or out at sea. You hear it too unless your sealed windows keep it out. Overcast, rain coming. The curtains lift indicating an east breeze, and Freud sits in the window sniffing the sea and listening to birds. He hears robin, song sparrow, house sparrow. Seagulls beyond the houses like a field full of blades of grass. In the gaps a gasoline motor on a fishing boat, assuming it's a fishing boat.

I'm too excited, agitated. If you're going to die now, there's something I ought to tell you. I need to tell you because if you die, we're going to be inundated, you and I. Already I feel the pressure on the dam. We're going to be swept into the torrent of World Bereavement, and we'll forget everything. I need to tell you like a tree to hang on to while the waters rush by. If I can remember what it was.

9

Second letter.

Mother, this excitement I feel, it doesn't fit. I need advice. I need advice on what to do if this ends. If I'm obliged to stay on this island, and where I can go if I don't.

My God! All the people coming and the things I have to do. I should have been up. He must be dead by now. I shouldn't have slept.

––––––––––

ABEL JEFFCOAT: *A speech*

Written Friday morning for possible use on a future occasion.

A few words for my good friend Thomas Westerly, who passed or is passing or will shortly pass away. I last saw him at dinner last week wearing a jacket and tie, still pretending to be alive.

I shouldn't call him friend, since we have nothing in common. But I'm in a sentimental mood tonight. I met Tom three years ago, when I moved here. I bought my house, which you may have noticed, the big one near the harbor entrance which pays your taxes. Tom and his wife invited us to dinner. As much a newcomer and even more of an outsider than I, he thought he was upholding your famous Island hospitality, him with his gullible old heart. I know better. I asked him, Why did you retire to such a godforsaken place and he said, what the hell, it's an island. He'd been looking forward to an island all his life and never thought how you people who live here might regard him.

Him with his idealistic ideas, this ex-president of a university which you'd think was the top of his profession, pinnacle, acme, he was ashamed of his success. He told me so himself. What crap. You should know about life in the universities. It's the only place in the world where the labor looks down on the management and if you go from labor to management they call you a sellout. Professors live the Life of the Mind and actually feel scorn for Deans and Presidents. That is, they pretend they do. My friend Thomas had it both ways. As President, he looked down on the scholars and scientists and teachers who never got to be President. As professor-at-heart, he looked down on his administrative colleagues, Deans, Provosts, other Presidents, and included himself for the finer scorn of it. However, if he hadn't made it to president, he could not have afforded to live among us, you and me. It takes money to be rustic and romantic.

Tom and I, we're opposites. Diametrical. He's all that liberal stuff you'd expect from one in his position. It's built into the profession. Mondale, Dukakis, Clinton. ACLU. Have you read his speeches at River City University? Affirmative the action, dismantle the hegemony. Recycle the environment. Recycle integration. Iran the Contra. Hire women. Diversify the diversity. Recycle the canon. Ban the skinheads. Hire gays. Thank your personal God he was President of a college and not these US and A. Recycle the faculty. Keep down the right wingers.

You think I don't mean it but I do, him and me, we come out of different worlds. He's intelligentsia, I'm philistine, in spite of which you'll find he's all heart, the bleeding kind, whereas I'm all head, the hard kind. I'm business, corporate America, he's academe. He's geology, which means exhume the fossils. I'm bottom line, which means melt them down.

One thing I'll say for him. He wasn't any good as President of River City University. Can't say I blame him. A non-profit institution is an absurdity to begin with, and university administration is a contradiction in terms, but if that's where you put your bottom line you might as well save the top line for yourself. Don't look him up in the history books. He did the best he could, and it's not his fault. What am I saying? Of course it was his fault, but who cares when you're seventy-plus years old and dying? At seventy it don't matter if half your life was stupid. What matters is being seventy, and circumstances contingent upon that.

The difference between him and me is that he was President but I was Board. If I'd been his Board, his job would be to come to me hat in hand, and mine would be to say No.

You ask, How did you two get along? I'll tell you. In retirement you don't care. He didn't mind that I'm a dirty capitalist. That I screw the poor and suppress the arts and exclude the blacks and vote Republican, and built myself a fortified house on an island miles out from a vengeful world. Now he's retired, he don't give a shit about principle. Never did, really. He thinks he's a good man, has his heart set on it. We can indulge him in that.

What we do, we don't have to talk. We play chess. We're matched. Chess is a quiet game, good for friends, especially friends who have nothing in common.

God damn. How to end? I hope he don't die, but I suppose he will. That's a damn shame.

ANN REALM: *To her husband Frank*

Good news. It looks like (I hope it is) a false alarm. He had a good night, his speech is back, he talked to Mother, he knows what happened. I'm in the waiting room down the hall: vending machines, cigarettes, soda, ice, microwave, gucky ice cream on the table. I haven't seen him yet because he's having procedures.

Somebody named Mrs. Grummond met me (tiny plane, a dozen passengers, bumpy under the clouds, the shore, the islands, the dark jelly sea, triangles and diamonds of sunlight). Rain and her driving make me nervous. She talks. How famous *you* are, watches you every night. She doesn't know I'm famous too and I don't tell her. How nice, she says, moving to Europe so far away from your poor old parents. Assuaging my guilt, of which I have none.

There was a confusion about what happened to Dad. Mrs. Grummond said something which I couldn't understand,

12

and then in the hardware store where I went for light bulbs Mr. Canay asking after my father wanted to know where he was hit, which was odd. Well, strokes hit you in the brain, so I said, Brain, which made his eyes pop. Brain? Brain? He was hit in the brain? My Lord, he didn't realize it was that bad. I said I never heard of a stroke hitting anywhere else and he said, Aw he's got a stroke too? He must of got that from the shock, and I said, What shock? He said, Why from the shot, and I said, What shot? and he said, Why Sam Truro's shot, and I said, Who's Sam Truro?

It was like I was behind the times. He said, Don't you know who Sam Truro is? and I said, Should I? and he said, Sam Truro's the nut who shot your daddy, and I said, Who shot my daddy? and he said, Sam Truro, and I said, When? and he said, Yesterday afternoon, he went to the hospital, and I said, First I ever heard of it, and he said, What you didn't know your daddy was in the hospital? and I said, Of course he's in the hospital, and he said, So what's the problem? and I said, I never heard about a shooting, he had a stroke, and he said, So he got the stroke after he got shot, and I said, My mother would have told me a thing like that, and he said, She didn't?

Well, Mr. Canay said, Maybe she didn't because everybody knows it, it's in the paper. He said, You ought to write it up, it's a good story for the media. I said, I doubt it, my father was not famous outside of River City, Ohio, and he says, I mean Sam Truro, and I said, Why him? and he said, Because he took his wife and two children hostage in his house. How a man can take his own wife and children hostage Mr. Canay don't know but he done it. Called the editor of the newspaper, Town Clerk, police, I'm holding my wife and kids prisoner in my house, until or unless you meet my demands. What demands? Mr. Canay don't know. It makes me think if you could take *me* hostage for a ransom of a few thousand dollars from the city of Boston.

According to Canay after Truro has given his message to the paper and is sitting with his rifle by the window, and the police have a car out front to keep an eye on things, along comes Dad. Walks right up to the Truro house. Neighbors standing around, one warns him, don't go there, man. I know him, Dad says, so Sam Truro sticks his head out the window and yells, Stand back, granddaddy. And Dad—my source is Canay, who's a narrating enthusiast—Dad says, You in trouble son? You need to talk? And Canay says Sam says, Don't son me, granddaddy, and Dad perhaps don't hear because he's old (says Canay), and Sam Truro waves this big long gun in the window and Dad says, What's that you got son? and Truro says, It's a gun, and Dad says he always thought there was better ways to solve problems, and Sam says, you bullshitting old university sonabitch, and Dad askin' for it goes up the door with his hand on the doorknob, You don't mean what you say son, and Truro out the upper window with the gun pointing like screaming I told you not to son me old idiot, and bang goes the gun and down falls Dad while Truro shouts to the neighbors, Come get him, and they run up while he covers them with his gun. The ambulance carts him off to the hospital and now he's critical and Canay says if he got a stroke on top of getting shot why that's too bad, a lot worse than I thought. And he says that guy holding his own family hostage, don't you think the Boston media and TV folks will come down here like you don't get that kind a story every day just anywhere?

I told him your field is international relations and mine is science news, but Canay he says media is media, so I told him I would tell you, which I have now done.

I found it in the paper with Dad's name, so I asked Mother. She said it was ridiculous. Then she started thinking and I could see her thinking when we went to the hospital. We sat in this crummy little room, I with my letter, Mom knitting (she talks to herself, I never noticed it), and when the doctor came, she asked him, You didn't find any bullet wounds, did you? Well that unsettled the doctor quite a bit until I showed him the paper and he laughed. That's the press for you, he said, which I resent, though we all know there's all kinds of press.

Mom says the Doc (his name is Eastcastle) asked her the extraordinary measures question last night. I asked how she replied and she doesn't know. Today she says he's so much better, the question is, what's the word? What word? I say. The word for what the question is. Moot? I say. Moot, she says.

Philip comes tonight. Patty tomorrow. Henry can't decide. Nobody knows where George is. Since Dad's improved Mother wanted to call them all and tell them not to come. It's too late for that, I say. We'll have a nice family visit before I go.

––––––––––

ANN REALM: *Dialogue*

Late afternoon, Thomas's room in the hospital.

Lucy: My doesn't he look better?

He's propped up. His lips are drawn back exposing his teeth, cheeks concave, eyesockets bruised. The shape of his head is the same as always, more fore and aft than side to side. His eyes dark and large look at Ann.

She thinks he is going to speak, but he doesn't.

Trivial conversation between Lucy and Ann.

Abel Jeffcoat enters with a copy of the *Island News*.

Jeffcoat: Here's the story you old fake, did you see the paper?

He reads the Truro story to Thomas, who doesn't seem to understand.

Jeffcoat: What have you got to say for yourself?

Lucy: It's utterly ridiculous.

Thomas (*speaking at last*): Hello Ann.

Ann: Hello Dad.

Thomas: You made it back in time.

Ann: I came back to see you.

Jeffcoat: In time for what, old man? Great to hear your voice.

Thomas: What's he talking about?

Jeffcoat: Me? This newspaper story which says you were shot. Were you shot?

Thomas: *(inaudible)*

Jeffcoat: Were you shot by Sam Truro?

Thomas: *(as if puzzling out a math problem)*

Ann: Mr. Jeffcoat, my father is not well enough for jokes.

Mother: This is nonsense.

Jeffcoat: Sometimes people don't know when they've been shot. If the doctors have no reason to look no one ever knows.

Thomas: Was I shot?

Jeffcoat: Paper says you were. That's why you're here. You old liar, you old fake.

Thomas: Why?

Ann: Why do you insult him at a time like this?

Jeffcoat: Didn't mean to insult you, old man. *(Laughs)* Ain't it a bitch, that dumb reporter.

Ann: How did such a story get in the paper?

Jeffcoat: I looked into it. I went to the police. Your Daddy was there. Sam Truro did take a shot at him.

Mother: He got shot?

Jeffcoat: Shot *at*. That don't mean he got hit.

Mother *(frantic)*: *Did* he get hit?

Jeffcoat: I doubt it. Ask the doctor.

Ann: We did ask the doctor. *(To Thomas)* You tried to talk to that crazy man?

Thomas: What crazy man?

———

Austin Wright

ABEL JEFFCOAT: *What to tell Lucy and dialogue*

The source of this narrative is the young policeman Oscar
Bale who told me in the police station how he was sitting in
the police car in front of the Truro house, keeping a quiet
watch as instructed not because this Truro had actually done
anything but because he had threatened to. There had been
a bunch of people around whom the police kept back from
the grass because Truro had his rifle in the window, and did
pop a shot into the ground every so often a while. But eventually they got bored and wandered off, leaving not much of
anybody but the cops along around two-thirty of yesterday
afternoon when the old Thomas comes down the sidewalk
and stops and looks at the house. There's Truro in the window with his rifle and old Thomas on the sidewalk looking
at each other. The policeman warns the old man, who don't
seem to hear. Stand back, dangerous territory, something like
that. Instead Thomas turns and shuffles up the walk to the
house. The madman yells, waving his rifle around, Get away
from here, go back. The policeman shouts him back too, but
Thomas goes on his shuffling little steps disregardful. Like
he meant to go right up and open that door and walk in and
sit down and have a neighborly conversation, talk him out
of it like he was trying to talk a rich man into bequeathing
his fortune to the university. He gets half way up the walk,
with something peculiar or unbalanced about the way he
walks, and Truro screeching like a kid on the roller coaster,
something like, Who do you think you are, God? Then bang.
The first shot went into the dirt to Thomas's right. The second ricocheted off the walk at his feet. It was such close
range the shots looked like deliberate misses. Finally Thomas stops. Looks at the ground like he don't know where he
is. Here the policeman intervened like this was his entry in
competition for the medal of heroics. Got out of the car with
his pistol, calling to Truro, Hold your fire while I get him.
Went right up that walk with Truro's rifle pointing at him.

17

Took Thomas by the arm, turned him around, and walked him back to the sidewalk. Got him into the police car. Meanwhile Thomas has stopped speaking, not a word. The way he looked, cross-eyed, the policeman could tell he was some kind of sick. Head lolling around more or less. No reply when asked where he lived. The policeman radioed the station, which sent out another policeman named Roger, who recognized him. It was Roger who brought him home.

Lucy: A little disoriented.

Jeffcoat: That he was.

Lucy: Why couldn't the reporter get it right?

Jeffcoat: Fallacy, ad hoc propter hoc. Is that the one, Thomas? What did the reporter know? He knew Truro took a shot at Thomas, because that's what they said when he investigated the noise. He heard the ambulance, discovered that's Thomas too. Ergo, if Thomas got shot at and is consequently in the hospital he must have got hit. When the reporter went to the hospital to ask about Thomas's condition they told him. He never thought to ask why Thomas was there because he thought he knew.

Ann: You must get them to print a retraction.

Thomas was speaking.

Jeffcoat: What's that, Tommy boy?

Thomas: Sam Truro.

Jeffcoat: That's the guy.

Thomas: Is he here?

Jeffcoat: What?

Thomas: Can he get in?

Ann: Why he's scared.

Jeffcoat: It's all right, Tom boy. You're safe. He can't get in here. He can't even get out of his house.

Lucy: How can anyone take his own family hostage?

Jeffcoat: Easy.

Lucy: He must be very frustrated.

Jeffcoat: Hostages, it's a cliché. He's trying to make news

with his limited resources. He hasn't got anybody else to take hostage, so he takes his family. He doesn't know hostages are out of date.

Ann: They should print a retraction because if they don't and somebody writes a biography.

Doc Eastcastle came in. Put his hand on Thomas's foot. Thomas do you hear? You to stay in bed, understand? Don't get out of bed, you got that?

I wouldn't say he's got much impetus to get out of bed.

———

PHILIP WESTERLY: Anticipating a memoir

Waiting for the ferry Friday night, to tell how you tried to put some of this into a poem. How you often wanted to write one, but never could. Can't say you haven't tried, how you used to chop your thought up into pentameter lines and let it go at that. With no place to write, do it in your head, anticipating the green notebook.

> No other person waiting on the dock
> For the last ferry of the night knows who
> This person is, nor how he named himself,
> Nor what has happened to those names,
> Specialist, ophthalmologist, eye man,
> Since he came out to watch his father die.
> Anonymous around the dock, he peers
> Blindly, squints in the dark to organize
> The lights, red, green, and white, and find
> The ferry in the gap to take him to
> The black hole where his father used to be.

Explanatory notes in the notebook can tell how you got the idea and every choice you made, pentameter scissors trying to make something out of your wait, you with your ancient and long exploded literary ambitions. (Noticeably empty words in the first line and maybe the last? Black hole too lurid?)

You need a form, if not poetic something else, to take care of listening to the waves slap the pilings below your feet, about this seaport you have never seen at night but only in the bright vacation summers full of the bright visiting daughters and sons of two marriages, as well as the bright children of your bright brothers and sisters, and all that institutional and organizational family picnicking cheer uprooted from around the country and repotted in this chosen outpost off the coast for the fatal final years.

Then it was always daytime and summer full of harbor and bay and sailboat buoys motor launches fishing boats and the great white ferry to the Island blasting its horn like a poet.

Which makes a contrast to the black hole where your father is, requiring something different for the wind blowing on the dock from the harbor bay island, the invisible ferry still an unsuccessful inference among the specky lights, undecipherable, while the sloshing sloshes expectantly around the pilings. More.

> This island cast a late deceptive shade
> Whose insulation kept the summer green
> Canceling other seasons of the year,
> And made an island of the man himself
> With no such thing as winter or bad news.

If that's a shade of green better, it's still cursed by poetic varnish which not only slicks down the slosh of the waves and neutralizes the bad feeling (whatever that is) but lies about it since it's not the Island canceling the seasons in your father's good long life as though summer had no end but your office which has snipped off your father's winters to comply with the work and vacation needs of your computer.

Here comes the ferry now, a row of lights warm and shifting across the dark, blocking the miscellany of background lights but still not constructible into a recognizable boat.

Then while the closing ship gains shape above the dock

with white sides catching reflected light, and white decks shiny in the light of caged bulbs, and the last returning passengers from the island look down to watch the landing process, you can make it pentameter by chopping up at every tenth syllable

>Then while the closing ship gains shape above
>The dock with white sides catching reflected
>Light, and white decks shiny in the light
>Of caged bulbs, and the last returning

passengers etcetera until you hit the middle of a word, at which point you must

change the words around, while the night keeps shattering the pentameter iambs and memory boxes, and the broken point skitters in the reflection of the light buoy across the wrinkled harbor surface

maybe free verse

ANN REALM: Diary

Friday, May 20. Fly Isl. DESC tiny plane bumpy jelly sea sun figs. Grummond. Rain.

CONFUSION Canay/Truro. Shot/stroke? = stroke.

NEWS: TW OK. Hosp. Jeffcoat fatass fake prole talk, Truro hit/miss TW, dumb reporter, brave cop. Retract paper.

PW here: talk late. Ophthal, money/waste life, age. Lit vs career. Poetry? Memoir? How interest rdr mem dull life? No help dull life, one retina after another, no lit either.

NE bedrm. DESC smell old sweet freshwood house, salt sea nearby. Damp gritty desk. Dark out, rural stillness rare. Real world still? Freud on bed, send sleep Mom.

PART THREE
SATURDAY

LUCY WESTERLY: To the editor, unwritten
After an insomniac night.

This is to protest the reference to my husband, Thomas Westerly, in your article about the Sam Truro hostage case. Apart from the fact he was not shot—an error you will correct—I object to your calling him controversial. Although there were controversies at River City University during his presidency (as during all regimes), your singling him out by the adjective is not neutral reporting. The word "controversial" is not neutral. It insidiously exploits its aura of euphemism to denigrate, enabling you to slander under an appearance of objectivity. Not only that, your usage implies the "academic world" has judged him, a claim you lack authority to make.

What do you, writing in this isolated place, know about the academic world? What do you know about River City years ago? What do your readers care? We came to retire, to get away from controversy, to live the last years of our lives in peace. My husband is ill in the hospital. We have friends here. No one would know there was controversy in his life if you hadn't said so. Your language incites pointless curiosity and reopens wounds to nobody's benefit in nobody's business.

You force me to repeat what I hoped I would never have to say again: my husband has nothing to be ashamed of. He did good work at River City. He was a good man and he was loved. How many wives will say that much about their husbands?

———————

PHILIP WESTERLY: To his sons David and Charles

In Thomas's study while waiting for Lucy to serve lunch.

Writing from the Island, where your grandfather's had a stroke. I came thinking he was dying, but he's better now, lucid but weak. He has a private room on the third floor, a picture window with a view of the parking lot. The harbor's on the other side, out of sight. I visited him and we spoke of family and island news.

I want you to think of your grandfather as a truly good man. The real thing. There aren't many in the world. In this evil cynical world, a person can still be good. If you don't believe it, let him be your example.

Writing on my laptop, which I brought with me. I take it everywhere I go. I'll use your grandfather's printer, which I hope is compatible. I expect to hear more from you, Charles, about your fiancée. I'd like to meet her, though I'm sure you have chosen well. No one would know that from your description, though.

Say hello to your mother for me. Tell her that my father liked her and still does in spite of everything. He does not hold grudges. If she wants to send a message I'll be glad to

The letter wasn't right. He pressed F10 to save it if he should decide to finish it later. Meanwhile, other things.

What to tell in a narrative. A battle of father faces. New father shrunken with cheekbone knobs, teeth sticking out like rabbit or troll. Old father with brow and mild watching eyes full of intelligence, and live humorous mouth.

In the hospital room where he was propped with a tube to the back of his wrist, squirrel cheeks, loose hospital sleeves, body immobilized whose shaded eyes moved from one to another. Lucy, Ann, Philip. When we told him who else was coming to visit, he felt like a fraud. He'd have to die to make their trips worth while. We laughed, noting for our notebooks all jokey words, lest it turn out to be his deathbed. We talked about Jeffcoat, the Truro case, bourgeois things, while he squinted trying to follow. After a while he interrupted. What am I trying to remember? he said.

What is it? I don't know, Daddy.

I've been trying to remember something. Oh yes.

You remember?

I've been trying to remember why Mr. Truro shot me.

He's shooting at everybody, Daddy. Not just you. You went up to his house.

He had a reason, he said.

His face was full of mental effort. What am I trying to remember? he said again.

About Truro?

I remember. I want to talk to Philip.

The others went out and you wondered how to write about being chosen without sounding like a child.

Do me a favor, he said.

The possibility of doing a favor, not just for your father but for your dying father, though his living presence reduced the idea of death to a figure of speech. His fine old face, pale, his nose came to a fine point, his intelligent eyes full of the goodness named in the letter to your sons.

My papers, Thomas said.

Thomas has papers. A career like his could not be had without papers. They'll remain.

You want me to take care of them? Don't worry about it.

I need to worry about it, he said.

Why?

Authorization in my desk, he said.

I'll take care of it.

The discomfort in the face was not satisfied. Weed them out.

Weed out your papers?

Some aren't fit.

You want me to destroy them?

Some.

Which? Since Thomas did not understand, you amplified: Are there certain ones you want me to get rid of?

Do it.

Which ones?

Use your judgment. You have my permission.

You want me to read them and decide?

Don't read them.

How will I know which papers to destroy?

I rely on you.

Dad. How can I decide which papers to destroy if I can't read them to find out what's in them?

You're my son. My good son. My wise son.

Listen to me Dad. May I look at them in order to judge?

As if suddenly noticing something on the opposite wall, he said, Why I remember.

Remember what, Dad?

Why Sam Truro shot at me.

No Dad, it had nothing to do with you.

He was shivering. Cold?

Got the shakes.

Shivering like excitement without antibodies. Like glee

without joy. Help me sit in that chair for a while.

You're not supposed to get out of bed.

Stretch my bones.

You're not supposed to get out of bed.

When Ann and Lucy came back, he looked dead, face gray, though breathing heavily with mouth open. We talked, but he did not listen. Put your father's validation in the notebook along with the context to assure its accuracy, still valid to dismiss your errors at the age of forty-six, to extend the string of fathers and sons in a clear line indefinitely back past history into the cave—fathers praising sons and sons and sons to authorize your own father's voice telling you that you deserved and had earned what you had become.

He opened his eyes like a bloodshot hound. Get me some—

Some what?

He couldn't find the word, and Lucy went for the nurse.

MELANIE CAIRO: To Dr. Parch

Henry Westerly came to the Island on the one o'clock ferry. He stood with his cane on the upper deck by the pilot house in the wind, while his wife observed him, collecting notes for Dr. Parch. She was Melanie Cairo of the Tarrytown Cairos, keeping her name in the modern way. Dr. Parch was Henry's psychiatrist, upon whom Melanie rested her hopes. She collected observations for a letter she planned to write to Dr. Parch prior to an interview she would like to have with him. The interview, not yet scheduled, became more important the longer she waited, for she hoped that when it came, Dr. Parch would solve her problems.

Dr. Parch, *she said, continuing from where she had left off,* it's about Henry's hat. A felt hat which he always wore, had worn for many years, giving to his lopsided face an aura of old movies. The wind around the pilot house was too much, he held it by the brim over his ears with both hands. He loved that hat like the old part of himself.

We were going to the Island, because his father was expecting to die. We had an argument. I'm sorry about that, I don't like to argue with Henry. We had not said anything since Stony Hill, we only undertook the journey because Lucy asked us to. There was Henry, elbows on the rail, holding his hat with the brim pulled down like earflaps and his cane tucked under his armpit, looking at the island, which was still distant, a long blue line with patches of white sand emerging into sight, and he said something which I couldn't hear. So he said it louder: My father's dying over there. I thought it was grief, so I said, Well maybe it's not as bad as we think, and he said something else, and I said, What? He said, My father is a dead hand like Aristotle. Shot by a barbarian.

Like Aristotle? He said, The dead hand of Aristotle held science back for twenty centuries. He delayed human progress two thousand years.

I didn't know what to say, so I didn't say anything. Meanwhile he said, I never liked my father. Somebody had to do it.

I was shocked. I thought he loved his father. He used to talk about him, what a good man he was. I thought they all loved each other and his father was a nice sweet gentle man who was not cut out to be a college president. But Henry said, He never liked me, so I never liked him. This upset me, it scares me when people jeopardize their dearest feelings by saying false words. He said his father never gave him credit, he preferred the older siblings, he was insensitive, prejudiced, thoughtless, smug, his father never saw him. He never saw me, Henry said.

He wanted me to respond, so I said, You don't mean that, Henry. Which I shouldn't have said.

All this time glaring at me with the ferocity in his eyes, he hung on to his hat pulling it over his ears until suddenly he noticed it, like getting a look at himself from outside. As if the hat was telling him he was a liar. Is that possible, Dr. Parch? Or was it that something funny about how he looked with the brim pulled down tickled some unmatured girlish impulse which made me giggle, though actually I didn't giggle, I didn't even smile, I swear to you, for I knew how terrible that would be, and I did not, though Henry must have thought I did. Whatever it was, if he had detected the possibility of a giggle or was just seeing himself, he tore off the hat, looked at it, cursed and flung it. Flung his hat, his sign, his very Henryness, as if it were, what? What, Dr. Parch, I have tried to think. As if it were *me*? As if that very Henryness had metamorphosed into me, so that when he flung it away he flung me? Or do you think I am making too much?

He was careful to fling it inboard toward the deck cabin, but the wind caught it. It skittered back along the deck among the lifeboats. He waved his cane at it, and I, knowing how important it was, chased it, but it disappeared through the railing at the stern. He limped along and together we looked at the broad green-white track the ship left, where I saw it one last time, a black speck among the eddies like the end of *The Secret Sharer*.

Dr. Parch, I thought for a moment he would jump overboard, which would be the same for him as throwing me overboard, and I wanted to cry. There stood Henry staring at the sea with the sandy shore and trees reduced to the thinnest strip of hazy blue receding. I said, Poor Henry, we'll get you another.

Fuck you, he said.

Among the things I've learned to accept in dealing with Henry, Dr. Parch, is not to expect appreciation. My words were not well thought out. I did not have time to test for tact, the right healing thing to say when Henry has lost his dear hat and is standing at the edge of the ship in the dazzling wind, looking like a lost doggie at his vanished self: I

knew *exactly* what he was feeling, and all I meant was that I
sympathized, blurting the only comfort I could think of at
the moment, which was, We'll get a new one. I should have
expected the reply I got: Fuck you. Does this mean I should
not offer what comfort I can? Withhold myself, let him endure his pain coldly ignored by his wife? The reason he says
fuck you is because I've deprived him of the opportunity to
accuse me of coldly ignoring his pain.

But Dr. Parch, it does pay off, my policy of patience and
sympathy. He is, after all, capable of shame. I simply have to
wait. After this incident he sulked ten or fifteen minutes.
(Actually, I don't know what to make of his mood today. I'm
accustomed to think of Henry as having just two states. One
is depression and the other is the timid sweet residue of Henry
at his best. This afternoon gave me a glimpse of a third state,
a different Henry, with an evil eye. The devil in him. It's as if
someone had told him how much I'd give for a return of the
original Henry, that he took to punishing me with a smile
out of Satan, horns and sulfur.)

We were still at the rail watching the wake, mesmerized,
ten maybe twenty minutes, when he turns to me and says,
Stop worrying that I'll jump overboard.

I protest: What gave you that idea?

Better for you if I did, right? he said.

No, Henry, I said. It's an insult to attribute such a thought
to me, Dr. Parch, though the idea did occur to me. That's
when he flashed the evil smile. You could see the candle behind the eyes and teeth.

I don't blame you for loathing me, he said.

Nobody loathes you, I said. How feeble that sounds.
Loathe is such strong language, so strong it means nothing.
I've denied it so many times my denial means nothing. I know
when he says I loathe him, he means he loathes me. It's what
I call Melanie's Rule, learned through hard experience: ev-
ery adjective or crime he throws at me is actually himself.

It's a useful principle of human nature, Dr. Parch, did you know that?

It could have been worse. After I said, Nobody loathes you, he could have got us into a long circular discussion of who hates whom and why, in which he trips me up on every point to make me feel bad. But he didn't. We turned and as we watched the Island closer, the lighthouse on the point, the cottages in the trees, the sheds by the harbor, I saw his mood change.

Not all at once. First, he said, Maybe we can rent a boat and go look for it.

Unfortunately, I missed the precise tone of that remark. I should have realized it was his idea of a reconciling joke. I said, Wouldn't it have sunk by now? So he gives me a look and says, Ugh. Ugh! to me, the ultimate word of disgust? Fortunately, it was not a major setback.

We were coming in close, and he said: I'm scared.

That was creepy because he gets scared of such terrible things, like committing suicide or killing me.

I shouldn't have said what I said, he said.

I thought he was taking back one of his insults, but no such luck. He said, What I said about my father. I shouldn't have said such a terrible thing. I'm always ashamed of myself.

Well, Dr. Parch, I can live for moments like that, the thrill of vindication with Henry by the rail, head bowed, full of shame. How good when he turns thoughtful and sees himself as he is. I can afford magnanimity, and I tried to erase the recent past by telling him: You didn't say anything about your father, you only thought you did. I was afraid he would say, Fuck you, again, but he accepted it, and it was as if the incident had not occurred except for the loss of his hat. The lost hat would remind him.

He stood beside me looking at the village on the shore and said, I wonder if he's still alive. They'll have him full of tubes and pumped full of drugs. The idiot doctors are trying to keep him alive, the idiot family is cheering them on, and he's wishing them all to hell. Don't you agree?

Because I care about the truth I said, I don't know why I should. I try to show him a realistic view of things whenever I can, to keep him stable.

We were pulling up to the landing. I looked on the dock and saw no one I recognized. They had not sent anyone to meet us, and I was afraid Henry would take offense, though I knew it was because they were at the hospital. I went down the stairs with him, holding his arm. I was thinking if he has to be depressed, it's good that he's feeling ashamed, for he's a lot easier to manage when he sees himself as others do.

NEWS ITEM

Abel Jeffcoat found this item in the afternoon Island News, *took it to the hospital and read it to Thomas.*

An attempt to rescue the wife and children of Sam Truro, the bank teller who has been holding them hostage, failed last night when a burglar alarm went off and warned him of the rescuers' approach. Police had hoped to invade the house on Shoal Point Drive and take him by surprise in the early morning. The attempt followed a demand by Truro late Friday for twenty thousand dollars and a safe conduct for himself, wife, and children to Switzerland, Sweden, or "some other free country."

Last night was the second consecutive night during which Truro and his hostages have been sealed up in his house in a siege that began Thursday morning. According to Sheriff Haines, "No one knows what is going on in there. We see him in the window with that rifle. Sometimes he shouts at us. We don't step onto his lawn because he takes pot shots when we do. He's taken up to a dozen shots since he hit the professor on Thursday." The reference was to Thomas West-

31

erly, shot by Truro while trying to approach the house.

Last night's raid was attempted at 2 a.m. in hopes Truro, who appears to be holding his hostages singlehanded, would be asleep. The house was dark except for a light in the living room. Officials don't know where Truro keeps the hostages, nor under what restraints. Several deputies surrounded the house and crept up under cover of darkness. The alarm went off when a deputy tried to pry open the kitchen door with a knife. "It sounded like a regular old siren you could hear through the village," a deputy said.

After the raid Truro was heard shouting out the window. "Get away from them doors," he is said to have said, "or I'll kill them all."

"We figured it a real danger he might hurt someone," Haines said.

Witnesses from a neighboring house Friday reported seeing Truro and the two children eating in their dining room. Haines said, "No one's sure the whole family's not in on it. Only we don't dare take a chance." He said the shots from the window do not seem intended to hit anybody. "If you step off the sidewalk, he'll shoot the ground in front of you," he said. "If you wander away, he'll pop a shot into the ground to bring you back."

No attempt is being made to negotiate with Truro. The demands raise questions, Haines said, about the seriousness of the whole exploit, which he termed a "charade." "He asks for ex number of dollars and safe conduct to a free country, which I guess means we're supposed to find a country that will let him in. Safe conduct for his wife and children, which is the people he is holding hostage. Wants that in exchange for freeing his hostages, which he will then take with him on a pleasure trip."

Officials are divided on how to deal with the case. One group wants to attack and overpower Truro. This was the policy adopted last night, frustrated by the alarm. Sheriff

Haines, on the other hand, believes Truro should be ignored. "If people would just not pay no attention. If those people standing across the street would just go away." When asked why he didn't remove the policemen on watch, Haines replied, "Because the danger to Mrs. Truro and the little children. As long as he keeps shooting out the window, we need a brigade to warn people away."

"Who knows what [expletive] is going on inside that house," Haines said. "I hope to God nobody gets hurt."

――――――

HENRY WESTERLY

had nothing to say. Not because his mind was empty. He would talk if he could, but his words were sticky like glue. Usually he did not notice when he was not speaking. But in the hospital room he noticed. This produced a flood of language, but there was a dam between it and the outlet to speech, so he turned it instead into a letter to God.

Dear God:

Are you trying to make me laugh? So he wasn't shot after all except by you under the pretense of natural causes, and here we are again with the stuffed idiot reading his newspaper to the zombie, while the family gapes at the dead TV, the picture window, sink and faucet and oxygen line, avoiding each other's eyes.

I'm silent because I lack speech energy. Every word needs a long inhale and exhale which I can't control, leaving me out of breath before the word is done and requiring another breath to finish the sentence. I'm not trying to be rude. It's the energy needed to gather thoughts and choose out of the stream of words the word worth uttering, like scooping fish with bare hands, and the additional energy, once you have caught the word, to squeeze it through the vocal chords.

Meanwhile he goes on reading about the genius who

trained his gun on his family to shock the neighbors into some realization of the stereotypes by which they live, not noticing how his voice droning on (laughing as if it were funny) has merged with the sick man's disease, energized the invading cells inside the old body, taking over.

How do you like that, Thomas, he says. Ain't that a crock?

If I had breath to speak words as free of effort as he, wasting all that precious life force in imbecility? No one is even curious why Thomas went to see the madman when he was on the verge of his stroke. I could tell this story if I had the breath. Love,

Henry

———————

THOMAS WESTERLY: Papers as read by Philip Westerly

Late in the afternoon, when the women were in the kitchen and Henry napping, Philip went into his father's room, leaving the door open so as not to arouse suspicion. In the archaic study, the old wounded desk, globe dark over the bookcase, gooseneck lamp spraying light over the file cabinet, swivel chair, rule and paper cutter, scissors, the rest of the room in twilight, books in shadow.

Also two large file cabinets with four well-oiled drawers, full of hanging files. These contained folders with papers stapled and loose, mimeographed documents, reports with glossy covers, crammed. The dividers between the files had headings:

AFFIRM ACT. ATHLETIC. BOARD. BUDGET.
COLLECTIVE BARG. FACULTY. MAKROV.
PRAISE AND GLORY. RECOMMENDATIONS. STUDENTS.
HOUSE. ESSAYS. THOUGHTS. UNIVERSITY FINANCES.

Somewhere here the papers his father wanted him to destroy. He flipped through the tops of the files. An absent dialogue: What do you want me to do? Am I supposed to read it all? My patients will be waiting for me.

In the file cabinet on the right was a divider labeled FAM-
ILY. *There was a tab in front,* HENRY, *then* PATTY, *then*
PHILIP. *Take a peek, someone says, find what your father
really thought of you. He lifted the* PHILIP *file two inches.
Tops of letters, old carbons, later xeroxes, fatherly typing:
After we go back to the Island, maybe we* Don't waste time,
he said. He looked in the back, the thick file labeled UNI-
VERSITY FINANCES. *The thickest files were full of busi-
ness, ignore them. The job was still impossible.*

*He pushed the drawer shut, then reopened it because he
had seen a thin folder in front with a yellow flag:* LOOK
HERE IN CASE OF DEATH.

To Whom It May concern, in the event of my death:
Please heed this request. Before anyone looks at my papers, I wish my son Philip to go through them and select
what in his good judgment should not be retained. If Philip
is not available my daughter Ann may act in his place or my
other children in descending order of age.

———————

MELANIE CAIRO: Dialogue

*Dinner table, Saturday night. Seated at the table: Lucy, Philip,
Ann, Henry (Westerlys) and Melanie (Henry's wife, a Cairo).*
    Lucy: He still might die.
    Philip: Probably.
    Lucy: Even if he pulls through, there's the underlying—
    Henry: That's why we're here.
    Lucy: What will I do if he dies?
    No one wants to answer.
    Ann: Didn't you make any plans when you came to the
Island?
    Lucy: Of course we did. We have everything worked out
with Mr. Haseltine at the bank.
    Henry: Well then?

Lucy: I didn't expect it so soon.

Philip: Yes, it's too soon. He's only seventy-two.

Lucy: So disappointing.

Henry: Three score and ten or whatever.

Lucy: We had six years here.

Ann: Six good years.

Lucy: Six good years. I can't complain. I was hoping we could live until eighty. My father lived to eighty. My mother lived to ninety-one. My grandmother lived to ninety-seven.

Henry: I don't want to live past fifty.

Lucy: I'll be sadly disappointed if I outlive you my dear boy.

Ann: Listen Mother. What plans do you have for what to do next?

Lucy: I don't remember. Yes, I do. I'll stay in the house. I have friends. My garden. I won't impose on you children.

Ann (*after a silence*): If Frank and I weren't moving to London.

Lucy: Don't think of it.

Ann: Maybe some kind of alternating arrangement. More silence.

Lucy: We put my mother into Sunset Leaves.

Philip: No need to worry about that for a good long time.

Lucy: Let's cheer up. We're talking as if he were already dead. He won't die.

Ann: Well actually Mother—

Lucy: The stroke is mending and there's always remission. He's had lots of remission, he's very good at it.

Henry: If he doesn't die now, you'll have to go through the whole thing again.

Ann: Henry.

Lucy: What will I do if he dies?

Henry: You just said.

Lucy: No, I mean what will I *do*? It's been so long, I can't imagine it. I always thought I would outlive him. It's so disappointing.

Henry: Looks like you will outlive him.

Lucy: There was Doctor Eastcastle's question. That was shockingly premature, don't you think?

Philip: You mean the extraordinary measures question?

Ann: There's only one possible answer to that.

Philip: Does he have a Living Will?

Lucy: What's that?

Henry: That's the euthanasia thing.

Lucy: Not euthanasia. That's going too far. I didn't authorize that, did I?

Ann: Not euthanasia Mother. It's just a way of making your wishes known, not to drag it out when it's hopeless.

Lucy: It's never hopeless, I won't have anyone calling it that. Does the doctor think it is?

Ann: The doctor has never said what he thinks.

Lucy: I hope I told him the right thing. Maybe I should tell him I've changed my mind. Should I do that?

Ann: You did the right thing.

Lucy: If he dies, I don't want it on my conscience.

Ann: It won't be on your conscience, Mother.

Lucy: It's so terrible.

Henry: What's terrible?

Lucy: It.

Henry: Life, you mean?

Lucy: No I don't mean that.

———

THOMAS WESTERLY: As skimmed by Philip Westerly
In his study Saturday evening.

To whom it may concern: Elaine Sine has been a loyal worker in the University President's office for the last eight years   because of your great distinction and accomplishments in molecular biology great pleasure to invite you as our LeClair Distinguished Faculty Lecturer, a specially invited annual by a famous scholar for which we can offer a fee

    unbelievable, no way I can rearrange my understanding of the case to give credence. It doesn't add up. Doesn't compute, in the language of the day. What is disbelief, I ask, a mal-correspondence between what you're accustomed to expect in the normal course of events and something outside, won't fit, like metric and English   call attention of the Board to this practice. I have sent a directive to the Provost asking measures initiated to stop it soon as possible, but the Board must realize entrenched habits

    all my life a memoir. Perhaps two memoirs, maybe more, the difficulty finding a form, where to go next what to include postpone, it is hard to write anything

    a fine novel just finished. Ordinarily no time for novels but this time fortunately, roughly epistolary, though not sure what principle of inclusion exclusion, series of call them *epistoles* in which everything seems to be a form of writing, recognizable as such, if not letter a journal entry or other standard forms like dialogue narrative or lecture or suppose to emphasize constraint on experience by writing don't know

    To whom it may concern: Ronald Guernick has been a loyal student of mine in graduate courses for three years, unusually bright imaginative   I have to recognize this a job for which I am by personality and temperament not fitted. Requires outgoing skills, salesmanship (calling on people for money, nothing more repugnant), whereas always sensitive easily hurt. My weaknesses, which maybe will be my advantage, if I don't accept the offer the question will always remain as source of possible regret, how would I have done as President of River City University?

    seldom so angry, or only do I tend to forget emotion after passed? Amply justified though well aware how an emotion like anger when it once gets a foothold is a living creature embryo or weed in the garden it wants to live grow develop an instinct for selfpreservation, it resists any attempt to pacify or resolve it creates imagines even worse offenses on which to thrive even worse outrages to fury, which is how I feel at this moment with enough sense to warn me be careful think it over wait a day but how flat and dull and humiliating to contain myself and wait to cool off

as if nothing really happened until it was written down. This seems like madness, tourist with a camera, and if I am mad the insane one victim of language, obsession with writing. Consider the peculiar nature of it, a blocking out of thought, tying it up like a box score after a ball game, the whole game reduced to an ordered collection of symbols, as if all my thought were to reduce experience to a box score, and yet impossible to think without

too vulnerable, easily depressed when things not well, I suppose this is another case not a suitable personality for the President of a University. Oh the advantages of a leather hide sit down and figure out the rationale of my quiver and tremulating echo when things go off a little, why such an inside shake. Analyze each case, but that's probably not the right way, it's what I do whereas the really thick-skinned ignore, disregard, apparently don't have any such inside waves   with great regret I must tender to you   In this I have to say, I must say, I'm obliged to say, it must be said, you have to grant, you'll grant me this one mitigating mitigation excuse alibi circumstance factor not beyond anyone's control not to make any excuses alibis, a political situation out of control forces of radical forces forces out of control factions and divisiveness   I must now I am obliged now herewith with the greatest of regret my resignation beyond my control my political base

with all due respect believing this bill should not be paid until your workmen have rectified the situation, in simple language: The job has not been done.   have always loved that part of the beaches of my childhood but never could some day afford to live on the Island, but when we retired just so happened this nostalgia trip in the offseason available on the market by the luckiest of breaks within the price range would never been able to afford were not my three otherwise mostly unhappy years as President said to each other unbelieving in our good luck and paid the downpayment then and there and   Eugene Makrov is the most brilliant man male or female whom I have ever known

To whom it may concern: Robin Walleye   when I hear cynical talk about the wickedness of man how vicious we intrinsic awfulness are drops of scum marring the serene face of nature, then I often think of my father innate gentle truly good man

loss of the sheen or aura of excitement that floats through the memory of past quality the present lacks   always an anxiety in the opera or great mountain view or the thrilling dinner honored guest the future yet to unfold your belly digesting your last meal no matter how exciting the event the eventual threatening fart or cramp or shit and when my next chance to go to the bathroom

Don't forget Mother too sweet loving tenderness her songs, naive though she

whether he exists or not, a linguistic question loaded since the phrasing implies a pre-existent answer, so the question becomes the following meaningless one: does this thing whose existence I have postulated by giving it a name exist, which tells you nothing since the postulation is only a linguistic formulation anyway, so we need to consider over again (reconsider) what real need the question is trying to answer, and whether that real need itself is not ultimately just a linguistic formulation

fatigue, I have no explanation

PHILIP WESTERLY: *Dialogue*

Thomas Westerly's study, Philip skimming through Thomas's files. Enter Ann.

Ann: Hey, what are you doing?

Philip: Looking through his papers.

Ann: How come?

Philip: He asked me to.

Ann: What are you looking for?

Philip: I don't know.

Ann: What do you mean?

Philip: He asked me to get rid of anything unsuitable.

Ann: Censor them?

Philip: Yes.

Ann: You're kidding. Why you?

Philip: Because I'm the oldest.

Ann: That doesn't make you the wisest. So what are you supposed to find?

Philip: Damned if I know.

Ann: He didn't say?

Philip: Use my judgment. That's all I know.

Ann: Would you like help?

Philip: He asked me to do it.

Ann: Oh.

Philip: You can help if you want to.

Ann: Does this mean Dad has secrets he's ashamed of?

Philip: Maybe just things that would embarrass others.

Ann: Does it scare you?

Philip: A little.

Ann: What have you found so far?

Philip: Nothing. I'm overwhelmed by the amount. I wish I knew better what he has in mind.

Ann: Maybe you can ask him tomorrow.

Philip: He wouldn't tell me when I asked him today.

Ann: Maybe tomorrow he will. Go to bed, it's late. Don't worry about it.

Notes.

If he has something to hide, why should I care? Everybody has things to hide. That's why we have skulls, to keep things from getting out.

Not everyone writes them down, though. Is that the problem, if he saved his mental garbage in a trail of writing?

What would a man like Thomas Westerly choose to hide?

Love Affair. Which I'd rather not know. Why shouldn't I know, if it came out all right? A rival to Lucy. Would it trouble me to learn that my secure and happy childhood, when the only problems were my brothers and sisters, was not secure and happy after all? Dangerous things that I didn't know, with a residue of painful letters.

University politics. Conspiracies, intrigues. If the secrets are other people's stored for safe-keeping in his files, then this creepy worry is pointless. Go to bed, Philip. There's nothing for your notebook here.

The question of how I might feel about what I might find suggests this odd question to me: what if my father is no different from me? This question filled me with alarm, giving rise to another, namely, why should it fill me with alarm? Why should it frighten me to think my father was no different from myself?

WILLIAM KEY: *Narrative*

Two more on the late Saturday ferry: Patricia, third of the Westerly children, and her amicably divorced husband William Key the lawyer, coming from New York. They carried their heavy bags up through the village, turning by the museum, down Peach Street to the Westerly house with all windows lit, where they went in without knocking. Henry and Melanie in the living room watching television. Well look at you, exclamation points greeting them, mostly from Melanie, who called the others, bringing Philip from the study, Ann and Lucy from the guest rooms they had been fixing, with more exclamation points. *The narrative is by William Key, formulated but not written.*

Immediate discussion where they should stay, indicating to William that they did not yet know about the divorce. The three upstairs bedrooms were occupied. William said they should go to the Inn, but Lucy suggested the sunporch with the cots if there's enough bedding, which there was, and Ann wanted to go to the linen closet right away, but Lucy said, Wait a while, they just got off the boat.

The point of view is William Key's. His official connection to the family having been severed, although they do not know this, his perceptions are sharpened as he sits among them in the living room feeling regret. He feels obliged to prove all over again that he is a decent and honorable person, and he makes a point of participating in the talk, which is otherwise carried mostly by Patricia, Lucy, and Henry's strange little Melanie, while the other men, Henry and the usually talkative Philip, seem rather reserved.

The point of observation is the piano bench at one end, where William sits, gouged under the ribs by the piano cover, closed after his soft middle on the keys had spilled musical discord into the room. Curtained windows on the left, opposite the tawny deep sofa which contains Lucy and Ann leaning back and Patty leaning forward. Coffee table by their knees. Melanie on the wooden straight chair in the dress with large solid-color flower prints. A remembering look on her face, which embarrasses him. Philip with his neat speckled beard in the father chair, Henry in the wooden rocking chair by the magazine table. Potted flowers. Shelves with pitchers, figurines, china animals, ceramic pots. Painting over the fireplace, sand dunes, surf vaguely delineated, brought from the university president's office, somebody's gift. The yellow cat, whose name he remembers with some scorn is Freud, goes from one shoe to another, sniffing around the room before settling on the window sill.

The words in William Key's mind have no particular destination. Their object is to gather such things as will soon be deleted from William's life. Words and pictures. Not quite voluntary, a moment of unusual detachment he did not seek, which makes these people of the family he's casting off look like strangers. For the first time he notices a Westerly look shared by everyone in the room but Lucy and Melanie. Ann, Patricia, Philip, and Henry: pointedness of face, convergence of lines and planes to the tip of the nose, enhanced by small-ness of chin, projection of lips as to kiss, recession of brow, all of which might be represented in caricature by a cone, which to create the proper effect must be decorated by eyebrows. The cone is diverted differently in each, by puffy fat in Henry, by a dignified half-gray pointy beard in Philip, by intelligent dark iron eyes with a light like swords or picks in Ann, by Patty's moist and fleshy lips which in other days, but never mind. Together they recall by indirection the old geologist in the hospital, his ravaged but humorous old eyes replaced in the young by earnestness and strife. Lucy is different. Her eyes are bruised, mouth squashed from the sides while the expressive lips don't know if they are crying or laughing. Is there anyone else? Yes, the outlander Melanie Cairo whose eyes bulge.

How does William look in such a crowd? He prefers his own looks, normally handsome with a small mustache, to those of any Westerly.

Talk of ferry schedules, rooms and bedding, with nothing for him, William wants to escape. There's a snack break to the kitchen. He must go for a walk. He goes out the sunporch door, which Patricia will leave open if he comes back late. He feels Melanie looking at his back as he goes.

He steps out to the sidewalk. Quiet of the island night. Clarity of air and sky, clusters of stars never seen in New York. A faint music and enclosed male voice, TV from the centers of civilization leaking out a window and dispersing. He walks back toward the village. Past firehouse with open door, a dim red light inside, Inn with lights on the front porch, museum dark. Shops are closed, though some shop windows remain lit. The street goes straight to the harbor.

Straight to the public landing, which is a square dock sticking into the harbor with a summer house in the middle. The harbor is black. He goes out and stands at the farthest edge from the village which twinkles hesitantly in trees. He looks up, examines for a while the full sky, constellations learned as a child, known and named by Greeks and forgotten by him. Nearby, the ferry dock, where looms the dark hulk of the steamer that brought him. Beyond that, the harbor mouth, a black gap between the red and green marker lights far out. On the other side of the dock there's a long pier lit all the way, with a large fishing boat and voices. He goes back to shore and out the other dock to see.

Illuminated by a floodlight, men in a hurry shovel what look like marshmallows but must be shelled scallops from a bin on the boat into bags, weighing these on a scale, then swinging them over to the dock, where they are packed in ice (all in haste to arrest the decay) and stowed in a truck.

Whence they'll be taken (William explains) to the airport under contract, to be shipped to Boston and transferred by prearrangement to planes for Cincinnati and Minneapolis and Atlanta in time for the early morning markets where they'll be tossed on trucks going to the deluxe restaurants which will serve them tomorrow night sauteed or poached or covered in sauce to people with napkins and silverware, buying by credit card like you and me.

That's Commerce for you, go the words in his head, as if to prove to another voice that the Island has business other than Tourist business. William recognizes that the destinationless words in his head have been organizing into an argument, with one voice representing himself and another the Island, or, more likely, some advocate like the old dying Thomas, that's who. That was the voice speaking when he first stepped out of the house and looked at the sky and when he looked at it again on the public landing, rebuking him for the skyless and starless life he had chosen in New York, not too different from that of a mole or ants in an anthill. His father-in-law's voice (not knowing he has become an ex-father-in-law before turning into an ex-person), chastising him for being out of touch with earth and the conditions of our being, represented by the clear island air and the sea where life began.

The other voice, William's own, replies with vigor, chastising the father for his escape from the civilization he was born into, the issue being not what human was before it was human but what, being human, it is. This voice attacks Thomas's island for being an island, taking advantage of the sea to keep out the world, poverty and injustice and crime. This voice (which cites William's service as a Civil Liberties lawyer to protect him from guilt) compares the vanity of Thomas's withdrawal to that of an old king crawling unburdened toward death.

The argument takes shape as William watches the commerce of the scallop fishermen trying to meet their deadline, thereby proving that the Island is no mere playground but actually produces things. No credit to Thomas for that, however, which for him as for William is merely part of the background, neither Thomas nor William having credentials as scallop fishermen.

Such are the mood and words of William Key as he strolls ashore again, turning left to loop the long way back to the house past the hospital. A new-looking brick structure of two stories, larger than any other building here though small as hospitals go and architecturally out of keeping with the aggressive New Englandism of the rest of the town. Lights in the front and the first floor windows, the upstairs dark, it

46

turns William's attention to the man (as opposed to voice) who's dying in there.

This makes him sad. The judicial voice in William proposes that Thomas be forgiven for old age and illness, that he be allowed such pleasures as remain to him. This judicial voice tasks William with the reminder that ugly old Thomas was the Westerly William liked best, including the daughter he married—a turn of argument which brings him back to the other problem, the question of What Do They Know?

What do and don't they know? The question depends on another, namely, what has Patricia told? Which recognizes the awkward fact that they never did decide what to tell her family—neither while the negotiations were going on nor (an oversight, a foolish carelessness) when they came for this visit. Why not? No doubt, things being officially amicable, he relied on her to deal with her family and felt a compunction against quizzing her.

In a diagram of information flow, the source point would be Patty: if she has not given the Westerlys the news, they won't have it, for it's unlikely her friends or children would tell them. Patty then, did she or didn't she? The evidence is that she did not, for no one has alluded to it in any recognizable way. Never underestimate the power of embarrassment however nor ignore the possibility that she might have told one person or another under some meaningless pledge of secrecy, which would be confusing now to the person so pledged in view of the complicated fact that although divorce proceedings have been completed they still share their valuable New York apartment mainly because they have not yet found suitable accommodations in the city for both of them. There's also the question, which is nobody's business but theirs yet short of which no knowledge is complete, of what she will say the reasons are.

It would be unfair to him if she told them his reasons without giving hers. But even if she told all, there's worry in not knowing how they'd take it—which is why he's been on the watch tonight for looks sneaked at him, glances, signs of reassessment, relabeling. But how safe is that? Though they've been family for seventeen years, he's never known enough to know how fiercely this family of individuals might turn into an expulsive force if they identified him as a foreign body.

The drift of his words narrows like a stream between rocks moving toward Patty as destination with the question he must ask after all, what he should have asked before they came, with his decision to come contingent upon the answer.

Something in the dark far ahead attracts his attention, and he sees he thinks a young woman step onto the sidewalk from the shadow wearing, it is hard to tell, a patch of white, something dark, a flash of unspecifiable nakedness. Coming toward him, making him surge before she disappears, leaving nothing, a trick of his mind or a cat in the street slipping into the bushes. She leaves a dreamy yearning, longing, which produces then in his mind a montage of women floating and circling and swimming around him in filmy and transparent dresses and robes falling back, and skirts opening around luminous thighs, and shorts and bras and halters, with eyes shadowed and gentle smiles and fingers stretching out and touching lightly, and voices soft and sweet, and bellies clothed in silk swaying silently toward him. Familiar friends in William Key's mind. They come vaguely and abstractly to give him the stiffened courage he needs to keep calm and do his work in the world.

Past the hospital his attention is arrested by flickering light on the branches, which explains itself when he turns the corner as the flashing blue and white lights of a police car down the street. The car is parked by itself, just sitting there as if someone had forgotten to turn the flashers off.

He looks a long time, trying to decide whether to investigate. How strange it is, in the safety of this remote place on a dark insulated night, to see this signal of emergency and violent correction flashing away where no one can see it while everyone sleeps. But it's far down the road, and since it's late William ignores it and returns to the house. If it's important enough for him to know, he'll learn about it in time.

––––––––––

ANN REALM: *Diary*

Saturday, May 17. NEWS. TW talk +/- weak. Sigh ah God.

ENTER HW + MC. HW 0, MC bigeyes fuss flap. Cause HW depress:? MC chirp. Hosp jerk Jeffcoat/Truro siege + whocares?

PW snoop TW files. Reject AR help.

ENTER late PK + WK. Q P/W on/off?

DESC HW bad, overweight, sallow, bulge buttons belly, pants hang belt tight below summit paunch, danger drop off, limp worse, cane. Note MC erosion.

PART FOUR

SUNDAY

LUCY WESTERLY: Composed in bed

Sunday morning, Lucy Westerly writes to ask her dead mother the time. Six-thirty, her mother replies, plenty of sleepy time yet.

Lucy reminds her mother of all the people in the house, filling it with energy. If any come early, she must be ahead of them in the kitchen, for guests need breakfast before they can do anything. She'll be busy this morning, one after another, places to set in kitchen and dining room. How many will it be? She counts members of her family and their attachments, two and two and one and one, or one and two and two and one—adding up to what, eight or seven, her brood, her litter? Happily she feels the sun and breeze helping her count and recount the fertility of her life until she remembers why they came. But even that's not so bad if Thomas's stroke heals quickly and the remission holds, making it a joyful reunion.

Austin Wright

ISLAND NEWS: *Correction*

In a news item Thursday about the Sam Truro hostage case, it was incorrectly reported that Truro wounded a man who had approached his house. The correct version is that the man who was wounded has not been identified.

WESTERLY FAMILY: *Collective narrative*

I'm going to church.

That's Patricia, coming into the breakfast room in a flowery dress, where the others have been talking idly without leadership. The narrative is that of a collective precipitate from the observers in the room, the common denominator in each as they wait for an indefinite Other, projected by most minds present as the One who knows what they will do next, but has not told anyone yet. Patty's announcement annoys the collective, but since there was no advocate of another plan, it meets little resistance.

God I totally forgot, Lucy says. We must go to church.

Yow, Melanie says. I've got to get dressed.

You don't have to go, Lucy says.

I always go, Melanie says.

That's Melanie. To the group as a whole Lucy says, No one has to go. It's only the Unitarian church.

Patricia says, I'm going to the Catholic church. The Unitarian isn't Christian.

Since when did you become religious? Philip says.

They won't know you, Lucy says. I don't know any Catholics here. Unless they haven't told me.

Anyone is welcome in the church of her choice, Patricia says. You go yours, I'll go mine.

Ann the good daughter says, I'll go with you, Mother.

Are you going with Patty, William?

I think I'll stay behind.

51

Henry decides. I'll go too, he says.

A miracle, Ann says. He goes upstairs to change into a suit. In the bedroom his wife Melanie says, What are you doing?

I'm going too, Henry says.

You don't believe in God.

What do you know what I believe or don't believe?

When they're ready in the living room, Ann says, You've got so much company, I think I'll stay behind after all. Do you mind, Mother?

Lucy doesn't mind. I don't believe in it, she says apologetically. Thomas and I never went before we came here. The music is so restful. The sociability.

William says, I've changed my mind. I'll go too.

With us or with Patty?

With you.

How nice, William.

Their going splits the collective: Lucy with Melanie, Henry, and William; with Patricia also, who will turn off when they come to the Catholic Church; leaving Philip and Ann behind.

Watching them go down the sidewalk, Ann remarks: What's with Patty and the Catholic church?

She's always looking for radical things to do, Philip says.

THOMAS WESTERLY: As read by Philip

Sunday morning in Thomas's study while the rest of the family except Ann was at church.

MY BIOGRAPHY

How happy and fortunate I was. My happy childhood, good parents, those long years of indolent pleasure, the sunny beach, calm green water rich blue beyond, the summer haze with big philosophical thoughts about time and history in the stillness of the hot morning sand. The holiday river, Hudson with brown Palisade cliffs peeking through the woods like teeth, tar shimmering along the railroad tracks in summer heat, the Day Line excursion steamer skimming upriver, yellow stacks, flags, crowded decks.

On the other hand, involuntary memory like belly cramps in the opera house listening to the greatest singers in the world with gas. The world as seen by Thomas Westerly, Thomas Westerly as seen by the world. The beach against Thomas Westerly's concocted self. Praised for your reliability, your refusal to panic, your steadiness, you had always been wary from the moment you walked into the drugstore holding the hand of your skyscraper father and walked out beside a skyscraper man you thought was your father until you looked up and saw with shock a man with a hat like your father's whom you had never seen before, who knew you no more than you knew him.

My father rejected introspection because of the sour taste in his mouth.

Is it possible not to feel superior to what you were?

Start over.

PHILIP WESTERLY: *What to tell Beatrice*

In the hospital anteroom after lunch, while waiting his turn to visit. Patricia writes a letter, Henry fidgets by the Coke machine.

Weather report: Thursday rain. Friday overcast. Yesterday sun. Today fog. Fog in the village and over the docks while the others were in church and he was in the study reading his father's papers. Make verse.

> Went walking through the village to the docks
> in fog while they enjoyed the clarity
> of church. The fog affirmed the fogginess

of things, post office, house, the fogginess
of faded colors, shallowed depths, ambiguous
boundaries.
Never mind that he had been not walking but reading in
his father's study. Later he went with them to the hospital,
chilly despite his woodsman's jacket, her birthday present.
Tell how the fog

> from the sea made me see the sea it came
> from like the end of time: how the ground swell
> older than life stumbled and died upon
> the dangerous shelter reefs with bloody plumes.
> And how the green wash from aquarium depths
> subdued the timid gardens in the mist:
> the frightened crocuses, the daffodils,
> fruit trees, spare, white and pink and blue denied.
> A dead lobster lay on the garden path.
> How it got there was a mystery.

Give her this scene when it's his turn to visit. The older
man staring where the walls meet the ceiling moves his foggy
eyes occasionally toward his son.
How are you feeling today?
Not so hot.
Pause.
How's Freud?
Freud's fine.
Dreamy silence. A sudden question. Does anybody call
me that?
Call you what?
Ole Doc Westerly.
What?
Ole Doc Westerly.
Did somebody call you that?
That's what I'm asking you.
Not that I know of.
A man came in with a chef's cap and Groucho mask.

Mop and pail. Said "Ole Doc Westerly's agonna die." Three times.

(Philip outraged.) He said that to you?

It stands to reason. I'm ole. Ph.D. Westerly. I must be Ole Doc Westerly.

That's ridiculous, Dad.

Imagine being Ole Doc Westerly.

After a moment he said, It was Sam Truro. He was the one.

He's shut up in his house.

I need to see him. I figured out what's bothering him. I need to explain to him. I need to make amends.

Sam Truro? Amends? Sam Truro's a madman, and you don't owe amends to anyone. Rest easy, Dad, relax, relax.

Eyes move slowly from the corner of the ceiling to the door to the toilet to table with flowers to television set up on the shelf. The television is off.

What?

Did you find my papers?

Yes.

Did you?

I looked at a few.

Did you?

I'm not sure what you want me to do with them.

Do it. Good boy.

———————

HENRY WESTERLY: *Narrative*

His version of the story Abel Jeffcoat told on Sunday afternoon to Thomas, who may or may not have been listening.

This girl, seven or eight or nine, wearing a dim green dress, her hair scraggly, her legs thin, her knees dirty. The door to the house opened, the people watching across the street saw it and called to each other to get attention. Look, the door. The little girl stepped out, scared, on the upper step not knowing what to do. The door shut behind her and she looked back surprised, then at the sidewalk, at the people across the street, as if between two sides in a war.

They heard his hysterical voice from the window: Go on, Dinah. They'll take care of you.

They said she looked like sucking her thumb, though actually her hands were at her sides.

Tell them you're sick.

People asked each other questions. Should we get her? Will he pop us? Call her. Comfort her. Tell her we're friends.

One of the women called out: What's the matter honey dear? Come on over, we'll take care of you.

A man yelled, Hey Truro! You want us to get her, don't shoot. The girl cried. She said, I'm going to throw up. She heaved. They heard the man from the window: Not on the step, dummy! The bushes! They saw her bend over the bushes beside the steps and heave again.

A woman ran forward. Another cried, Liz, he'll shoot you! Liz, who was large, said, I'm going to help that child. She had a voice like a chain saw.

They watched, and three deputies raised rifles aiming at the window, while Liz ran up the walk toward the girl, with no sound from Truro, no sight of him. When the girl saw the fat woman, she wiped her mouth and shrank back. They saw the woman hold out her hands, and heard the cicada buzz of her whisper, though not what she said. The child was afraid, cowering. But after a moment she gave Liz her hand and they came down to the street while the deputies kept their rifles on the windows lest the man try to pick them off.

When they got to the sidewalk, this Liz explained to the deputy Oscar Bedloe, He turned her loose because she got the throwups, poor little thing.

Best take her to the Hospital.

Hospital for a tummy ache? I'll keep her. Hospital can't

give a poor child what she needs.

Haines will want to question her.

She went down the street, holding the girl up by the hand, the girl jumping to keep up. He wants to question her, tell him to see me, she said. Her voice was like a power mower.

PHILIP WESTERLY: *To David and Charles*

In the sleepy hospital afternoon while they take turns visiting. He works at the gummy table where Patty was writing before and wonders whom she was writing to.

Grandmoose is visiting Grandpear and I'm waiting my turn, writing by hand because I don't have my laptop. David can forward to Charles with apologies.

What do you know about Grandpear? I remember him young in Chicago where he was a geology professor. My childhood is Chicago and my Chicago is he. He inhabits the Lakeside and the Midway, the Museum of Science and Industry, the Brookfield Zoo, the Aquarium and Art Institute. He taught me the library and took me into his study and as a result I still feel his presence in the order of the alphabet, in footnotes and endnotes and every outline which steps down from I to A to 1. I feel it in the beauty of the physical text, the sweet smell of galley sheets, the economy of proofreading symbols and words like dele and stet. I learned from him the laws of evidence and the ideal of clear writing: bad writing is not just writing, he said, it's bad thought. Analysis and synthesis, the left and the right, science and the humanities—concepts I tried in my turn to teach you.

His grandsons should know their grandfather's career. Some will tell you he made a mistake to leave teaching for administration. You'll hear things about his presidency at RCU, perhaps you already have. Much of it is biased and unfair. Remember instead his reputation for tact and sympathy. Trust your own impressions to refute the jealous rumors.

He was broad minded and true to his principles.

His troubles came from things beyond his control. A bad appointment to a high position. His Provost, Gene Makrov—I won't go into it. A deficit problem. A university president has to raise money like a glamorous beggar or salesman. It was against Grandpear's nature. The last straw was a faculty strike. He was not fired but resigned on principle because he would not take the line the Board wanted him to take.

He was too sensitive and honest to be an administrator. Too perceptive of the universal ambiguity. Everything I know about morality and character I learned from him. The virtues of civilization? Reason, integrity, sympathy, imagination. Be skeptical of all claims, all assertions, all. Question the culture of the day, but do so with an inquisitive and generous spirit.

PATRICIA KEY: Letter

Begun in the hospital waiting room in the afternoon and finished at night on the sunporch under a shaded lamp.

I intend to tell, though my father's illness may distract them. Don't know if I'll mention you yet. Best to go slow, implicate William first. Then bring you into it, let them get used to that. Only after that will I tell.

Even with my liberal and tolerant family I need to move carefully. My mother is the question (my father's wrapped up in fate). Henry will attack whatever I do. Philip is a snob. George is not here. Ann has the right attitudes, which doesn't mean a thing. They all have the right attitudes. What good is that if a real and living black man shows up and wants into the family? I can't predict. No one will try to embarrass you though. Not intentionally, I mean.

This morning I shocked them by going to Mass. They bribed their consciences by going Unitarian. I haven't told them about God. It will upset them. Spent the afternoon at the hospital. My father glares. His remaining life will be all in the shadow, which is nevertheless as much life to him (with his mind full of the lives he has led) as your life to come on the street or mine with you. What will God do with him? Depends how much allowance He gives to good intention and ignorance.

I object to your reincarnation theory, however. Why do you want to believe that? Myself, I'd rather not, unless you can explain it better. You say my belief requires reincarnation, but I don't understand why.

Is it based on the conservation of souls? Or space: if each living entity has a soul, there's not enough space for all of them, therefore they must share? Or how wasteful to have so many one-shot souls, like those of small babies or fetuses who die with no time to develop. Or is it a question of what to do with the souls of the dead while they're waiting around for heaven, so you figure they must go into new bodies? What worries me about reincarnation is what happens to all the recycled souls if the world keeps getting worse? It is getting worse you know. Another thing. My father's soul when he dies goes into somebody else. Who then will I meet when heaven comes and my reunion with my loved ones, and they've all changed into other people? Or animals. Or is it that you don't believe in heaven and that's what your theory is about?

I'm not trying to discredit, I just want to understand.

Bedtime in a corner of the sunporch where we've been assigned to sleep (in separate cots), writing in a little circle of light surrounded by dark. I've been listening to Henry, back from a walk. He's obsessed with a local crime: a man locked his house and took his wife and child hostage, while the police sit outside not knowing what to do. William is out too, probably looking for something that doesn't exist.

If the family disapproves of you, to hell with them.

HENRY WESTERLY: *Narrative*

He has two guns, a carbine and an automatic revolver with six bullets. He sits in the deep chair in the living room by the fireplace—a chair that reclines flat out—carbine on the table by his right arm, revolver in his lap. His wife Georgette and his children, Dinah and Roger, sit opposite. Each is hand-cuffed to a chain which is padlocked to the radiator stem. They move their hands about, stand up and stretch, but they can't move away, either to each other or toward him. In this way they spend the days and also—with some modifica-tions—the nights.

After some time has passed, Roger, Dinah, or Georgette must go to the bathroom: I have to, Daddy. I can't hold out much longer. So he gets out of his chair with the revolver in one hand, the key to the handcuff in the other, comes over and inserts key in lock, protecting himself by putting the gun to his child's, or wife's, head. Warning: Hold still, I have to get the key. These are tricky moments, the coordination of turning the key while holding the gun ready, yet as the hours pass and turn into days he becomes more adept, while they, nervous about his coordination, take care not to upset him.

One wonders, are these children, this wife, really afraid he will shoot—their daddy, this husband—if they don't do what he says? According to Dinah they are afraid because he keeps saying he will. Don't get thinking I'm afraid to, he says, and they know, because he is their daddy, what he says, he'll do. His wife Georgette tells him he is a bastard and a son of a bitch, but she too does what he says and advises the children, in fact screams at them, to obey. Your daddy is crazy, she says. The son of a bitch is bats, you do just what he says.

When one goes to the bathroom, he keeps the door open and stands guard with the carbine lest anyone pick that mo-ment for a diversion. Relieved, the child comes back, and once again holding the revolver to her head, he locks her to the chain.

According to Dinah, they eat regular meals three times a day. Georgette cooks out of cans or serves frozen dinners long stored in the pantry and freezer. She sneers, What happens when we run out? His answer is calm. If we're still here, he says, we'll call the supermarket. She laughs at him. You'll see, he says. They'll deliver when I tell them to.

He releases her to cook. He props himself in a chair between living room and kitchen, where he can see both the children handcuffed to the radiator, and his wife moving around between the sink, the shelves, and the stove. He uses the carbine for this. Does the thought occur to him that she might throw a pan of boiling grease at him? He keeps enough distance, with his rifle ready. She makes the meals as simple and quick as she can, and when they're ready, he releases the children and they sit at the dining room table. They sit there with the wife, and he sits on a high stool at the end of the room, overlooking them with his carbine. He has his own meal on a shelf next to him, taking care as he eats never to relax his watchfulness. When he drinks his milk, his other hand touches the gun, always ready, and he looks over the top of the glass as he drinks.

After the meal, she washes the dishes—again under watch—and when she is finished he handcuffs her back in her place. In the long intervals between meals, he keeps the television on. He has put it against the wall between him and them, and they watch the talk shows, soaps, sitcoms, news, and commercials together.

After the first night, perhaps because the children got so whimpery in their discomfort, he had them bring down the two canvas cots from the attic. This according to Dinah. They set up the cots next to the chairs where they were handcuffed. After this they could lie on the cots or sit in the chairs as they preferred, while remaining handcuffed. At night when they settled down to sleep, he would handcuff their feet to-

gether as an additional precaution. His wife says, You son a
bitch. She says, You've got yourself a divorce, mister, and
that's not the least of it. She says, You just see what you've
got on your hands when we get out. He grimaces and tightens his lips. All the more reason not to let you go, he says.

He has the whole house rigged with burglar alarms—
every door, every window. To prevent anyone sneaking up
from outside. Must have put in the alarms beforehand. Makes
you wonder what his wife thought, his neighbors too, and
the hardware man, making his house a fortress on this sup-
posedly peaceful island, last outpost of harmonious law-abid-
ing civilization. With what excuses did he justify this
paranoia? One thing it proves: he knew what he was going
to do before he did it. The burglar alarm lets him sleep too,
gun in his lap in the reclining chair and hostages handcuffed
hand and foot, knowing it will wake him if anyone sneaks
up. What if they come from two sides? Suppose they come
from both sidewalk and woods, creeping up to both doors,
windows as well? The burglar siren will sound and give him
time, if not to shoot the invaders, to shoot his hostages—
which is what hostages are for. Just what they want to prevent. So he sits, sure how well he has guarded himself against
threats. By now they've been at it more than three days—
seventy-two hours of siege. Despite his arrangements for sleep,
he has grown haggard, his cheeks are sallow and thin, his
eyes ringed with black, dark, heavy. His mouth has the sag
of despair and bitterness. He waits and waits. Though he
has made every arrangement for sleep, he can't do it.

He waits in the perfection of his arrangements. His wife
has quit her threats. She too is haggard, face stretched, lines
deepened. She does what he tells her to, and depends on her
eyes to remind him what she has quit saying. When Dinah
got sick, she said, Your child is sick, are you going to let her
die? And screamed at him. She screeched as loud as she could
screech, and he picked up the gun and pointed it at her fore-

head, trying to say, Shut up! and there was a moment when the children thought he was going to shoot her right there. Then Dinah threw up again, which distracted both parents, and he unlocked her handcuff and took her to the door and pushed her out. Go on, he said, go get someone to take care of you.

He has communicated with the outside world once or twice by shouting out the window, but generally he avoids this because of the danger of a sharpshooter trying for a quick one to the brain. He makes his demands mostly over the telephone, talking to the secretary at the bank where he used to work. He knows his demands are ridiculous—he must know, how could he not? Suppose they do give him money and safe conduct—what would he do then? Would he know what to do? Would he be satisfied? So he sits and waits while his wife sullenly watches, no longer repeating what she used to say: This is the end, brother. You really blew it this time, man. As he waits he thinks, trying to remember, if he can, what he originally had in mind.

The above is Henry Westerly's reconstruction as he walks the harbor Sunday night, made on the basis of conversations and gossip in the shops and streets during the day just past. He thinks of it as writing, but he doesn't know who to write it for.

PHILIP WESTERLY: To his father in the hospital

You didn't say what to do if others want to help. Last night I let Ann join me because I couldn't think how to stop her. Tonight Patricia too, and now we're three searching your papers for whatever you want to protect us from.

To himself: Why am I scared? Secrecy implies scandal, bribes, vulgar affairs. But what is the danger here? I know my father. Forty-six years established should survive the shock of a secret file. Yet the father I loved was an image always correctable against the original while the original lived. What will prevent some escalating deformation if that original dies?

There are many reasonable and innocent grounds for secrecy. A man in Thomas's place, professional and patriarchal, would have confidences. The real question, Philip, is this. What's wrong with you that needs such perfection in a father?

———————

THOMAS WESTERLY: As read by Philip
Sunday evening, while Ann and Patricia also read.

MY BIOGRAPHY

The present moment (watching the keys on the keyboard making words while out the window on a hazy recently raining midday a white pickup truck has been sitting for a long time in my neighbor's drive) is all memory kept alive by the future it contains. My neighbor's drive, saturated with future because I know that unless I die or am called to lunch, I will continue to see it just the same five minutes from now. Whereas my memory of Circle Avenue where I was born has no future in it, so that's past. Elimination of the future is what turns present into past.

My biography, then. Let it remember the future that kept the present present in the past. Where can I find this past future? In people. In places. That's where the future lives if you can remember it.

But in a person the future is adversary, an opposing consciousness you have to reckon with. A place invites, a stage where things will happen. So write my biography about places, free of people, free of time, a memoir of futures.

In this present present the future sputters in my screen. I am sixty-four years old, said to be at the top of my career. I sit at my computer by my study window, looking at the street on a bright and hot day. The haze has burned off. The pickup truck is gone. Parked cars reflect the sun in a knify silver glare. A man in shorts has the back of his compact station wagon open, working on it (he's gone now too). A small breeze stirs leaves, I hear a sparrow or two (but the birds are quieter now, the molting season, all birds are depressed, they say). The papers on my desk flutter. I am wearing shorts, to which I changed late this morning after pulling vines and weeds. I have poison ivy on my arms, and the remains of a bee sting itching at the base of my thumb.

THOMAS WESTERLY: *As read by Patricia*

Self-evaluation:

My primary identity has always been geologist teacher appropriate for a candidate high university administrative. Institute of learning learning learning the highest value reading and study nature and man. Regard writing understand the professoriat, faculty inside out, faculty mission, the Pursuit and Transmission of Knowledge, what men (and women) men and women, people, have learned, what they know: science. Have known: history. Thought: philosophy. Felt: art. Science leavened by humanities.

My putting this academic devotion to intellect first not disregardful of the executive importance of university presidency, or that I am ignorant disregardful of an institutional institution, a great organization of a number of complex and diverse. A business. My experience as Provost, following experience as Dean, began experience as Department Chair. Surprising even myself of native talent, which have used native intelligence to develop, organization, staff, people skills. People skills.

Every member of the staff, from the top down to the lowest, janitorial, secretarial. Custodial, bookkeeping, long range projections.

On that particular occasion, not to boast but simply by way of, I gave orders to money raising, as said the whole job of a university president a salesman, obviously a presidency has more important duties of leadership such as I have suggested in the first part of this but clearly not to negate the importance of which I believe my experience shows I am capable of and willing to perform to my highest capacity

---

TESTIMONIALS TO THOMAS WESTERLY: As read by Ann

Just to thank you for your support beyond the line of duty I never expected.

Please forgive a mere student from writing a letter for the extraordinary kindness which caused a total turn around of my career prospects and choices.

He came, he saw, he understood.

Misunderstood. Quite contrary to the common stereotype of university brass, intelligent and understanding.

Lord God, how you'll be missed.

I speak from the bottom of my heart.

I have to tell you no one in this otherwise rather dreary little university can match you, you alone made this worthwhile to me and raised above the level of the ordinary.

Do not believe the bad things people have said about you. I know better.

I write this from the bottom of my heart.

Honor, respect, admiration, even, dare I say this? love.

From the depths of my heart.

Who taught the beauty of the rocky earth on which we play.

Misunderstood.

Hardly what you'd expect in this academic jungle pit of vipers cobras and rattlesnakes, a mongoose among the moccasins.

Plumb the deep mysteries of the heart, many thanks and may you long prosper and prosper long in your island of retirement.

————————

ANN REALM: *Diary*

Sunday, May 18. DESC fog out reluctant clouds low dark damp, air = sea.

Church goers w/o AR. PK Cath, news? PK = PK. HW waddle. "Waddle" = bloat fat depress.

Lunch LW dizzy so many children forget why.

Absent GW doghouse. LW: Canada, Maytime woods? Brr. LW mod world: "If George camp, + nice young lady?" *Nice*: afterthought. Protection. LW adapt 70 yrs ago inconceiv. Learn youth 20 yrs, unlearn 50, imposs. Nice young lady = wanton hussy whore share GW sleepbag vs healthy still budding woods, mountain streams, moral fish, good moral trout and bass. Compare PW/me learn/unlearn in 20 + 20 yrs, if GW "nice young" not lady but man? If say GW + n.y.m. see LW relief ("oh well if with friend") versus own numb dreary tired usual.

Hospital alternate visits tho TW talk everybody 0 except PW: Old Doc W, assault/dream? Rankle papers, get busy there.

PAPER SNOOP: PW + AR OK then PK nose butt OK OK fam peace, read[3] hunt skeleton. Find HUSHNEWS, danger. TW nar (Code: *Killdog*) scandal? Do? dele? hide? steal? OK steal tomorrow. X PW.

PW fear, show letter/sons tribute TW like no brothers/ sisters, TW perfect Fount Virt, risky PW danger fall, what say? + fulsome papers Wow[3]. Well, hide & pat back, okay, no blame, stick together, poor PW need TW, need bleed, not know need bleed, bros sis mutual boat.

PART FIVE

MONDAY

THOMAS WESTERLY: As composed by Lucy
Monday morning in the car

About this drive you are taking around the Island without me. Because of the change in the weather. How the
rain last night, blurring the streetlamps as the wind blew.
Which looked like the end until this morning when the rain
stopped, and you saw how clear after the cold front, sharp
and distinct the trees and roofs and the glimpse from upstairs of the harbor between the maples, and the white trim
on the houses across the harbor. On the grass before breakfast and the bud-green like a veil with tulips, you took the
weather for a sign of how much better I am, which is why I
write to you now.

Even Henry has hope, the weather joy driving you around
the Island without me. Past the flower trellises, lobster sheds,
mansions whose widows are remembered in rooftop balco-
nies. You forgot me, but I forgive you, with Ann driving and
you, and Patricia in back with morose Henry and Melanie.

Philip didn't come, nor William. The road joins Shoal Point Road at the junior high school, then by the shingled windmills and golf course to the sandy plateau, with crests of naked sand and miles of dune grass above the beach. Tell me how the sea trembles in the irritating light. From the lighthouse down the back side of the Island, miles of beach facing the ocean, full of history and pre-history drowned in the unbroken sea between here and Europe and Africa. While on their own beaches Europeans and Africans watch you.

Tell me also your return across the middle island past the reservoir and scrub woods to the crest where you see the ferry with its yellow stack turning the buoy and you skirt the town back to Shoal Point Road past the Truro house with a single policeman in a parked car, and into town past the old hotel and the hospital where I can't see you because the road is on the other side from my room. You write this letter from me not because you are thinking of me and everywhere you go you hear me in the cold frontal air but because if I die I will forget it all myself.

Philip came out to meet you when you got back. You are wanted at the hospital.

PHILIP WESTERLY: *Anticipating a memoir*

We six march to the hospital, two abreast through spring streets by lilacs and hyacinth, a bright morning with a cold breeze, wrapping sweaters and spring coats not enough to keep warm. Interpreting the nurse's telephone voice, You folks'n come over soon's you can come over.

So to the hospital, the plain brick rectangle facing the street, the automatic doors. The usual information desk and usual elevator, yesterday's waiting room with the table and the vending machines, to stop at the nurse's station for news. Plump Miss Hansen down the hall, Oh here you are, hi there. What's the matter, is he worse? Mr. Key's with him.

The room shaded from the bright morning. My father lying in the bed on his side, back turned. William Key in an armchair by the window with a newspaper, looks up. I went for a walk and decided to drop in, he says. This looks like it.

HERMAN EASTCASTLE, M.D.: What to tell the family in the waiting room

Hours, maybe minutes. You should have been called before. Someone lapsed in her responsibility. That won't do.

Not that it would make a difference. He's been unconscious since one o'clock this morning. Someone should have told you.

Last night about midnight, he got out of bed. Got up and went for a walk. Right out of the hospital he went, right out into the street. No one noticed. He unhooked himself from the IV and climbed out of bed. Went out into the hall, escaped and was never missed. It's not supposed to happen. He got past the nurse's station, where was everybody? Midnight, three people on duty, and nobody saw him. Tending to patients in the middle of the night? Coffee break, I don't know. Reading the comic strips most likely. Down in the elevator and right out the front door, nobody to stop him. No one's at the information desk at that hour. Maybe the security guard was having a coffee break too.

A policeman brought him back, one of those men watching the Truro house, which is where he went. Why he went there rather than home is a mystery I won't attempt to crack. The policeman noticed him in his hospital tunic, not even a bathrobe. Confused. Didn't answer questions. The policeman got him into the car, no resistance as if glad to be told what to do. The policeman brought him back. No one in the lobby, but he found the security guard, in a neighborhood bar I presume, who got a nurse, who was doubtless waking up from a nap. He hadn't even been missed. They put him in

70

a wheelchair and he passed out. Would have fallen but the guard caught him. He's been unconscious ever since.

Before he passed out he apologized. They tell me he apologized a lot. He apologized to the policeman and to the security guard and to the nurse putting him into the chair just before he conked. I'm sorry. I don't mean to put you out. Sorry to be such a trouble. That's what they tell me.

They called me and I came over. There was nothing I could do. It won't be long.

MELANIE CAIRO: *Dialogue*

They're two at a time in Thomas Westerly's room. Now it's Henry and Philip and I in the waiting room.

Henry: Twice. Twice he went to see Truro and twice he got a stroke. Which was the cause, which the effect? Did he get the stroke because he went to Truro or did he go to Truro because the stroke was coming on? What did Truro mean to him?

Philip: Looks like you'll never know.

Henry: He meant something to him.

Philip: Which you'll never know.

Henry: Are you on my back?

Philip: You never could accept fatality.

Henry: I have a better sense of fatality than anybody in this family.

Philip (*laughs*): Do you remember this, Henry? Riding out to the Indiana Dunes on a hot summer day, looking forward to swimming. Dad was telling you about death. You didn't like it. Everybody dies, he said. *Everybody dies.* I remember him. Every living thing: bird, dog, lion in the zoo, the great elephant, the whales in the sea, the flicker killed by the cat, the flies on the wall, mosquitoes on your arm, squirrels in the street. And people. Old people. Young people, if they don't die young they grow old and then die. Well now,

71

you thought that was unfair. There ought to be exceptions for good people. You wanted to know if I would die. Yes Philip will die, he said. But Mommy won't die, you said. Alas, she too, he said. And you too? you said. I too, he said. *When?* you said.

Henry: I don't remember any such thing.

Philip: I do. I won't let you die, you said. Oh but I will, he said. You don't remember?

Henry: No.

Philip: You saw the logical conclusion. *I* won't die, you said. Sorry, no exceptions, he said. You asked, isn't there anything we can do about it? It's how things are, he said. After spring there's summer, then fall and winter. Then spring again. Does that mean you'll come back, you asked? No, he said, it means you'll grow up and have your own children. And someday you'll tell them the same thing. I'll never tell them a thing like that, you said.

Henry: So I never had any goddamn children. You're making it all up.

Even now Henry thought he was being put down like the little brother and was probably right.

Suddenly there was a blaze of light exposing everybody's skeleton, and Dr. Eastcastle came in.

Chorus: Oh Doctor Eastcastle, there you are.

Eastcastle: He won't last the day. But he doesn't feel a thing. It's the best way for him to go.

RUPERT NEWTON: News as read by Henry in the waiting room

The Sam Truro case entered a new phase Sunday afternoon with Truro's demand that a former handyman and schoolbus driver be brought to meet with him. The shy scholarly-looking bank teller who has been holding his wife and child hostage telephoned police late today to announce his new conditions. Apparently withdrawing his previous request for money and a safe conduct, he asked now "for one thing only," a meeting with a man whose name he said was Angel Vertebrate. The Vertebrate referred to is a former schoolbus driver, believed to have left the Island some weeks ago.

Police said Truro would not say why he wanted to meet with Vertebrate, except that he wanted to negotiate his demands through him. His words, as quoted by Sheriff Haines, were, "You get him and let me talk to him." When informed that Vertebrate had left the Island, Truro replied, "Find him and bring him back. I won't negotiate with nobody but him."

Police sources have no knowledge of a connection between Vertebrate and Truro. Vertebrate, a mainlander who came to the Island about two years ago, is believed to have worked in Gordon's Hardware, and he drove the schoolbus last year. His address while on the Island is unknown nor is it known when he left or why. Asked if they intended to track him down, a police source said, "It's pretty hard to find somebody you don't know where they're at but we'll try."

―――――――

LUCY WESTERLY: *To Thomas*

When I came in after our drive around the Island, you were on your side, head raised, back to us. The nurse said you were unconscious, not asleep. The difference is that you can be wakened from sleep but not from unconsciousness. I've seen you asleep often, your hair which used to be dark and wavy but I got used to it white and thin with scalp showing through.

The nurse said you'd been like this since she came on at seven. The doctor showed up and said it won't be long. You don't feel a thing, be glad for that. A matter of hours, maybe minutes. I don't know if I was relieved.

All morning by your bed. Others took turns, not I. You didn't notice or couldn't say if you did. Two nurses turned you over. They pulled the curtain and one had a big ass pushing the curtain when she bent, and they grunted like a sack of coal, huffing and leverage, and when they came out you were facing us, propped with mouth open, eyes closed, a long slow rasping breath, making it easy to believe you were dying, though not easy.

I tried to tell you I was there if you needed me, though I suppose your thoughts were gone. If you were not having nightmares, you were thinking about file cabinets or politics or Mother Goose and the candlestick.

I told myself Thomas is dying and this is a big moment, but it didn't seem that big, like I had resigned myself long ago. For forty-eight years I've known one of us would die first and I used to wonder who. With both of us healthy, no serious illnesses, no heart attacks or cancer, all the talk about old age and care was hypothetical until three months ago. When we moved to the Island I thought maybe we were destined to live to a good old age. I really did.

I never did know, still don't though I'll find out soon, how grief stricken I'd be if you kicked off first. Not to disparage our marriage, but I thought there might be some ratio between grief and relief. How much? Seventy-thirty? Eighty-twenty? Maybe even fifty-fifty, it's so hard to know. Don't mind, old friend, for I suspect you felt the same. We knew each other well, and though there was love, it wasn't all love, as you know.

Lately it's different, though. The old issues are dead and not interesting anymore. I'm sorry I criticized you. You criticized me too long ago. Somewhere, at some point, criticism stopped. I hardly noticed. It happened about the same time that we began to share our most humiliating physical problems, also without noticing. Bowels. Smells. Itches. Hemorrhoids. There's little we don't know about each other.

The death that do us part caught me by surprise after all. You're seventy-two. Your open mouth, faint and weak breath, closed eyes frowning, not feeling a thing, you did look like a dying old man. That's what you looked like to the rampant young nurses in and out. Perhaps also to your children and certainly their mates gathered to watch you go. By any objective standard. Not to me though. You looked like Thomas disguised. Thin white for thick dark hair, chalk whitewashed on the naive pretty face. But the shape of your shoulder unchanged for forty years gave the disguise away and made it impossible to believe.

The nurses turned you back again. The doctor returned. A matter of minutes. Eleven thirty. I wondered about lunch. I wasn't hungry but I would be soon, and the others would be. The question was whether a matter of minutes was enough minutes for shifts to the cafeteria and back in time.

The nurse snipped the IV tube. They were letting you go. I didn't protest. Did you want me to?

Were you aware who was in the room? I guess not. At ten after twelve, I looked at my watch. I saw it first. Barely perceptible like the poem about the good man passing mildly away while sad friends argue has the breath gone yet, the sign of your shoulder, lift and fall, which I had been watching. It stopped. I asked Ann, whispering because it was a big thought. Maybe, she said. Henry, Not yet. Melanie, Yes. Call the nurse. The others from the waiting room, Patty, Philip, William, stood looking along the wall, while that shoulder rose slowly once more and paused even as the cheerful little plump nurse leaned over you, and the doctor entered, looked, nodded, and left.

Before you died I went and touched you. You probably didn't notice. I thought if I don't, I'll never touch you again. On the bony shoulder, then the emaciated hip. The forty-eight years moved like an electric current. Your back was turned. I thought of kissing you, but in front of the others that would have been a display. So I put my hand on your shoulder and hip and the forty-eight years passed back and forth between us.

I looked again after you died. You frowned, your eyebrows dark, mouth open. I thought how rare to die with eyes closed, then realized the doctor or nurse had closed them when leaning over to see.

My grandmother, my father, and my mother all died with the mouth open. Each time the time ended and new time began, but nothing like when I saw you looking just like them. I thought, You are dead. The words kept saying it: Thomas is dead. Repeating and repeating, stuck, trying to make something of it. Then someone added the number forty-eight years. That helped get them moving again, since the finiteness of that number reduced to zero the infinitude it had been. My whole life was changed in that instant moth-like from life into episode. My marriage was reduced to an episode. That was a help, to be able to say that, better than being stuck in the same words all the time, at least.

So I decided to write and tell you. I expect to feel grief, for the notion that you and I are a finished episode will be hard to bear. It hasn't hit me yet though and in the meanwhile there's the house and the visitors and all the business I have to attend to.

PATRICIA KEY: *To Pete Arena*

Just finished watching my daddy die. Another stroke. We took a ride around the Island, which is one of the conventional things we do when we visit. We were riding around the Island when he was dying and we didn't know it.

He was on his way when we got there and never woke up in mortal body again. I watched for several hours to observe his struggle with mortality, but I couldn't find much hard evidence. He made chalky sounds and crackling noises. Death rattle, I thought, but it sounded like phlegm in his throat.

Nurses turned him over. I studied his face, which showed discomfort or eternal agony, depending on your point of view. Mouth open for oxygen or God or both: Dear God, help me breathe the oxygen of heaven. Like that. Like birth, the shift from umbilical nourishment to outer air, only quieter.

I thought dying people struggled more. My cat and dog both got a case of the shakes before they passed away. Which really is like birth if dogs and cats have souls, which I haven't decided about yet. So I was waiting for Daddy to scream like Ivan Ilyich or Dean Harrison of the graduate school. But it was quiet, how gradually he faded, the breathing subsiding slowly until there was none.

I considered three possibilities: One, if the soul eased out of the body peacefully because he was a good man despite his faults, God sparing him agony as a reward. But I never approved of God punishing and rewarding in this world, however much He may have done in the past when His lessons had to be taught. If the reward is given in heaven, why should it also be given on earth?

But maybe the agony was inside where we couldn't see. Sealed off in his mind, pains and visions and horrors. Why do people think dying in one's sleep is peaceful? How can it be when sleep is so unpeaceful? Dreams are horrible things full of life, especially dreams about dying. I hope I won't die in my sleep, considering what a thicket of wilderness my sleep usually is.

Third and worst, if the stillness of Daddy's passing meant there was no passing. No birth pangs, because no birth. If only selected souls are saved, and Daddy was denied because he had no faith, which he didn't.

I tried to find with my nerves some manifestation of liberated soul in the room. I found nothing. Of course I shouldn't. That's the essence of soul: it's immaterial. If it's separated from body it should not be perceivable by another body like me. So be not distressed. But that's not wholly true, for faith depends upon intuition beyond body. Intuition of my soul and others transcends the body, how else could I be so sure of these intangible things?

Meanwhile, your theory of transferable souls. If Daddy's soul left his body in the quiet moment of his death, by your view it went (or soon will go) into another body at the beginning of life. That's the procedure, right? It's Daddy's soul until he dies; then it migrates and becomes someone else. When this new person grows up he (or she) will have no memory of having been Daddy. That's the norm, no residue of memory remains. Otherwise your reincarnation of souls would have been recognized as fact centuries ago.

So, my question. If Daddy's soul on leaving his body really does forget everything and takes over its next body with memory washed clean, how can you call it Daddy's? If it can't remember him, why isn't it just another new soul? In which case, Daddy's soul isn't immortal at all, it's dead. But if that's true, why talk about souls at all? Seems to me your reincarnation theory gets rid of immortality. If Daddy no longer exists in his soul, how does your doctrine differ from those who think life dies with body in the atheistic void?

I know you have an answer, but until you explain, I prefer to think of Daddy's soul as uniquely his and let it slip gently out of his body into eternal disembodied life *as Daddy*. In full possession of his mind, his thoughts, his memories, everything that endures, stripping away only the transient earthly desires and fears. And to tell the truth, now that a little time has passed, I realize that I did indeed feel him rise quietly out of his body, which was shrunken finally into a pile of old bones and dried guts. I heard him rise, felt him look around, almost saw him turn and whisper or breathe on each of us with a promise of future reunion and reconciliation. Okay?

Austin Wright

ANN REALM: *What to tell the survivors*

In the room where we went and waited and watched, talking like any other day, a natural part of time, where I saw the external manifestation. The sunny room full of unmentionable history was too simple to understand. The bed where hundreds of strangers had lived or died, with a curtain rack for strangers' bathing, dressing, bedpans. A movable hospital table for trays, thermometers, cotton swabs. Though it was unlikely that a majority of his predecessors had died here, some certainly had. His propped head, unresponsive to us in changing groups, Mother, Philip, Henry, Melanie, Patty, William, and myself.

The damage inside was severe, communications ruined in the flooded part of the brain and reduced oxygen flow aggravating the damage. Memories still flashed, but cut off from each other, available only if you had a way to get across the barriers. If you did you could probably still find Chicago and River City University. Names and places, students and colleagues, enemies who forced him to resign, friends who supported him. Such names therein might ignite flashes in the chambers, the walls would light up for a moment. Likewise pictures of the Island and house and harbor. Me too and the others, Lucy on her throne, still present despite the sleeping exterior silence. You'd find everything illuminated by light of the blood, but the chambers were inundated. The memories were sinking under the water like china and silverware in the sunken *Andrea Doria*. If like Philip you wanted to ask a question, it would be hard in that drowning machinery to find a dry switch that would work.

The increasing faintness of breath meant less space in the lungs open to the air. Less oxygen was available to circulate and what there was circulated more slowly. The brain struggled to keep its lifelong treasury of memory lit, but as the available oxygen diminished the light faded. The screens on which Thomas's memories were projected dissolved in the liquid, and the slides containing the images shriveled up and disappeared. The chamber walls collapsed like soaked cardboard. A vicious circle developed in which the weakening power to breathe weakened further the power to breathe. This weakened in turn the power of the heart to move the already almost inert blood, allowing the flood to rise still higher.

At some point in the morning the flood reached the oldest memory cells, and the brain shut down, curling up like a fetus not knowing what it was. When the flood reached the breathing centers it caused a short in the machine's rhythm. I don't know which faltered first, the breathing circuit or the heart circuit, but their mutual faltering reinforced itself and both circuits stopped. Unfed, the heart could pump no more, and despite seventy-two years of habit, it stopped.

At once everywhere in the body the sluggish already useless blood stood still, and in an instant a change spread through the whole organization. Universal panic, every part, every cell, groping for sustenance, and finding none, giving up. This was the moment of Thomas's death.

The fine assemblage fell now into a clump of parts, a simulacrum of the corporation that had sparked with spirit and personality for seventy-two years. I looked at him dead, a statue of who had been there. I knew he would not stay in that condition long. Rot began when the life stream stopped moving. Decay inside was already dismantling the parts.

Who was this Thomas who died? Suddenly he was past tense, all past, nothing but past. I found myself quietly out of the continent of time in which I had lived and into a new one where nothing had yet happened to give it history, and everything was strange and empty.

The decay of external memory which he imparted to others has already begun like the body, and the only tangible thing is a thin trail of writings he left behind. These like a track in the woods, nothing in themselves, good only for the way they stimulate the hunter trying to reconstruct what went by once. Not sure I want to do that, since some of the tracks are bloody. Most likely I'll have to cover these and invent the creature myself. I won't have even that chance though, if I go to London and let Philip hide his writings in a safe.

PHILIP WESTERLY: *Anticipating a memoir*

Back of his head with what Ann called its fore-and-aft shape (remember that shape going to the University when he was young and jaunty), hair white, short. Go around the bed with Lucy to look. Open mouth, closed eyes, hairy eyebrows, a frown. Look at Father trying to think no Father there. No effort to think it, for though he's evidently there evidently he's not.

His body a photograph of the moment of death. At that moment his mouth was open and he frowned the discomfort of his last few days. Left on his face by life leaving.

All the recent turmoil exhaled from the open mouth. The last four months remembered in the open mouth, to the hospital and home and again and back, to prolong normality with breakfast lunch and dinner which he could not eat, fever and pain. More than that. The turmoil of his retirement expelled and exhausted in that gape. Turmoil not known as turmoil until expelled. Brought up and expelled from all old time, exhaled from all the past, the controversy, the presidency, the dead speeches, letters, meetings, ceremonies. The unknown turmoil vacated from youth before my time, invented by my imagination from clues and vented through the mouth like an echo from a vault.

Lucy bends to touch the dead shoulder. Already it's getting cold. When she turns around, tears. The surprise of not realizing this is the time for tears. Not knowing what time it is except that it's precarious, like an overloaded rowboat.

PHILIP WESTERLY: List

1. Hospital: a) Dr. Eastcastle, death certificate. b) Hospital depository for belongings. c) Thank nurse.

2. Bank. Glassman: will, trust fund, safe deposit box, savings and checking accounts. Make appointment, Mother's income, what she needs to know or do.

3. Church. Minister (Dawson?). Service, dates (Friday?). Ceremony, music, speakers?

4. Undertaker (Gregory Morticians, OK per Dawson). Church service, lot bought. Don't get suckered on the coffin. Visitation (Thursday?). Embalming (embalming?) included, taken for granted. Limousines. Get estimate now. Gravestone? Mr. Cage in The Marble Halls. Check, does Gregory collect body from hospital?

5. Home, notifications, telephone the VIPs. Who's a VIP? University. Where's George? If you can't reach him, to hell with him.

6. Call Beatrice tonight. Fly, bring girls, important for them. Let Beatrice call boys, pay their way. (That means she'll have to tell Louisa. Okay? Would Louisa come? Don't ask, but okay.)

7. Older generations: call and put Mother on. Uncle Carl, probable. Aunt Edna not (Florida at her age). Nor Fred.

8. Patty and Ann, call your own children.

9. Island Inn, reserve X rooms and beds for overflow.

10. Others: Cousin Charlie (Cleveland: Alzheimers?). Is Cousin Marie still living? If so, where? Dr. Balsam in River City. Ask mother re Makrov. Island friends: Jeffcoat. Grummond.

11. River City News. Island News. New York Times.

12. Obituary.

————

Austin Wright

THE WESTERLY FAMILY: *Obituary*

Thomas Westerly, geologist and former President of River City University in Ohio, died today at Island Center Hospital at the age of 72. Dr. Westerly had been a resident of the Island for six years.

A familiar figure in the social and political life of this community, Dr. Westerly was born Jan. 2, 1922, in Sherwood Forest-on-Hudson, N.Y. His father Philip Westerly was professor of biology at Columbia University. His mother, Ann Jenks, was the daughter of the astronomer Oswald Jenks. As a boy Dr. Westerly anticipated a career as a scientist and studied geology at Dartmouth before earning his doctorate at Chicago after the war. He taught geology at Chicago for many years before going to River City University (Ohio) in 1968, where he was named chairman of the geology department in 1972, dean of the college in 1978, provost in 1983 and president of the university in 1985. He retired in 1987 and moved here in 1988.

Specializing in paleontology, Westerly was noted for his fossil studies in the southwest Ohio region. As an administrator he was admired for his sympathy and interest in the concerns of students. Noted for his liberal policies, he supported the right of students to bring unconventional speakers to campus and defended their artistic freedom against censorship in the community. He advanced the cause of racial integration and worked to improve the situation of faculty women. He strengthened the University's Liberal Arts college by hiring internationally known scholars, and by developing a climate of reward for research and good teaching.

He believed strongly in humanistic learning, especially in a technological society. He regretted that his duties never allowed him to write a book, though he produced several significant articles. A sensitive and inquisitive man, he also wrote unpublished essays of a philosophic and poetic kind.

This was his hobby and he encouraged his children to write whenever and however they could. He believed thought was possible only through writing and reading and deplored the television culture which he considered to be the chief threat to civilization as we know it.

In his retirement on the Island he distinguished himself as a member of the Library Board, of the P.T.A. though he had no children of school age, of the Nature Society, which profited from his professional expertise, and the Board for Clean Beaches. Though shy and reticent, he was particularly liked by the younger generation as organizer of church picnics.

He is survived by his wife, the former Lucy Sycamore; his brother Carl, retired professor of English at Stanford known for his work on the novelist Fisk Purser; his sister the late Beth Coates, professor of biology at West Carolina University; his aunt, Edna Forsyth of Sarasota, Fla.; his children, Philip, an ophthalmologist, of Ithaca, N.Y.; Ann Realm, wife of the journalist and international correspondent Frank Realm, lately of Boston, Mass. and now of London, England; Patricia Key of New York City; Henry, a social worker from Stony Hill, Ohio; and George, a free lance writer, author of "Jungle Depths," who lives in Ontario. He is survived also by thirteen grandchildren.

Visitation will be on Thursday evening from 8 to 10 at Gregory House. The funeral will be Friday at 2 in the Unitarian Church.

Written by Philip Westerly, Henry Westerly, Patricia Key, and Lucy Westerly. Sent to the Island News, The New York Times, *the* River City Post, *the* River City Enquirer, *and the* Sherwood Forest Bell.

Austin Wright

HENRY WESTERLY: *To God*

As you know, before dinner we gathered in the living room to compose the obituary. It was Philip who remembered to do it. He thought we should collaborate, and he got the card table and we sat around it, three of us, Philip, Mother, and I. Melanie and Patty were in the kitchen cooking the dinner, to spare Mother. Melanie was glad to stay out of it, but Philip called Patty in every so often to take a look and make suggestions.

The scribe was Philip, who proposed most of the phrasing (worrying a lot about newspaper style and subordinate clauses), writing it down and reading to us, so that we could make contributions. He was concerned about dates, though Mother knew most of them pretty well. She wasn't sure when Father graduated from college so we left that out, and there was an argument about which year he became Dean at River City, but Philip remembered it was the year he went to Europe, so that was all right.

When Philip asked if we should say anything about Father's childhood, Mother wanted to mention his music and the sonata he wrote, but I objected, I thought it would sound silly in a dignified notice, considering that nothing ever came of it, so Philip left it out. When Philip asked for characterizations of his work, Mother mentioned racial integration because he got praised for it, but most of the language about how liberal he was and the good things he did was Patty's, who came in from the kitchen and reeled it off while Philip copying toned it down. The phrase about defending the arts surprised me, but Patty reminded us of *Oh Calcutta*, so we let it stay.

If you see as deep into hearts as you should, you know I thought they were laying it on too thick about Father's liberal good deeds, especially that about developing a climate of reward. It could provoke a sarcastic reaction. But do you see deep enough to know why I didn't object? (When I talk to you, I never know how much I say is superfluous because you already know it.) It's this: I didn't want to call attention to myself, not right now, not in what might be thought a criticism of my father. As it happened, Philip raised the same objection, but Patty said it was important to correct Father's reputation after all he had been through, and so they kept it.

Philip thought we should say something about his geological work, but it was hard to think what. Mother wanted to call him a distinguished scientist, but Philip wondered if we could since he hadn't written any books. He compromised by mentioning articles, though none of us knew what articles Father wrote, but he must have written some, since he couldn't have gotten tenure if he hadn't. It was Philip who wanted to add the stuff about his unpublished writing. Mother protested a little and wondered what unpublished writing there was, but Philip said it was an important part of his life and she said, If you say so, dear. I made a casual remark (I was trying to participate so that people wouldn't think I was brooding or distracted) about Father's pestering us to write things down, and Mother said that should be included, and Philip agreed because it followed smoothly after the unpublished writing. So then it occurred to me this would be a good opportunity to speak of the threat of television to civilization. This surprised them, which alarmed me. What Philip said was that he didn't know Father was concerned about that. And it's true he didn't make a point of it, but I'm sure he believed it in his heart, just as I do. And whenever I think of the destruction of civilization there's always an image of Father in my mind, so I believe my belief came from him, an inheritance, whether or not he stated it in outright words.

It was Mother who put in the stuff about his life on the Island. Philip wondered about the Nature Society remark, how much the members appreciated Father's professional expertise, which Philip was afraid might seem condescending. Especially as there are three other retired professors in the Society. Mother insisted they did appreciate him, and Patty came in saying if they didn't they should, so Philip left it in. She leaned over his shoulder to see what he had written, and laughed (and God I still don't know what to make of it when Patty laughs in that tone) and said we should also include the church picnics, so Philip added that, throwing in the young people on the Island because he was afraid it would seem an anticlimax and undignified otherwise, though I don't believe anyone here knows any young people on the Island.

When it was done, Philip read it aloud and asked where to send it. I thought we should send different versions to the different papers: River City wouldn't be interested in the Island news, and *The New York Times* would prefer another slant. But Patty said the papers would rewrite the obituary to suit themselves, and Philip was damned if he would write separate ones, so we ended up agreeing it wouldn't make any difference. There was one logical booboo about the survivors that slipped by. None of us noticed until it was too late. I hope the editors fix it and it doesn't make anyone laugh.

Then dinner, seven of us at the table. You know how uncomfortable it was. Everybody talking about triviality. What a nice man Dr. Eastcastle was, what a fine job he had done for Father, being careful not to look at me. I mentioned this character Angel Vertebrate sent for by Sam Truro, but it was hard to sound natural. I wonder if you noticed how carefully they treated me, as if they knew but were willing to protect me. I could tell by how they glanced at me, as well as from the gentle tone in their voices speaking to me even when it was as trivial as pass this or that or would you like a roll, poor Henry, that sort of thing. Looking at me with carefully veiled incredulity, as if they realized again they didn't know me and were trying to figure out who I was in this familiar appearance. My question to you: how can I deny it if they don't accuse me?

In the evening I went out for a walk. You know what I did, don't you? Later I met William Key, who'd been out looking for a pickup somewhere, I suppose, the bastard.

––––––––––

ANN REALM: *Narrative*

Coming into the house she watched her mother, seeing with her own eyes what her mother saw, how every material thing was changed by what had happened in the hospital at 2:10 p.m. Transformation, Thomas's things, everywhere altered: her mother saw this without a word. First the wheelbarrow on its nose by the garage door where he had left it two weeks ago. Indoors: his upholstered recliner which many had carelessly occupied while he was in the hospital, now occupied by a ghost. The magazine pile: *Time, Nation, Review of Books*. White toothbrush in the jar next to Mother's green, his shaving mug, brush stiff with streaks of white residue. Male shoes under the bed. Hall closet, the red plaid jacket, the dark suitcoat on a hanger, the brown checked wool sweater.

In the study the computer is off, full of programs and files for somebody to go through. The calendar shows May, in which we still are. Framed photograph of a bird, a great horned owl, idiosyncrasy, bookcase full of his stuff, idiosyncrasies. His stuff everywhere.

There's a yellow blanket on the couch in his study, folded into a square. It must have been used for something, I don't know what. The laws of property have been suspended. A living body has been converted into a trail of residue, ash.

Analyze the difference between these things today and yesterday. How when he was alive his property was tangible character, exuded presence, a material body emitted by his biological body and spread about, so that to touch something belonging to him, to pick up a book or open his file cabinet, was equivalent to touching him, violating his person. How he expanded, his nerves reaching from the hospital where he lay breathing into the house and to what he owned, a network, tent, mesh, an airy body. It still floated around them after his death, but empty, a property corpse extended from the biological corpse. The corpse enclosed her mother and herself and all the others as they returned to the house. It folded around them. Yet nothing was changed, everything was exactly as he left it. That's the point: if it had changed it would not be corpse.

How dead the file folders look, the antiquated typed papers. Like a lifeguard looking for a drowned body, she takes the manuscript up to her room to read after everyone has gone to bed, as if that could revive the dead.

HENRY WESTERLY: *Narrative*

In the Ahab 'n Abigail Bar on Nautical Street, Rupert Newton talked Truro. Showed me the news for tomorrow's paper: Angel Vertebrate, sought by authorities as a possible mediator in the Sam Truro hostage case, located this morning as a hotel worker in Provincetown. Heard his name in the news and called to offer assistance. Will come to the Island tomorrow. Truro has been informed. Truro: will negotiate with no one else.

And then repeat the facts. It is now four days since Truro, a teller at the Island National Bank. Etcetera.

In the bar on Nautical Street talk about Angel Vertebrate. Newton quotes Truro: You get me Mr. Angel Vertebrate who drives the schoolbus. I want to see him. Negotiate? the Sheriff said, giving Truro the word for his vocabulary. Yeah, negotiate. I want to negotiate with Mr. Angel Vertebrate. I won't negotiate with nobody else.

Rupert Newton's researches into Angel Vertebrate. Who came here from the Cape as a construction worker. Hardy: I remember him. Got tired fast, that guy. Reservoir project, then schoolbus, night watchman in the high school.

Muscular, long hair. Mustache, blond. Little talk. Guys remembered him on the baseball team when he came out to play, tried second base but no match to McWheel, used as pinch hitter, couldn't hit curves, couldn't hit fast ball either, struck out both times, quit. Yeah, Bowman said. Long hair sticken out his baseball cap. Funny name. Guys hooten when he struck out.

Neighbor (Harriman) thinks he did gardening on the Truro place last spring. Digging, planting, starting a hedge. Wore a pony tail. No shirt. Remember him at the back door, drinking water out of a dipper. Heard his name, thought it was a joke.

Daughter (Dinah Truro, staying at the Froehlich's since her release) says Angel used to come around. Her words, "He used to come around." Calls him Angel. That's his name, she said. How often did he come around? A lot. Did he come to see your Daddy? He come to see me. You? And Mommy. When would he come, evening, mornings, afternoons? Afternoons. When your Daddy was at work? He come to see me and Mommy. He liked me and Mommy. When he came did she send you out to play? Yes. Did she really? She sent you out to play? Sometimes she did.

Rupert Newton bought Henry a drink. After talking to him for an hour, Rupert looked at him and said, Who the hell are you? I'm here for a death in the family, Henry said. Yeah, who died? My father, Thomas Westerly. How come I didn't hear of him?

Henry Westerly on his late night walk. Even at night you can tell it is a white house. A plain box on Shoal Point Drive, just before the sidewalk ends and the speed limit goes from 25 to 55. Square with a steep peaked roof, two front windows on the second floor, two on the first, one on each side of the door, which is centered perfectly symmetrical. At night the lawn is dark, but the last streetlight illuminates a circle of the sidewalk. Two deputies remain on guard, sitting in their cars, their rifles sticking up, watching.

In the house, the light is in the downstairs window, where they say the living room is, to the right of the door, and another is in the second story window on the right. A half hour ago, the deputy says, he passed in front of the living room window. Now for a moment he appears in the second story window. One of the deputies raises his rifle and sights. After a moment the man disappears.

Whyn't you shoot? the other asks.

The first deputy laughs.

A man says to the passerby: They say they sit down together for meals.

It's a publicity stunt.

An extortion racket. Five thousand bucks and a safe conduct, for Christ sakes.

Wish somebody'd give me five grand and a safe conduct for my wife and kids. I'd let em keep the dog.

WILLIAM KEY: *Narrative*

Turning the corner at Nautical Street, William Key sees a chunky human shadow moping along. The shadow stops, turns around, totters his way. Man drunk, William thinks, and crosses city-bred to the other side. The man stops and looks at him with a purpose which tightens William who thinks this kind of thing shouldn't happen on the Island. Brace himself with no weapon.

At that moment William recognizes Henry, lame but not necessarily drunk, and in the same moment Henry turns to go away. Stops though, and William realizes that Henry realizes he has been recognized. Also clear Henry wanted to avoid him as he wanted to avoid Henry, but it's too late for both, and they meet in the street.

What are you doing out?

Taking a walk. You too?

Can't sleep.

Stop for a drink?

No thanks. Smells like you had one.

I suppose so. Quiet night.

Fuck it.

What?

Never mind. Guess I'll go home.

Guess I'd better too.

There's the hospital.

Too bad today. I really liked and admired him.

Yeah? So did most everybody.

Not you?

What do you mean? My old man. How could I not love my old man?

———————

THOMAS WESTERLY: *As read by Ann*

Late in her room Monday evening, the house quiet. A printed manuscript that looks like a story. She's uneasy about reading more father's secrets, but decides she'd better take a look. Thumbing through she sees three or four chapters. She won't have time to read them all.

WYOMING 1

The inspiration for the following narrative was my discovery by accident of a name in the Island telephone book. I was looking in the G's for a carpenter named Greenough. I saw this:

Glade Harrison J So Village

That's the name of the man Penny Young married fifty years ago after which I never heard of her again. A name, a combination of names, rare enough to mean something. If not the man himself, then a relative, a son, nephew, or cousin. The listing doesn't say if this Harrison Glade has a wife, much less whether she would be the same as the wife he married in 1942, but the odds were good, I thought, or at any rate fair. And if Penny Young herself were not living in the South Village as Mrs. Harrison Glade, the number provided a nearly sure way of finding out what had become of her.

Like nearing the end of a quest I had not known I was on. I found the forgotten memory skittering in the discarded trash of my mind. I thought, all I need do is call this number, ask for Mrs. Glade, and if she responds, ask her. Are you the former Penny Young? Did you go to Wyoming to study field geology in the summer of 1941? Did you return East that summer in a car belonging to Thomas Westerly—whom you called Tommy? Did you kiss this Tommy Westerly in the back seat while Turley drove, to mark yourself in his memory as the first girl he ever kissed, though you were at the time engaged simultaneously to a cowboy geologist named Jule Foss and an Amherst man named Harrison Glade? The latter of whom you married the following summer.

A year has passed since I saw that entry in the telephone book, during which time I did nothing. The new directory repeats:

Glade Harrison J So Village

A general address in the South Village, where I seldom go. I have not seen his name anywhere else. I have looked for it in the paper, the obituaries and citizen lists, who owes taxes, attends school committee meetings, runs bake sales. Selectmen and board members, the name of Harrison Glade, or of Mrs. Harrison Glade. If I saw him I wouldn't know him, for I never met him, but I have looked searchingly at the women in the village, strangers who might be the right age, in the streets, the shops, post office, library, wondering if I would recognize her or she me.

In 1941 she was twenty-one. That makes her seventy-one now. It's impossible to imagine Penny Young, who kissed one man while engaged to two others, as seventy-one. I went up to the attic, the scrapbook with the picture. Glazed like glass, faded but not discolored. Through the glass I saw her on a clump of Wyoming grass, wearing a thick plaid shirt and cowboy hat, heavy pants and boots. She sits by others with her elbow on her knee, looking up at the camera over her right shoulder. She's next to Mimi, who shared her cabin and came back East with us when it was over. The grass slopes up into a field with another ridge. Geologists walk on the ridge.

It's rest time after lunch before returning to work. She squints as she looks up. Her hat is pushed back a little, and a few loose strands of hair cast a shadow across her forehead. Squinting in the sun gives her a shrewd look, brows contracted, thinking things over. As I look her frozen expression seems to change, passing through possibilities: annoyed or pleased, surprised or not, friendly or indifferent. The expression is stripped of its past and future. The picture implies the motion of rest on the grass, the ongoing conversation in which she was sufficiently uninterested not to mind looking when I showed up with a camera. Fifty years later her image still looks up where she left it before going on to pursue the rest of her life.

I have two other pictures. In these she smiles, posed, ready, wearing a sweater in one while sitting on a log next to Jule, and in a light summer dress in the other, standing on a corner in Iowa with the group who came back with me. The smile in the pictures is opaque, anybody's smile, an ordinary pretty girl of the time.

I try to circumvent the opaque smile, looking for her in the memory of snack stops and restaurants, away from the blaze of the road, in the shade when I moved into the booth beside her, recomposing her eyes as large, as dark and blue, as friendly. Before her, I was in love only with the movie star Vivien Leigh.

If she's alive still, she'll have been through the same years as I and witnessed the same history. I could call the Harrison Glade number, find out if she's there or who knows about her, perhaps talk about the amazing coincidence of living three years close by on the Island without knowing it. And wonder what she remembers.

My own memory is amazed, how easy to close the gap of fifty years as if it were no gap at all except the tremendous aging of a whole life. I went to Wyoming full of wonder and surprise to study geology in the field. Why should I want to study that? I was nineteen, inside myself looking out, thrilled by the view. Growing late out of a sweet solipsistic childhood, interested in birds and stars and imaginary countries. I was supposed to choose a serious career, and to prove I was serious, I chose the earth. Geology, hard and full of rocks, to curb my dreamier tendencies.

But Wyoming in 1941 put color into everything and painted the hard geologically serious world with romance. Take the car, my father said. Go West, where I had never been, the West of legend and movies, full of Henry Fonda and the Grapes of Wrath. So I went with Stone and Turley from Columbia, down to the Lincoln Tunnel, across Jersey, through traffic into Pennsylvania, which was already West for me, following route numbers on the shields, road maps in our laps. We found the newborn Turnpike, which had no speed limit at that time, thinking like the *Titanic* how new and safe it was.

Closing the gap I remember 1941 less different from 1991 than my children might think. Trees, fields, houses, roads, telephone lines, just like now. Cars and traffic, speed and speed limits. The landscape was less populated, with fewer houses across the fields, the towns and cities proportionately smaller, but I didn't know it then. I didn't know the railroads would disappear, not when there were always tracks visible across a field, along a river edge, entering a town, and sooner or later a train with a steam engine, at speed or coming into a station, where cars were parked and people waiting.

No jet trails but otherwise the same sky, the same clouds, the same clear blue, or gray and gloomy days, mist, haze, towering or sliding cloud banks, rain and drizzle. Farmhouses and townhouses. Fewer suburban subdivisions, fewer real estate developments, no shopping malls, no office parks, but that too I didn't know. No television, but there was a shared culture of movies and the radio which we read about in *Life*. Stars and brand names. Jack Benny. Benny Goodman. Clark Gable. Coca Cola. Ivory Soap. Shirley Temple. Juke boxes everywhere, diners and cafes.

Four days we drove, meals and gas and nights in tourist cabins. Hot dog stands and billboards. The Burma Shave signs were evenly spaced along the roadside:

SHE KISSED THE HAIRBRUSH/ BY MISTAKE/ SHE THOUGHT
IT WAS/ HER HUSBAND JAKE

The rough mountain ridges of Pennsylvania settled into Ohio. The sky bore down on flat Illinois above the high tension wires and tiny distant farmhouses by tiny distant clumps of trees. Flatter still in Nebraska where a far tree ate up five miles without changing shape or size and a jack rabbit did fifty on a dirt road detour. With songs and stories in the screaming window wind.

In 1941 the war had done terrible things but had not reached us yet. The future was vague. It was either the previous year's New York World's Fair, subtitled The World of Tomorrow, with rocket ports, automatic doors, plastics, and Superman capes. Or it was France fallen, England bombed, civilization at an end under a thousand years of Hitler. I didn't want to think about it, while pacifist friends argued with non-pacifist friends. The world increased on field trips, where the land moved out from our feet in colorful dusty waves, purple and orange and olive drab with sage brush or dry clumps of grass or no vegetation, ridges of layered strata where we climbed with our picks to pick and chip to see what's what. In cowboy hats and plaid shirts and geological boots, with notebooks and compasses, tables and tripods, we assembled at the tailgate of the trucks for lectures, and worked in groups of two or three over the barren bright lands, poking away, identifying and plotting. Then lunch, food tables on the grass, shaded by canvas on sticks, and the crew built fires under tripods for hamburgers, hot dogs and soup.

We worked in the Laramie basin and among the formations of Colorado and in the interior of Wyoming. We camped in the Dinwoodie Canyon, and by a green lake in sight of the glacier peaks of the Wind River Mountains. We saw abandoned mines and met rattlesnakes on the open mountain paths and worked a ridge of points and scarpments like the fins of sharks, magnetite which attracted the lightning when a storm came up. We bought Coca Cola at road stands, and at each new destination blew up air mattresses, and in the evenings played softball in the geological fields between the rocks.

In Wyoming during all this time Penny Young was Jule Foss's girl. That was the geological reality I had to put up with. In the caravan of station wagons, she rode in his car next to him, ate meals with him, lay on the ground by the camp fire, or disappeared into the geological shadows. But this wonderful thing happened. She reserved her trip home in my car, she and Mimi, and I had it to look forward to. I watched everyone pair off, including her and Jule, and waited patiently for my turn.

After six weeks, we came home, and this return was the climax of my Western adventure. I let my passengers off along the way until only Penny, Turley, and I were left. Then she kissed me, sitting in the back seat while Turley drove, some-where in Ohio. She kissed me and I kissed her all the rest of the way through Ohio, Pennsylvania, New Jersey, into New York. She told me she was engaged to both Jule Foss and Harrison Glade. I bore it because she was kissing me. It was only later that I minded, when she stopped answering my letters, and I learned that she had married Harrison Glade and never heard of her again.

Eventually I'll call. If Mrs. Glade is not Penny Young, too bad. If she has forgotten Penny Young, too bad. But if I wait until she dies, or until I do, it will be too late.

A break in the manuscript. The next section is labeled 2, but it's late and Ann needs to write in her diary before bed.

ANN REALM: *Diary*

Monday May 19. HISTORY: 2:10 pm TW die. LW, HW, MC, me. + PW, PK, WK.

PRE: Sightsee Isl while TW conk.

DEATHWATCH. Lung fld > O_2 loss brain content? What did TW know? Sink *Doria*, vicious O: $-O_2$ > -heart > -lung > $-O_2$ > -heart > die > rot. Sad[3].

LIFE GOES ON. Business, scurry calls, empty house, magic change *(remember, analyze ++)*. Property = character, dead prop = ghost.

FAMILY. Collab obit. 5 children -GW. Comment 0, mute GW. Lost? Reject? Reject father mother brothers sisters along with hetero? Reject past with hetero? Past hetero, down with it? Fam silence, does LW know? PW? Is that why, doubt it, doubt[2]. Forget it.

PAPER WATCH. Forget *Killdog* while trailing dead Wyo-ming naive old times (trains land BShave: Jake/hairbrush) romance West vs dull geol West symb what? Kid TW love VLeigh. Hard read deathday invis people. Cry damn.

Austin Wright

TOMORROW. > Boston ex crowds here: > Europe. New life. No funeral. Grieve solo. Cry damn[2].

PART SIX

TUESDAY

LUCY WESTERLY: Letter folded in another

Lingering in bed, fiddling Freud's ears, pretending I'm good, while others take care of things. Pretending I'm a bird. Song sparrow in the pecking dirt. Garden birds that fly no more than they have to. Up from the dirt to a low branch of the nearest tree, then another tree, one tree to the next, flap flap, hard on my arms. How is such a creature capable of the sustained effort necessary to cross the sea from mainland to island? How does he know when he sets out with no land in sight that trees and a hospitable garden with cherries and worms are on the other side of that fog?

Meanwhile all that thumping upstairs. So maybe it's Ann I'm writing to instead,

Dear Ann,

who'll be setting out in a plane opposite to the birds later this morning. Up packing already. Making me think how much time to get up and eat and go to the airport with you, meanwhile writing to tell you not to feel guilty for not staying to the end. Of course you're right to carry out plans made without knowledge of unforeseen events. The important thing is you came. Be thankful he died while you were here. To stay on and bury him is another matter. So don't blame yourself. Blame rather the husband (I am not talking about Frank) who would not allow his wife a few days' extra leeway to be with her dying father. It's hard to understand a daughter who would put the mundane concerns of her daily life above the unique and terrible crisis of a father's death. Just as it's hard to understand the feelings of a daughter who can abandon her native land to settle across an ocean, cutting off friends, brothers, sisters, old parents, as if it didn't matter never to see them again. It's hard to express (which I never have) my blank when you announced your London plan, nor your father's so adroitly concealed behind his generous good wishes, so don't listen to me. Cruel though it may be, you have a right to choose what's best for you and no one else has any rights at all. Good parents let their children go. You've been a loyal daughter, until now, if that will soothe your conscience such as it is. Thomas too. My problem is whether to go to the airport, which I'll be happy to do if there is no crisis elsewhere.

It's not Ann it's Thomas leaving me empty. How could I forget? I can't express the

express, reminded by his sweater, the heavy checked Indian one, on the back of his chair—not only tangible but still bearing a faint smell though they say he no longer exists, distinctive mild usually unnoticed not unpleasant, leaving his things around as if he didn't care about me, express whatever that is

---

MELANIE CAIRO: *Dialogue*

Leaving the bathroom, she goes downstairs, knocks on the sunporch door at the bottom of the stairs.

Melanie: All yours.

Patty (*behind the door*): Thank yoo-hoo.

Through the hall she sees Ann and Philip at the breakfast table. Lucy's door is shut.

The telephone rings as she passes. She hesitates, unaccustomed to picking up other people's phones, but Ann looks at her.

Melanie: Hello.

Male voice: Miz Westerly?

Melanie: Wait, a moment please. (*To Ann, covering phone*: Where's Lucy? Ann: Not up.) She can't come to the phone, can I take a message?

Male voice: Excuse me, this is Mister Osborne, Gregory Morticulture. If you would be so kind as to tell her he's ready.

Melanie: What?

Osborne: Professor Westerly, he's ready.

Melanie: Ready?

Osborne: Excuse me, ready for viewing. If you would be so good as to tell the lady, she can visit him any time now.

Melanie: Now, already? I thought the viewing was Thursday.

Osborne: Excuse me, isn't the lady going away today? We worked ahead of schedule to get him ready for the lady who's going away so she can say her last goodbye.

Melanie: Oh you mean Ann.

Osborne: Thank you. If you will tell her, when I heard she was leaving so soon I made a special effort. I thought she would appreciate having her last goodbye. Thank you.

Melanie: All right, I will, thank you.

Osborne: Thank you so much.

Melanie: I'll tell her, thank you.

Osborne: Thank you so much again.

Ann (*in the kitchen*): What? He got him ready for me?

PHILIP WESTERLY: *Scheduling*

The Present Moment: 8:37 a.m.

Scheduled Time of Ann's Flight: 10:05

Advised time to be in airport: 9:45

Time needed to get to airport: 20 minutes

Last safe time to leave house: 9:25

Time between Now and Last Safe Time: 47 minutes.

Time to get to Gregory: 6 minutes walk

Time to get ready to go: ask first, will other people want to go with Ann? If so, will they eat breakfast before they go?

Breakfast time minimum: 30 minutes. For seven people, expand to 45 minutes.

Henry, Patty, William, Lucy will also need time to get dressed. Dressing will occur simultaneously, not consecutively, but time elapsed will be that of the slowest dresser, not the average. Slowest dresser time: 25 minutes?

Time needed to view corpse with dignity: 10 minutes?

Time back to house: 6 minutes.

Time needed for Ann to pack: Ask her.

Time needed for Ann to pack: 15 minutes.

Wash? Bathroom? Add a little more.

If Ann goes by herself:

Time needed to finish her breakfast: 8 minutes (coffee to cool). Leave house 8:48 (already ten minutes have passed just talking and figuring this out).

Arrive Gregory's: 8:54. Add 5 for confusions.

Visit Dad: 8:59-9:09.

Get back to house: 9:20.

Pack, bathroom, goodbye. Leave for airport 9:25, last safe minute, and that's rushing things.

The only way for Ann to view Father is to go by herself, unless I run over there with her.

Question: If Ann sees him first and I see him with her, will others also want a privileged preview before the official display? Will feelings be hurt? Decide later.

One alternative would be to cancel her flight. Then she'd have to call Frank and cancel London.

Additional problem: Ann's not sure she can finish packing and do all that has to be done in fifteen minutes.

The telephone rings again.

Female: Mr. Glassman's office at the Island National Bank, can we move Mr. Philip Westerly's appointment up to ten this morning, Mr. Glassman has to go to the mainland and won't be back until Friday?

Time now: 8:50 a.m.

Scheduled time of Ann's flight: 10:05.

Time of Glassman's new appointment: 10:00.

Conflict.

Alternative: Glassman Friday 10 a.m. Conflict funeral morning. Alternative: Friday 3:00 p.m. Conflict funeral.

Okay Glassman today, let others take Ann to the airport.

Time passes. Ann is in her room. What's taking her so long? Time now: 8:54. Give warning, You won't have time.

Ann comes out, not ready. Can I take this manuscript of Daddy's? I want to see how it comes out.

What's that?

His Wyoming story.

Damn. Send it back when you're done.

William comes in. I'll drive you to the airport.

Somebody please apologize to Mr. Gregory.

Not Mr. Gregory, Mr. Osborne at Gregory's. Gregory Morticulture.

Time now: 9:25. Hurry hurry it's time to go.

Nobody's had breakfast yet. Some of us did.

Lucy doesn't want to go to the airport. Henry is still in his bathrobe and Patty hasn't finished eating. Melanie wanted to stay in the background. I have to see Glassman at ten.

So we stood by the door and said goodbye to Ann before

she got into the car with William driving, at 9:30, already five minutes past the Last Safe Time because in the end it took Ann almost thirty minutes to pack and say goodbye and everything on her mind before setting off to Europe, and she won't see any of us again for at least a year.

After she left, we found Dad's Wyoming folder that she had wanted to take on the kitchen table.

———

HENRY WESTERLY: *To God*

Let me remind you of the facts. By midnight of the night in question I was asleep. You can verify that with Melanie. He got out of bed in direct defiance of explicit instructions. He slipped out of the hospital, past the nurses' station, the security guards, into the street: were you leading him on? And then he went back to the Truro house. Do you intend to tell me why he went there, of all places, and not to his own home family and bed? I'm sure you remember also that it was the Truro house where he was first stricken. Where the bullet didn't hit him but he was stricken anyway, so what the bullet couldn't do, you did. Is it your plan to let me know why Truro so drew him like fatality, what he was looking for that made him go back or how he knew that's where he would find it—or do you intend to make me figure it out for myself? As for me, please remember when you go around accusing people that the first time he went was before I came, I wasn't even here and had never heard of Truro. And when he went back to that house in the middle of the night before last that's his responsibility or yours, for I was asleep in bed afflicted by this depression they say I have.

As for last night, I dropped in at the Ahab 'n Abigail because I heard voices, and a man talking about Truro. One thing led to another, but I was never out of your sight. Afterwards, I walked for an hour, for my health, to circulate my blood, dissolve the oily chunks and clear my soul of people.

I did nothing but walk. You saw me. I walked through the village and out the beach road by the harbor light. I swung back past the power plant and the tennis courts. I met William Key on my way back, walking by himself too. It's all right for him to walk alone at night, why not me? Because it's impossible to stay in this house. A point is reached when everybody merges into a single personality like a pot or stew, a steam bath of personality, and you simply have to escape. We went out independently, met accidentally, passed the hospital together, then came home. If you are uncertain about this, ask William. At home, Melanie had gone to bed.

As for this morning, I did say goodbye to Ann before William took her to the airport. No one waked me, it was not my fault I didn't get up in time to go with her, if someone had waked me I would have gone—if she had wanted me to. Yes it is my fault, I know. It's my fault to oversleep, but it was not deliberate, not selfish or callous or hostile. Selfish, yes I admit that. But not intended. The last time I saw my father conscious was Sunday, he did not speak to me. He did not speak to me. Of course I could have. I did not try to make him speak because I thought he didn't want to. I could have tried but I didn't because I thought that. You understand that, you can't accuse me for it. If they accuse me, they should out and so say, they should tell me to my face. They shouldn't tell you without telling me, so I can explain it.

I wept when my father died, you saw that. I point that out, if you didn't notice it, though of course you did, being who you are. Who else did? I never never never wished my father to die. The only time I wished my father to die was for his sake, the last day or two to terminate his suffering. He would have wished it himself, if he could have wished. I was reinforcing him. The only other times I wished him dead, if I wished him dead in years past, which I never did, but it was not literal. You can understand it was a manner of speaking, a metaphor for certain frustrations on my part, not to wish him dead, even if that's what the words of my thought seemed—seemed—to say, but to wish him, not to be silent, but to change his mind, this or that, I forget the issues. If I wished him dead for any other reason at any other time it was not a true wish but an idle thought, a curiosity about how things change, a mere question, like what would things be like if he died, like action in a movie. All life is change, surely you know that, you know it better than anybody, it's the way you set the universe up.

WILLIAM KEY: *What to tell*

At the Island airport this breezy morning after death, William Key's point of view pauses in the car that does not belong to him to watch the plane go. In a flash of sun it rises steeply and turns toward the sea carrying the chunky woman away. He watches from the car after the other visitors have gone, at the fence by the restricted area and the little private planes, while flags flap, weather vanes spin, the radar arm circles.

Alone again, he pauses outside the restricted area, not ready to return yet. The empty airport takes shape. There's a flat cinder-block terminal with tiles of opaque blue glass. A runway rising into the liquid distance. A line of scrubby growth on the monotonous edge. A blue sky with cotton puffs extending over where the sea must be. The cool air quivers from the released weight of the past half hour. The baggage-centered, ticket-oriented conversation recedes into a memory of politeness. The chunky woman's hearty civility, brisk and blunt, and his own kindness. Mutual courtesy, full of implications. He discovers the implications in retrospect. His sympathy and condolence for more than her bereavement, for the necessity of her sudden flight and exile. Her sensitivity, which he reconstructs from a momentary look in her gray eyes, to his intelligence and his difference, which she will never mention. Off to Boston she goes, on her way to London, full of brain and good sense and a knowledge he knows she has, shrinking into nothing in the sky.

Though he has never discussed anything important with her, he feels surprisingly abandoned, as if she had incorporated his intelligence into her own and taken it with her. He thinks admiringly of the fullness of her writing, with its analytical and finicky attention to detail, while she talks impatiently about what to leave behind in a move overseas. With cryptic meaning that eludes him, she says, Don't let Thomas's papers out. Then she's gone, leaving this empty point of view behind. It puts this viewpoint temporarily in a gap, open like a glimpse into hell, though the guessed horrors may be deferred and possibly deferrable for life or maybe even nonexistent, who knows? For twenty minutes he lingers in the gap, car parked by the fence after the other cars have gone, between the woman vanished in the sky and the strangers mourning in the house.

Patricia's hated sister, she never meant anything to him before, and she never will again. Only this once, when they found themselves mutually helping each other into exile, she became for him in retrospect the one true link to Patricia's alien family. He imagines in her and in the dead father together the family's integrity, though he never paid attention to her, and she had no importance. But in her departure he finds authorization for his.

When he gets back to the house, what's left will be only peripheral in a family to which he has only temporarily, it now seems, belonged. Seventeen years temporary, flown off into nothing. He confronts them again in their new strangeness. The white mother with the bird nose projecting from the shocked blue eyes, the skin like a veil with light shining through, hooked to a trembling machine powering the shake of her voice. The ugly fat man with the limp promoting depression like a law suit, mistaking for sensitivity the monomania that has made him simple, coarse, and crude. His wife whose yearning guilty eyes will give away the secret between them even when there is no secret.

And the man with the beard who fancies himself good. The steady one, who makes a profession of looking into the eyes of others. As if eyes could see, though blind to whatever the man's reasonable goodness protects: something scared behind the practiced modesty and ingratiating manner. William Key's viewpoint, expert in concealment, thinks the man in the beard believes he is hiding a guilty secret, like a Puritan minister with a veil, though no one but the man cares and the world would laugh if it knew.

When at last he drives back to town he resents the car. Lucy's car, which won't mind. It's big and drafty, a powerful old machine in need of a muffler. The steering wheel is higher than he likes, the brake pedal too loose, there's a vibration at high speed. The maps in the back fly around.

At the house, the family is dispersed, remnants sit idly at the breakfast table. That irritates him, he doesn't want to sit with them, so he'll take another walk. Where to? Having no plan, he finds himself on Main Street where suddenly he sees Henry again, ahead, coming in his direction. He looks around to escape but then sees that Henry has disappeared. Hiding from him too? William advances cautiously. There's the shoe repair shop and the silk imports store. Between them the office of the *Island News*. He glances through the plate glass window just when Henry, standing by the desk, is looking out. Their eyes meet, there's no escape. Wave, nod, go on. It's the kind of encounter that will oblige William to ask later what he was doing there, before he realizes from Henry's startled look that he'd better not.

PATRICIA KEY: *What to tell Pete Arena*

It leaves me wondering what will become of this family now. My prediction, it will split, never be a family again. My older brother and sister'll say we're too warm and close for that. And when it has happened, they'll pretend it has not. But if it gets too obvious, they'll blame us. By us I mean Henry and me, the malcontents. Henry they'll blame for not being cheerful and me for being me.

My father was too busy being university president and when he wasn't he was alone in his head, staring at the world on his computer screen, even when he was retired and supposed to be living life. My mother, you're a good American, you believe in mothers, but mine never approved of me. She was afraid I would fall into disgrace, pregnancy or worse. Because of where I stand on the ladder of roles. Third child, second daughter. She worries how things look and now I'll have justified all her fears by taking up with an African-American garage man. She'd reconcile easier if she thought you were middle class, but since you're not she'll judge by what you are doing to pull yourself up. Are you taking courses at night? She'll expect you to improve your social standing. She'll approve if she thinks you're trying to do that, because it means you know what your standing is. Better for her, therefore, more instructive, if you *don't* tell her about night school.

Since my sister is moving to Europe, you may never meet her. On the way to the airport, they talked about me. I know they did because I was their common link. She told him what a rotten sister I was (as if I were still her sister after seventeen years of marriage) and he told her what a rotten wife. I must explain my sister's dislike, for my family is different from yours: if you came into this room and sat down among us you would never notice that anybody disliked anybody. You don't understand a fight unless it's a fight. Whereas we Westerlys are full of peace and good will. I have never discussed with my sister her dislike of me, because she would only deny it.

The reason she doesn't like me is that I was thin. Because I was graceful in my body, lithe and slim, because I used to willow around chairs, and glide slimmingly across floors, and wander my hips and thighs in flower movements like stalks by the pond. Because I had a pretty face, my features smaller and softer than hers, and my cheeks were pink and I wore makeup and enhanced my eyes with eyelashes and shadow, giving me a stare like a slow loris. My sister didn't like me because I was flighty and had sex years before she did though she was three years older than I. Because I snuck out at night, smoked cigarettes in the woods, had marijuana, cocaine, beer and gin in my youth. She didn't like me because I knew she didn't like me, meaning I could see through her good will and family feeling and pretense of responsibility.

My older brother doesn't like me because I don't like him, though he doesn't know it. The reason I don't like him is that he never gave me reason to. He attended to his life, which had nothing to do with me. He was there like the Lord, giving no reason.

My middle brother and I formed an alliance against the enemies on both sides of us. On one side the older sister and brother, on the other the baby brother, who was everybody's pet, taught to sit and heel and shake hands until suddenly he came back from college full grown and gay from a scallop shell in the sea. Who's that, we asked? Don't worry, you won't meet him, he'll never show up in New York.

My alliance with Henry was imposed on us by the others as a booby prize. My older brother and sister telling us without words (you don't understand that but never mind): You belong together, stay out of our hair. Go play with Patty, Henry. Be nice to Henry, Patty. Later on I'll tell you why Henry doesn't like me. It's too sticky for your present stage of development.

111

My ex-husband doesn't like me because I am female. It took him almost all the seventeen years to realize this was a handicap. For long he thought he could handle all kinds, and it was worth two children before it became too difficult for him. After we reached agreement it got easier. He has his friends and I have mine. Now that he doesn't like me because I am female, he likes all females better, including me, and we get along fine, which makes it easier to part.

He says I married him to prove to my sister that I was not brainless. By marrying a brain, an intellectual. He says you are his natural successor, the reaction. Even though he has not met you nor knows the most elementary fact about you, he looks down on you just as you look down on him.

None of the members of my family has the slightest interest in God. They're superior to God, more intellectual, more sensitive, more upper class. Since I met you I've been trying to get over that tendency in myself. Some day you and I will have a fight. It's inevitable and will be the end of us. Unless one of us changes. That will have to be me, for you can't. Well, I'm trying. Hope for it.

———

HENRY WESTERLY: *What to tell Thomas*

They brought this Angel Vertebrate down from the Cape, expecting something heroic. Sole Authorized Negotiator. Select and special chosen by the protagonist himself. Brought from the Provincetown Hotel, and across on the first ferry of the morning. Accompanied by McSwan the deputy, he stood on the upper deck forward as the boat came into the harbor, hands against the rail. Dressed special for the occasion—for we have grown accustomed to thinking of him (this Hercules-type with long blond hair in pony tail, weight-lifter biceps) bare chested for construction work or tight-filled T-shirt for schoolbus driving, or at worst and alien to his nature stuffed into a white coat for busboying—but this morning comes Sunday dressed in a dark suit and a tie like a baseball player meeting the public, puffing up in the suit as he makes a point of inhaling the fresh sweet harbor air when the ferry pulls in and he casts his eyes heroically down at the dock to see how many people, reporters, thankful police, grateful relatives, admiring girls, have come to see him arrive.

Not many, as it turns out. Perhaps a single reporter (his name is Rupert Newton), who asks him an impertinent question or two why he was chosen by Truro for this critical function.

Trust, Vertebrate says. It's I'm an old friend of the family, the only guy he can trust.

Reporter asks if he has any plans, any tactics in mind to get Truro off the hook in not too humiliating a manner.

No comment, Vertebrate says. Have to size up the situation and see what we shall see, right?

Reporter asks if he would care to elaborate on his relations with the Truro family. Laborate blabberate, Vertebrate says. I'm the trusted family friend, what more you want? Always used me for sensitive jobs. What kind of jobs? See that hedge? Vertebrate says. Planted that, these here two hands themself.

They take him in the police car to the Truro house where Sheriff Haines briefs him. Tells him, your job is find out what Mr. Truro wants and persuade him to give up peacefully. You can say we'll be good to the wife and kids. Offer him loving care in the state hospital, but don't call it the asylum and be careful lest he think you mean the booby hatch. You can point out we can outwait him the rest of his life if he wants us to. You can remind him we have nothing to lose, it's his wife and child not ours, but we do have a natural concern and the law has a natural concern that no innocent people get hurt. You can't promise him anything, you can't promise he won't be prosecuted or go to jail or the booby hatch, you can't promise him no gifts or trades, but you can make it sound like we might be willing to give him something if you think it will loosen him up, without actually lying about it.

It's around noon when this happens. The sheriff's car and two police cars are parked in front of the house with a pretty good crowd standing around, mostly across the street afraid of bullets. Sheriff Haines calls with his bullhorn: Truro? No answer. Truro, we got Vertebrate. You want to talk to Vertebrate, Truro?

Reminds me of chivalric romances, the silence after the trumpet blast before the hero appears. The house is still. The bullhorn repeats. Silence again. Grumbling in the crowd. Someone says, Look! The eight-year old boy, named Roger, appears at the window. He is opening it. Looks back in and out. His faint little voice. Speak up, son, the Sheriff says. My daddy says—

What's that your daddy says? The bullhorn booms over the crowd.

My daddy says you send Mr. Vertebrate on over here.

Why don't your daddy tell us? Whyn't he come to the window hisself?

My daddy says you'd better no tricks.

A voice from the crowd barely audible next to the sheriff's boomer: Jump out the window kid. Stay close to the house. He can't get you then.

My daddy says no tricks.

The man next to me grumbles, Bastard too much a coward to show himself holding a gun on his own kid. Another man says, Publicity stunt. It's what you call public relations.

Angel Vertebrate starts slowly up the front walk. Very slowly, though his arms swing in bravado. Truro, Mr. Vertebrate is on his way. The boy shuts the window and disappears. The front door opens, and the boy appears in it. Angel Vertebrate hesitates. Looks back at the sheriff. Turns abruptly, someone speaking to him from the house, inaudible to the crowd. Angel Vertebrate walks into the house, and the door shuts behind him. The sheriff is heard muttering to the deputy, Christ I wonder if we did that wrong.

What Angel Vertebrate heard before he went into the house was probably a voice he knew: Come on in Angel, or I'll split both their heads in half.

On the basis of the evidence doubtless he looked up to face the carbine pointing at him, the man clutching it, snarling orders: Shut the goddamn door. Lock it, you little son a bitch, Okay now Angel, hands up in the air.

Why what's a matter Sam boy, I'm here to negotiate your demands. Don't you want to sit down and talk?

Up your hands you don't want you head blown off.

Sam, you're my friend. Ain't you my friend?

Off the jacket, come on now, quick. Off the tie, off the shirt. Move now, move. Undershirt too. Now the pants.

Sam? The pants?

Drop em. Underpants too. Take em down.

Sam, the lady!

Fuck the lady. You lyin doublecrossin skunk. Off em I say. Let the lady take a long look, it aint nothing she aint seen before. Now you can just take a seat right there, that one, while I handcuff you to the chain, and then I'll explain to you the rules of the establishment. You might as well know the rules since you've decided to stay with us.

I got tired and left in the middle of the afternoon. Just after I heard the sheriff say to the deputy, Seem like they been negotiating a long time. I dropped in later on Rupert Newton, who was writing the following:

The man brought to the Island for the express purpose of arranging release of Sam Truro's hostages was himself captured by Truro at the start of the negotiations today and has been added to the number of hostages. Angel Vertebrate, 26, former schoolbus driver, who had been especially requested by Truro to serve as go-between, came to the Island this morning from the Cape. At noon he approached the house to open discussions. Watched from the street by deputies and police, he was admitted to the house by Truro's son, after which no word was heard for several hours. That he had himself been taken captive was not revealed until five o'clock, at which time Truro telephoned the police office and indicated that Vertebrate was now his prisoner. No explanation was given, nor any new demands. "He's definitely not playing by the rules," Sheriff Haines said.

Today is the sixth day of the siege in which Truro has been holding his wife and son hostage. His daughter Dinah was released Saturday on account of illness. She has been staying at the home of Mrs. E. R. Froehlich on Water Tower Road.

PHILIP WESTERLY: Lists

People already here and where they are:
  Lucy Westerly. Master bedroom.
  Philip Westerly. Front bedroom, upstairs.
  Henry and Melanie Westerly. Back bedroom, upstairs.
  William and Patricia Key. Side bedroom, upstairs.

People expected, when, how, and where they will stay:
  Beatrice Westerly, by car, bringing Greta and Minnie Cordage plus Betty and Nancy Westerly. Arrive 2 p.m. boat tomorrow. Stay: Beatrice with me in the front bedroom. The others (four) on the sunporch. (That fills the sunporch.)
  Charles Westerly, by bus. Arrive 2 p.m. boat tomorrow. Sleep in his tent (if he doesn't forget it).
  Lucy Realm, from Philadelphia. Arrive 3 p.m. plane tomorrow. Must be met. Stay: Inn, single room.
  Gerald Realm, hitchhiking from Chicago. Arrive ferry Thursday, time unknown. Stay: Inn, Thursday only. See comment.

Larry Realm, by car, with Dolores and baby (Martha?). Arrive boat tomorrow, time unknown. Stay: Inn, one large room, two nights.

Angela and Tommy Key, arrive 3 p.m. plane tomorrow. Meet (same plane as Lucy Realm). Stay: Angela on sunporch with Betty, Nancy, and Minnie (this moves Greta to Inn to share double with Lucy Realm). Tommy: the old Westerly tent in the yard—next to Charles's tent. See comment.

Uncle Carl. Arrive ferry Thursday, time unknown. Stay: Inn single, Thursday only.

Aunt Edna Forsyth. Arrive 3 p.m. plane Thursday. Meet. Stay: Master bedroom, moving Mother upstairs when she comes and Patricia and William to the Inn.

Comments.

David Westerly not coming, too far. Note phone call of sympathy from him and Olga.

All three of Ann's children are coming, without either Ann or Frank. Point this out to Mother.

Where put Gerald? Too smelly for the Inn? Would he stay in tent with Charles? It'd be worse for Charlie in the tent.

Tommy and Angela are too old (14 and 16, right?) for cots with William and Patty. And by now Tommy's too old to share the sunporch with girls. He'll like the tent probably, being a boy.

Aunt Edna's unexpected coming confuses everything. I think she should go to the Inn, but Mother says if Edna comes this far at her age, she must stay in the house. Where? No guest rooms because she can't climb stairs. Can she walk at all? Sunporch, oust the children? Imagine Edna on the sunporch. Share the master bedroom with Mother? Two old ladies in double bed, one half dead? So it's Mother who decided to move upstairs and give the master bedroom to Edna. I objected to the sacrifice, the symbolic rending of Mother's life, but she was firm. This required kicking somebody else out of an upstairs room to the Inn. I would have ousted Henry and Melanie, since they have no children, but William and Patricia volunteered, solving that.

Mrs. Pixmire unavailable for cooking. Try Mrs. Jordan.

ANN REALM: *Diary*

Tuesday, May 20. Over black Atl > London. Pre go call view TW pre trip > choose corpse/trip. Nasty AR fly Lond headlong rushfut post TW die, coldheart. Goodbye TW goodbye all Lond away we go. Why vis crpse? Crpse crpse. Proof die, saw dead dead, what else, Morticulture Art? Mem TW/crpse compete. Scootairport WK, reason/feel breakrule Centuries Awe, circle vill harb tiny house downlook inside seefam LW PW HW MC PK griefrites + TW in unknown funhome prep for famgroup rit - AR cry in sky. Neghelp Wyoming + corpse + Atl + AR alone = lost = woe > cry. Farewell.

Damn forgot: Wyoming, *Killdog*. Find PW, heart attack?

THOMAS WESTERLY: *As skimmed by Philip*

His father's files again, pages that look the same as before though their source is now dead, and wondering if that changes his mission, still Philip looks for what he might have been expected to censor. Henry follows, then William Key, who asks if he can read the Wyoming papers Ann left behind. Philip is annoyed, soon everybody will be rummaging. Nevertheless he submits, lets William look, gives Henry files from the lower drawer, and takes some for himself. He skims and reads when something attracts his interest.

THE CLINIC

The man who screamed at the abortion clinic   *Shame on you. Blood on your hands in the wrath of Jesus*   God

118

the avenger   I drove off angrily thinking you know nothing
about   the balmiest sweetest day of spring, tulips and green
lace, when the neighbor's beautiful long-haired cat killed the
cedar waxwing   waxwing tragedy in life's revival while the
beautiful cat chews its beautiful victim under the beautiful
dogwood tree   tell life lives by killing life, all live things end
up food   required by the DNA   no argument on behalf of
vegetarianism   animal kingdom bias   on a spring day birds
and old people die in the bloom   the exuberance of death
God of Nature cares more for life than for me or any other
me such as you

ask him how the God who rejoices in life can deplore
death   rejoice deplore in equal time it balances   does God
of the woods and highway accidents recognize a category of
the unnatural   a species of natural   when mother mouse
ate her first litter, the children watched, try again mousey
tell me sir do you really believe this God believes in human
supremacy   why me more than the cedar waxwing or cat
on a spring day   poetry of the wilted rose, everybody knows
creative flux, the joyfully blossoming murdering God

thundering angry God the voice of human fear   to be
food in the wild march of life   it's a human not divine
crime, who   murder?   would believe God who created
murder for the sake of life condemn his chief instrument

THOMAS WESTERLY: As read by Henry
COMPULSIONS

When I was fifteen my father was tacking shingles on the
roof with his back turned. I was behind him with a hammer.
It was not anger or hate, but like a compulsion from outside
against myself and all I loved. It scared me and I thought if it
happened I would have to run down to the beach and smash
my head dead on the rocks. I had fears like that sometimes.
In the kitchen I saw the meat knife on the table, behind my

mother where she stood washing the dishes. I moved away, carefully, carefully across the room to be as far from the knife as I could. I thought if touched it even accidentally. And I wouldn't have the strength afterwards to push the knife into my gut so all I could do would be feebly to howl.

There was no hostility in these thoughts. They attacked what I loved most. It was the simple realization that at all times in the most ordinary day to day I had the power of life and death in my hands and fingers. A small push, whatever was required, no more than throwing a baseball or kicking a stone, which could change the world. Prevention depended on my restraint, which depended on my will. I couldn't judge my will and lived in fear lest the balance be upset in an off-guard moment. I thought I was insane. I imagined pulling out my hair, drowning my face in mud, screaming, above all screaming, for the horrible things I would do.

I got over it though never to the point of absolute certainty. Now almost sixty, I'm probably safe. I'm familiar with the connection between deciding and doing, the little push needed to turn a thought into a speech or an act. I had a bad moment at the commencement exercises when I narrowly avoided welcoming you new generation of idiots into the fellowship of educated assholes. But I kept my composure and was never in real danger. I know what it feels like, on the diving board before you jump, especially if you are afraid of jumps and water. But still I wonder, is the destructive impulse a part of me? Or am I what rejects the impulse, my refusal to act? My created self. What you can predict me by.

So I told Henry, when he was worried about his bad thoughts. I said, What you are is not what you think but what you do about what you think. It sounds good when you put it like that.

Unfinished. Henry growls bitterly. You should have told me, you old bastard. You should have told me your thoughts.

Next, in a folder tagged PROVOST, TOP SECRET, *his attention is caught by the word* SECRET, *a single half page:*

ATTENTION

To my wife Lucy and whom it may concern,
Forgive me.

You'll know what I mean by the time you get this. A terrible thing to do, I know that. I feel the cruelty as if I were you. I never thought my life would end like this, I thought it inconceivable. Believe me it wouldn't if there were an alternative.

I can't explain. The reasons are beyond us. Don't try to guess. It's not what you think. Think only this: I love you no less. I love you if anything more and you can construe even this as proof, if you'll give me the credit.

HENRY WESTERLY: Dialog

Hey, I found what we're looking for.
Show it to Philip.
William: What is it?
Family business, William.
William: Sorry.
Philip looks at me and hands it to William.
William *after reading.* Suicide note?
What else?
William *after handing it back to Philip.* What's the date?
Philip: There isn't any.
"Provost Top Secret." Maybe the Provost wrote it.
Philip: It's addressed to my wife Lucy.
William: What's the Provost got to do with it?
It's a screen. Obviously.
No one says anything.
The bastard.
Philip: Don't say that, Henry.

He had no right to do a thing like that.

William: He didn't do it.

He changed his mind? What a hypocrite.

William: He must have been unhappy. Whenever that was.

He was never unhappy. He was blithe, cheerful, optimistic. Always. Damn it.

William: Maybe it was that fight as President.

He loved that fight. He loved being misunderstood.

William: It would be nice to know when it was written. It could have been many years ago.

What do you think, Philip? You're wise and grown up, what do you say?

Philip: Don't tell anybody.

Nobody?

Philip: We need time to think about it.

Nuts to that. I expect to tell Melanie.

Philip: Must you?

William: I won't tell Patricia.

Philip: He wrote it but nothing came of it, thank God. He kept it to himself.

William: Maybe you should burn it.

Philip: I'll take it out of the file.

You're going to keep it?

Philip: Until we decide what to do with it.

William: Is this what your father wanted you to get rid of?

Philip: I doubt it.

It's his all-purpose escape, if and when the occasion should arise. I wish he hadn't written it. It's as bad as if he had done it.

Philip: No it isn't. Be quiet, Henry. It's over now, and he'll never have to worry again.

We won't have to, you mean.

———

Austin Wright

THOMAS WESTERLY: As read by Philip

When the others had gone to bed, the Wyoming narrative which Ann had forgotten to take. He read the title—

WYOMING 1

—and the description of Penny's pictures and the narrative about geology and going to Wyoming, and then another chapter before quitting for the night.

WYOMING 2

I used to treat my adventure with Penny Young as a joke. The joke was on me, because I was so shy she had to kiss me before I could kiss her. That's embarrassing to remember, so I made a joke of it. The joke was also on her, because she was engaged to two other men at the same time, though that seemed to amuse more than embarrass her.

Her word for me was "bashful," which was the language of the times. In 1941 there had already been a jazz age, a roaring twenties, a depressed thirties, a revolt of youth, but I didn't know about all that. Like every young man I was obsessed with sex, but I had not read Hemingway or D. H. Lawrence, never heard of Henry Miller, and still believed what my parents taught me. So did my college friends. They wondered and gossiped and made crude jokes to avoid getting laid. Like my friend Robinson, who did not want to lose it sordidly, only in some high exalted way. The West was different, though. In the field she wore a cowboy hat, a cardigan sweater over her plaid shirt, and heavy geological boots. Her intelligent eyes squinted in the sun, and I did not know what to expect in the West.

On the trip she wore light summer dresses. The trip took four days. I sat next to her in lunch rooms. When I was not driving I rode in back between her and Mimi. The silver dollar rolled, the moon harvested. Clementine, Abdul Abulbul, and the old gray mare. Lake Cayuga and Notre Dame, show me the way to go home. In the back, they held my hands, she and Mimi, their warm palms and fingers. She teased me, but I did not feel humiliated. Later, after Mimi was gone, she told me what she had in common with Mimi. We like to flirt, she said. I thought about *flirt*, its literal meaning, its possible euphemistic meanings, which frightened me.

In Sioux City on the second day, hot, in a large empty restaurant for lunch, dark with ceiling fans, the waitress served ice water, for the land was full of fever, the roads afire. I went blind. I could hear the talk, but I couldn't see. So she washed my forehead and my face, and in a moment I was fine, more than fine, I was full of ecstasy. I did not mention the fierce pain in my groin when I got out of the car to come into the restaurant. That was the result of the erection I had been fighting in the back seat for half the morning. This in turn was the result of her lying in my lap, looking up at me while she chatted. It was monstrous, and I could not keep from poking her, with acute embarrassment wondering if she noticed and wondering how she could fail to though she gave no sign. So that when we finally got out in Sioux City, and stood up on the sidewalk and I turned aside so as not to be seen, my testicles banged against each other like gongs, and I walked bowlegged to reduce the clang, while she stretched herself in the open air and breathed in the sun. That afternoon we went to the movies and continued the trip that night. She thought what had blinded me was the shock of the ice water after the heat. So she said.

On we went from Sioux City, dropping people along the way, while she sat beside me, leaned on my shoulder, slept on my lap, and my erection struggled not to be noticed. By the next afternoon, as she lay looking up at me, the invitation to kiss was so obvious it could not be mistaken, and still I failed to respond. At a road stop in Indiana, I heard her tell Mimi, making no attempt to conceal it: *He's not human.*

I was human enough to know what she meant. In the car again she lay in my lap, smiled, and closed her eyes. For miles and miles across the historic states of Indiana and Ohio, in the shell of the car on the fast two-lane highways, while Turley drove with Mimi beside him in front, passing cars, watching speed signs, slowing down for towns, stopping for traffic lights and regaining speed across the high flat farm lands, with the distant farmhouses and silos and barns and high tension wires crossing the horizon and railroad tracks accompanied by telephone poles thick with wire, for miles and miles she lay on my lap waiting for me and though I knew it perfectly well, I did not dare. What was I afraid of? That she would say like the woman in the poem, That was not what I meant at all? I was not human and could not believe the world I was in.

Then it was the third day of the trip, a sunny afternoon and always the wind shrieking by the open windows, tire and engine, a three-day scream of noise. And motion, lurching, braking, accelerating, and I with my head on the soft cushions of her thighs looking up while she leaned over me, grooming me monkey-style, looking for blackheads to pinch, her eyes large, lips half open in her amused smile. I wasn't human and I could see her reach a decision. Close your eyes, she said. If you close them, I'll give you a surprise. I closed them and for a moment felt the light double touch of velvet on my lips. I looked at her and she laughed.

How do you like my surprise?

Do that again.

Your turn now.

So she kissed me and I kissed her, and we kissed each other the rest of that afternoon whenever Turley drove, and all next day through Pennsylvania and New Jersey except when I drove. We kissed in the tunnels of the Turnpike and the traffic of New Jersey. We kissed in Sherwood Forest after Turley had gone, before taking her to my family's house, and again the next morning before delivering her to Greenwich and again six weeks later in the evening when I took her to the play and the following morning before returning her for the last time to Greenwich.

I took my understanding of kissing from her. Two lips touching two lips, mouths closed, touch light enough to appreciate the satin texture. The first kiss was short, though I learned gradually to stay with it. She said something about kissing more passionately, which I thought meant hold on longer and exert more pressure. On the last morning, by the beach road near Greenwich, I felt a third thing emerge between her two lips, but I did not open to receive it, thinking it an accident.

So how did we vary the endless miles of lip-to-lip? It was too new to need much variation. She leaned on my shoulder to sleep while the car jounced, her hard little head against my jaw, her silky soft hair. She was always there. When not kissing or sleeping, we talked. She asked me what I was thinking, offering the equivalent of her name for the information, as if my mind was treasure, and she told me about her aunt who wanted her to take the pledge, which she refused to do, not because she wanted to drink or get drunk but because she didn't want to rule out any experience. And the two boys she was engaged to, a dilemma, pretending to ask me for advice. Jule Foss in Wyoming. Harrison in Amherst. She would marry one of them next year, one or the other. I tried to locate myself in her scheme. What am I, Number Three? Better than Four or Five, anyway.

She disliked fuss, she disliked artificiality. She didn't like makeup, she said, nor hairdos or perfume, high heels or stockings. She took care of me, my blackheads. She looked at the bandage where I had sliced my finger against the flange of the trunk while packing the car. It was getting dirty and she told me to come to her room that night and she would change it. But I forgot. At any rate, I didn't go.

We let Turley off near Times Square in New York in the late afternoon. I called my parents and asked if they could put her up for the night. We ate in an automat and sat at a table with an old man who asked, Sweethearts? Friends, she said. Then a sentimental movie at the Paramount with a stage show featuring a trio in inky light and a lead singer as if he didn't care, what a beautiful voice, she said, what a beautiful tenor voice. During the movie, she snuggled and held my hand. When we got home, my parents were waiting up. Afterwards they said what a nice bright intelligent girl.

I wonder how much of this she remembers. The next morning I took her to Greenwich and delivered her to an aunt in a small house between others on a street up a hill. The aunt was a nice good middle-aged woman.

PART SEVEN

WEDNESDAY

LUCY WESTERLY: Composed in bed

Here comes the second morning of the new age. Eras we have known: Planting the Tomatoes (Chicago); War and Peace (Chicago Two); Rise and Fall (the Presidential Mansion); Autumn Etcetera (the Island). I don't want a new age, but who cares what I want?

Everyone tries to feel sorry for me. Some want me to be upset because we haven't heard from the University. Why bother, after how they treated you? Some are smug, those who think I've joined the group and those too young for it to happen to them. A few wives scared because they know it will. Maybe they're scared it won't. Most people treat your death as an event. Generally speaking, I don't like events.

Patty came into my room and asked if you and I still had sex. Not anymore, I said. I meant before, she said. I said that was a mystery, wasn't it? She took that as a negative and lectured me: all the columnists agree there's no good reason why people even a lot older than you. I asked was she advising me to have an affair and she took offense. All our kids want to know secrets. Knowing secrets makes the world meaningful, that's what meaning is, a secret disclosed. You and I had just five secrets disclosed, named Philip, Ann, Patricia, Henry, and George.

Ann ran off to London, she couldn't wait. All her life she has truncated things, like when she abandoned her degree to take that job. Yet how patient her writing is, so detailed and complete. But I guess it has to be, it's what she's paid for.

They are snooping in your papers. It makes me nervous. Who knows what garbage you left for anybody to read?

DAVID WESTERLY: *To Olga his wife*

Typically, they weren't expecting me. They put me out to the backyard to sleep, sharing a tent with Charlie, a thing I haven't done since Mt. Eldenberry, at which time I vowed I would never sleep in a tent again, certainly not with him. But that's where I'll be. What a crowd, sunporch full of girls, overflow at the Inn.

On the plane a regular family reunion, though nobody noticed until we landed. I recognized my cousin Lucy Realm but didn't greet her since she didn't recognize me. Is it my beard? Later she said she didn't say hello because she thought I was snubbing her. There were a couple of familiar-looking teen-age kids, and an almost petrified old lady who had to be carried from a wheelchair onto the plane and carried off when we got there. Nobody said hello to anybody. When we landed, Aunt Pat met me, only it wasn't me she was meeting but the two teenagers, who turned into her kids Angela and Tommy. They're the brats who used to break up chess games. So Aunt Pat says, David! Nobody told me about you, and Lucy Realm turns to me and says, I was wondering when you'd acknowledge me, and Aunt Pat notices the petrified old lady carried off the plane by four furniture movers and yelps, That looks like Aunt Edna. Why, it *is* Aunt Edna, while her kids are trying to introduce her to some black guy they met on the plane, whom she almost pointedly refuses to acknowledge, which makes me feel ashamed on her behalf.

Now I'm trying to write a letter in a corner of the dining room on a piece of my grandmother's sewing table, ignoring the board games on the dining room table and the talk in the living room and the people cooking in the kitchen and the other people thumping the bedding and cots around upstairs.

Aunt Edna's voice like a can opener keeps talking to nobody. I haven't seen her since Hatteras. She doesn't remember me. But she gave me a look and said, Every minister needs a wife. Do you have a wife? I explained that I'm a graduate student in English, and she said, I wonder if you know Professor Dingle. He was my father's favorite teacher, a very fine man.

I am highly susceptible to nostalgia. Thinking of my grandfather brings me back to their presidential mansion in River City, which I remember with a longing I don't understand. Hard to believe they occupied it only two years. I was fourteen. The big house with its tower and its river view and its front stairs, back stairs, doorways, such that it was never possible to look from one part of the house to another without being thrilled by anticipation. The memory of that house—lost by my grandfather when I was sixteen—recalls similar *anticipation* in other old things, like the forested cottage where we used to go before my father's divorce: the clumps of woody islands on the lake, the prospects of rowing among them, the hope of getting lost. And the beach after the divorce before he married Beatrice, enriched in memory by that same anticipation which I underlined above because it's the essence of all remembered ecstasy (yes) as well as the source of all the poignancy, the *unbearable* (yes yes, that must be underlined too) sadness in the memory of such ecstasies: the joy of expectation, the hope of fulfillment, embodied concentrated in the very shape of a house, a lake, a shore. Right?

Nothing in the present can compare. This island is pretty, but it's just a place, the sunshine is ordinary sunshine, the air is ordinary air, and the time is present tense. What else is there? Sex and love—that's what the present has to offer, right? I wish you were here.

If you don't want to keep this letter, please save it for me. I might want to use some of the writing later.

PHILIP WESTERLY: *Arrangements*

Necessitated by the unexpected arrival of David Westerly and the premature arrival of Edna Forsyth.

Call the Inn for additional room tonight.

Move Patty and William to Inn.

Move Mother upstairs.

Force Charles to take David into his tent.

Also this: *Call* the University (for Lucy). Ask: Do they know he died? Are they planning to send anyone?

BEATRICE WESTERLY: *What to tell Philip*

How we went for a nature walk when we saw dinner would be late and the bright day had begun to fade. For Betty and Nancy while you folks were having your drinks, and I never expected such a crowd. There was Larry Realm's Dolores with her baby, could she come along—a nice gesture since we are strangers until now, and I was touched she'd want to know me. Then in the back yard by the rose bush Angela and Tommy Key asked to come. Doubtless they were bored and anything to do is better than nothing. And Greta and Minnie seeing us and never wanting to be left out of anything, suddenly it was a party of seven if you count the baby. I felt like a tour guide. I said I would go slow because this was for Betty and Nancy and the smallest child would set the pace, and soon Greta and Minnie went on ahead though Angela and Tommy and Dolores stayed with me, ambling along politely and sociably at Nancy's four-year-old speed.

Our kids have nice cousins. Why would this fourteen year old Tommy Key tag along with a bunch of girls and babies? But he was quiet and courteous, close to us the whole way. We went through the back alley to the rocky beach. Looked among the rocks to check out the small crabs and hermit crabs in their shells. Starfish and schools of minnows. Out past the rotted dock along the sand strip. Plenty of dried seaweed. Tommy had a stick, finding things in the sand, crab shells dried and crusty the color of the sand, and kelp and egg sacs and seaweed coarse like vulgar spinach, and dead fish and dead horseshoe crabs. One dead thing after another, he kept turning them over without saying anything, as if making a demonstration. The dead horseshoe crabs were helmets with a spike, which Angela said was the oldest species on earth, from which Betty recoiled because of the spike and the prickly shell and the package of little legs inside the helmet like a tank, lying on their backs in the sand. Also human residue, egg cartons, picnics of the past, cardboard containers, fragments of red lobster left by people not the tide (I explained) as you could tell by the red shell. I prodded Nancy onward as we went, and the big girls who had sailed ahead came back to see where we were and sailed out of sight again.

I could see Dolores's baby getting heavy in her arms, which she didn't seem to notice. Asking questions about my work. How I got started, published, my first book. How I came up with Thumpy Puppy and when did I invent Milkweed Kittypuss? Work habits, when I do my illustrations, how much time on text, how much pictures. She wants to be a book illustrator of course, which is why she approached me. That's fine, don't mind at all and I gave her advice she probably doesn't need though she thinks she does. I dealt with her questions and never got to my own, which was why she doesn't marry Larry, since she has a family now, my niece-in-law without the law? I wanted to ask but I felt a delicacy and didn't.

We saw a bittern in the reeds. The old osprey nest in a dead tree across the marsh, nobody occupying it. Angela offered her binoculars to Betty who couldn't hold them still enough to see. White and gray seagulls clean as fresh laundry, as well as the dirty-looking younger birds. Some of the mature gulls were different, with black wings or black heads, and no one knew what they were except the herring gull, which Tommy knew. There was a marshy smell, a whiff of sulfur, more dead things around. Dead fish in a stagnant pond, Tommy poked it with his stick, Angela said quit that, Tommy said why should I? Then a dead flicker right in our path, the flash of useless gold, the white back feathers, the strong neck broken and twisted around. Upset Betty, who wanted to know what killed it, which I didn't know, and Angela said Ugh, and Tommy turned it over with his stick. Flickers are always getting killed, he said. Then into the woods, the sandy path between lichen rocks, the struggling little evergreen and little oak trees, while we looked at the olive birds darting about like mosquitoes and heard a white throated sparrow. I called attention to the sound of the quail, bob bob, bob white, and the children held still and Tommy whistled an imitation.

The crows cawed echoing from the tall pine beyond the golf course, and a somber mood came over us from the darkening sky. Cirrostratus, I explained the high clouds full of ice spreading a veil across the sun, the brightness fading, the twilight will be long and lusterless, and rain tomorrow.

Timidly, as if she were asking about love, Angela asked if I believed in the reincarnation of souls. I laughed, which was tactless of me. I guessed some boyfriend had been trying to impress her. I told her it's an old idea with metaphorical significance. Plato used it. I said how you need metaphors to express what realistic and literal language can't express, and that's how it is with reincarnation. But what's it a metaphor *for?* she asked, making the mistake of assuming a metaphor says something which you can say some other way. I went along anyway to suggest that in so far as reincarnation was a metaphor it was probably for the bone-feeling of universality in human experience, empathy and oneness with others and our pasts and the human heritage and transcendence of our selves, and a lot of bullshit. I avoided saying that I'd be mighty cautious about getting involved with anyone who believes literally in reincarnation—if that's what was on her mind.

Dolores's baby began to cry so we started back. We found a gold and black furry caterpillar for Nancy, who played with it the rest of the way while it gradually shrank until there was nothing left. Then she cried, criticizing me for not warning her though actually I did warn her. So we were a bit grumpy by the end, but that's natural because we were healthily tired, and on the whole it was a good time and a good thing to have done.

———

ANGELA KEY: *Diary*

The best thing today was Aunt Beatrice took us for a nature walk. Down behind the house to the beach and back through the marsh and woods before town. I think I'm in love with Beatrice. She is so slim and tall and graceful. Like a dancer, every move slides. Pretty like the Virgin Mary, I'm not kidding. She can protect me from anything. Nothing upsets her. There was my stupid brother doing his morbid act, finding dead things and trying to shock us, and Beatrice just smiled as if that's what nature is, which it is but Tommy is too dumb to know. There's something wrong with him on this trip, I don't know what, something on his mind, he won't say. I don't think it's grandfather's death. Aunt Beatrice, though. How beautifully she talked to me, addressing herself to me, her whole attention, when I asked the Pete Arena question. She almost saved him without knowing. I could have melted.

Better not tell Axel. He'll think I'm perverted. He's wrong, it's not like that at all.

PATRICIA KEY: *Composed at dinner*

To Pete Arena. Here I sit containing my fury as we eat while Mrs. Goslowly helps Mother. How dare you come to the Island without asking me? Didn't you realize I might be meeting people on that plane? When I saw *you* coming up the tunnel, your black face, jeans, plaid shirt, talking to Tommy and Angela, I was shocked. With my nephew David right behind you not knowing and my old Aunt Edna in front of you and here you come full of big boy scooting past my poor old aunt in her wheelchair like a snail in the path of your ignorance. And the nerve to grab me in front of my relatives who don't know you exist.

You forgot that. Nobody in my family knows you exist. They think William's still my husband, sharing my room, same bed. (Queen size, forget it.) What am I supposed to say about you?

Your ignorance of decorum, that's why I scowled and pretended not to know you. Against my deep grain you forced me to make my kids lie. I had to whisper them not to know you. Lie to Aunt Edna with my kids watching. That humiliates me. I teach them to be honest and this is what you do.

What did you expect? Did you think I would introduce you? Even your call was awkward. There were people in the room. I pretended it was from New York.

Here are the rules. Keep away from the house. If we meet by accident, show no recognition. The funeral is Friday. You can go to it if you stay that long but sit in back, don't say who you are. If you spy on my family don't let anyone see you. If you have to be somebody, be a former student, come to pay your respects.

Your coming so prematurely, I could easily regard it as a breach of faith. I thought it was understood, I'll introduce the question to my family in my way. Nobody here knows you exist, let alone you're black. If you think you should present yourself and let them see for themselves, you'd better not. You laugh when I say my siblings are no racists and you're probably right, but that's no reason to bludgeon them. We need to be tactful, considerate, you included. When my mother learns the truth, she'll react. After her reaction she'll adjust. If I don't warn her in advance, she'll feel betrayed. It would be like introducing you to her in the bathroom when she's undressed.

Before she can get used to your distinctive color, she'll need to get used to the breakup with William and the fact that someone in your position exists. That's three shocks I'll be giving her. Even William doesn't know you're black. He knows everything about you but that. It will put his ACLU liberalism to an interesting test. He'll look down on me for picking you. He won't show it because of the hypocrisy, but I'll know and he'll know that I know and it will be part of the package of our parting. But he doesn't know anything yet. Do you understand?

MELANIE CAIRO: To Dr. Parch or Dr. Saunders

Hard to distinguish between his grief if he has any and his sickness. Quiet, lethargic, morose as usual. Or do I mean Dr. Saunders, Parch or Saunders in the living room with such a crowd I don't dare write yet, especially if it's Saunders not Parch I'm writing to. The distractive question of the other man, this man of last year's beach house, and me nervous and

136

fearful not of what he would do but of what I would feel. Since last summer I've grown to hate the memory, shabby and dirty in retrospect not seen at the time. Ashamed not for infidelity (no longer a useful term, the man soothingly told me) but for cheap excitement and obese emotion. I've not been able to expel the image of his secret sticking out like a red carrot through all that civic dignity and control. I couldn't recall what captivated me. Nothing captivated me. It was an opportunity to experiment on myself, but the instrument was crude.

I was surprised to be so jumpy about meeting him again. But when he arrived yesterday and I saw again the shielded gray look covering so much unsaid interpreting and recalled his hidden carrot of truth, why then Dr. Parch or do I mean Saunders my nervousness vanished and I felt secure.

I was determined that what happened once last summer back of the beach would not repeat this year, certainly not in the middle of grief, nor be mentioned or thought, erased from history as if it never was. I was determined that he conspire with me on this. But tonight as we sit here all these people in the living room and dining room, the young ones playing games, I've been aware of his eyes not looking at me knowingly and no longer with contempt if it ever was contempt, and there was the moment by the front door but only for a second as if to create an event. It was about the strain of taking care of my depressed husband, and I felt sympathy projected at me not like a carrot but a flame. So that all evening while I think notes for Dr. Parch I find myself thinking notes for Dr. Saunders about how it could be done again if that were to happen which I vow won't in the house or the Inn, but would a room at the Motel beyond the harbor be too dangerous, or might a safe wilderness be found along the beach like last summer or an empty beach house not in use at this time of year, and how much time might go unnoticed, what could be done with the husband, how could the wife be distracted? I try to dismiss the sentimental questions (how could you think of it at a time like this) because the fact is, I am thinking of it with him sitting across from me reading a magazine, and remembering we are the in-laws, the invited outsiders. Except that this was exactly what I intended never to think again.

But it's Henry I must think of, keep my mind on Henry, playing with the children, morosely. A child's game. I hear him animated, bargaining, calling to the cat that walks across the board, cooing, meowing, giggling, pretending not to be morose. This afternoon I heard someone crying in the house. It went on and on, oh oh oh, with intakes between the sobs. I thought probably a child, but loud enough to be adult so it probably was adult for only an adult would cry that loud, woman or man, how the voice rises and changes pitch under stress, and who here is capable of making a noise like that, crying away like the end of civilization.

The problem is, when I think of Henry I think of him, like one causes the other. And then I keep thinking he'll tell me, he'll find a way and when he does I'll know what to say. But I had resolved not to. As for Henry, what should I do, Dr. Parch or Dr. Saunders?

HENRY WESTERLY: *To God*

Let me ask you a question. Can God commit suicide? Can God be depressed?

Good, I thought not. God goes along all year doing what he does. The relief I feel today. Pray watch me not to make everybody ask what's come over me.

You saw last night when I read the suicide note by my father. Everybody was shocked, like a crime discovered at the heart of the universe. Philip and William, who wanted to classify it Secret with William going so far as not to tell Patty his wife.

But if Patty's his wife she's also my sister and that irritated me so I told her myself. You'd have done the same. This afternoon with the sheets on the sunporch before the airport. Well, she was shocked too. How conventional everybody is. Asking when he wrote it, as if that mattered, not realizing that the suicidal worm is a worm no matter when it pokes up through the ground. It's a deep way of seeing, and though it may require a mishap to bring it to the surface like rain, it's a worm in the ground nevertheless. She wanted to excuse it by a specific misfortune like presidential failure, but that won't do, this is character we're talking about.

Her problem was, she took it personally. Like by killing himself Father killed her. Because killing himself amounted to killing the world in which he lived, which includes her. It's also a repudiation of you as author and creator of life, and therefore of her soul and the immortality of her soul, that too. Then she realized that he didn't actually do it, which I say makes no difference but for her made it business as usual, and it was Poor Daddy all over again.

Nobody shared the relief I felt when I read his note. It settled a confusion of identity that's been plaguing me. Since you would never be suicidally depressed, it means he's just another mortal like the rest of us. Like say me. This isn't as naive as it sounds. I never mistook him for you. It's a question not of what I know but of the unseen connection. The underground conspiracy I used to suppose between you and him. I knew he was mortal, but I heard him in your voice.

Until last night when I saw it clear, the familiar vanity, the punishing ego full of tears and puff adder, curling to strike himself a venomous blow in his own serpentine neck.

I won't read his papers tonight. They read them like carrion birds. I'll sit it out for a while. I heard someone crying this afternoon with the house full of people, impossible to tell where from or who. Again tonight upstairs which stopped when I came out of the bathroom. I'd like to think someone is grieving for you, but it's only mourning Father, I suppose.

PHILIP WESTERLY: *Tribute*

My father as past, language, civilization. As Chicago, organized by him in the car and on foot and in everyday speech. As New England. As Ithaca where I live, which was mine until appropriated by him in his visits.

My father as the organized wilderness, arranging the red fox that escapes off the road under the headlight of the car and the skunk odor over country roads in summer evenings. The differentiation of bird songs, the divisions into phoebe and peewee, hermit and wood thrush, song and white throated sparrow.

My father as the modern world. The obsolete railroad locomotive, the internal combustion engine, the airplane wing, the jet engine. Attachments and luxury gadgets—windows that roll up by a push button. Glow of the dashboard lights in the dark.

My father as non-belligerent skepticism and genial doubt. Appropriate awe for the mysteries of life. Avoidance of simplified solutions. Common sense, horse sense, self-reliance. World in the image of the self-created self.

Omit this. My first wife Louisa, a rebel child of the sixties who was against parents, who fluttered and gave him hugs when we met and called him cute, who when I went into practice found me too conventional to be interesting, compared us. She said I was a mere pale copy of him. My second wife Beatrice assures me that's unfair.

How could I make myself without a model? What else is there but confusion?

140

HENRY WESTERLY: *Narrative*

So, Mr. Angel Vertebrate, Sam Truro says, you thought you'd stop by for a little negotiation. There they sit, each in a different chair, handcuffed to the chain, which is padlocked to the radiator post. Across the room is Truro, carbine in his lap, revolver on the table. Angel Vertebrate is naked, Truro's wife Georgette is disheveled, her hair scraggle wet across her face. She's ill, she refuses to look at her husband. There's age long frustration and defeat on her face, a look you see in the streets, the buses, the grocery stores on the faces of middle aged and elderly depressives, beaten by years which in her have been compressed into a few days. The little boy Roger rests his head on his wrist. He has been through all the comic books several times. He complains because the calves of his legs tingle, he can't hold them still, he kicks them out, he shakes his body, he makes birdlike and mouselike noises until his father says, Shut up.

So now are you satisfied, Mr. Angel Vertebrate?

Sweating in the leather chair, wiggling and easing his body around in an effort to loosen it up, Vertebrate says, I don't know what you want wimme, Sam. You tell me what you want wimme and I'll see what can be done. I never meant you no harm, Sam.

Georgette can tell you what kind of harm you meant.

Fuck you, Georgette murmurs.

You wanted to be a member of the Truro family, welcome to the Truro family. How do you like being a member of the Truro family, Mr. Vertebrate?

You got me wrong, Vertebrate says. I never wanted to interfere the Truro family.

What you think is Georgette if you don't want to interfere? Truro says.

I never meant nothing with Georgette. She's your wife, honesta God.

So now it's all out in the open, you, me, and her, and

your cock sticking out where everybody can keep an eye on it. I notice it ain't as interested as it used to be. Is that right, or did you always have difficulty with it?

You just tell me what you want, Mr. Truro, and I'll see that you get it.

Almost a day and a half has passed since Sam Truro took Angel Vertebrate into his family of captives. He has taught his friend the routines, unlocks his handcuff when he has to go to the bathroom, with the gun on him and the door open. Makes him wash morning and night, use the extra tooth-brush. Angel says he wants a bath, Truro says he can have one soon. The routine by which Georgette is released into the kitchen to cook meals has become habitual, but now that Angel has joined the group they no longer eat together as a family. While Georgette and Roger sit at the table Angel stays in his chair and gets his meal on a tray in his naked lap. (Evidence for this from neighbor boy Mick Haskins climb-ing up in the big oak next door.) After they are finished Truro eats by himself at the table, always with his eyes on the hand-cuffed group and his guns by his side. When they are done, whereas hitherto Georgette was released to do the dishes, now Vertebrate does them. He stands at the sink with his bare buttocks and an apron in front between his cock and the dishes, washing rinsing and drying while Truro keeps the carbine across his knee casually aimed.

Does Truro worry about the increased danger of bring-ing a strong bold man like Vertebrate into his kennel? Does it make him uneasy when he leans back for sleep in the night, wondering what new ingenuity this man from outside might challenge him with? Perhaps sleeping under such stress dur-ing the past week has trained him so that he can sleep even with his new prisoner in the house—well shackled, in any case: the mother and son each on a cot, and Angel hand-cuffed out of their reach further down the chain with only the leather chair to sleep in, or if he prefers, says Truro, the rug at the foot of the chair. Making doubly secure at night by shackling his feet together.

No doubt Truro wants to be most careful when he approaches Vertebrate to unlock him—the man is powerful and might make some violent disabling move. The usual way is to toss him the key and make him lock or unlock himself with the gun held to his head. When Truro comes close to inspect the lock, he keeps the revolver, loaded and cocked, pressed into the man's groin, as if that were a better deterrent than against forehead, and always he is alert to the quiver that might give warning of a sudden kick or swing of the heavy arms.

Why don't you just tell me what you want, Mr. Truro? Angel Vertebrate repeats. His confidence has not stood up under confinement, his voice has become a whine, almost a whimper when he repeats the question. The whimper pleases Sam Truro. It makes him grin. You'll find out, he says. You'll see.

Concealing no doubt the perplexity he must feel now that he has caught the fish he wants, has everyone in place, with the police and deputies outside, all waiting for him to demand something. But while they wait for this great thing he is now in the power position to claim, the fact is (isn't it?) he does not know, neither what he wants nor what he should ask for, he stands in an absolute perplexity as to what to do next. And so he too waits, as for a message that will come if he waits long enough, a message waiting on the rollers of unused time to be rolled into view where he will recognize it when the time comes.

––––––––––

THOMAS WESTERLY: *As read by Patricia*

Who came into the study and said, There you go, snooping in Dad's papers again.

We're doing this because he asked us to.

May I join you?

We can't prevent it.

It's a thin file labeled "Family memoranda." Her mother's name catches her eye and she reads every word closely.

August 16, 1968

Dearest Lucy, a note to thank you. No words can express my relief.

If you had stayed in Chicago, if you had allowed me to move alone to River City, no matter what arrangement we made for the kids, it would have been catastrophe for me, like death, regardless of the career. *I don't want to read this, Patricia says.*

I intend to be humble about your choice. You think I can't know what you're going through, the loss, the sacrifice. You're probably right. I won't ask you to tell me—ever—what happened. I'll accept and rejoice in the good fortune you have restored to me. *Banish this, Patricia says, my father to my mother. Stop it, both of you.*

And try to promise, with full knowledge how difficult such promises are to keep, that I'll be better for you henceforth, so there'll be less cause for history to repeat.

My gratitude and love,

Your Thomas

Another handwritten memo without a date. She tried to read but couldn't stop the shaky feeling left over from what she had just read and could only skim words off the top.

Lucy as for the two children let's break down the questions

Did anything actually happen? We could ask or spy or try to confront, but my preference

the biological question? if there were a tangible biological consequence yes that would be radical but if not

the anthropological question   yes, in all cultures, imply-

144

ing an absolute   however

docs a violation of the local violate the absolute or only local *What are they talking about? Everything she reads makes Patricia quiver on the page.* too old for innocent child play

I find it hard to believe they would actually do such a thing

your question, what we did wrong too late maybe nothing at all

some way to help them

dare tell them what we suspect   which could permanently destroy relations with our children

Be calm, Patricia. Philip and William are deep in their reading and will not notice if you put these pages back.

THOMAS WESTERLY: *As read by Henry*

Who did not want to read tonight until called by Philip: Hey Henry, I found a file on Sam Truro.

TRURO FILE

To: Sam Truro

From: Thomas Westerly, Provost

This is to inform you that I have personally reviewed the reports of Dean Schultz and the Academic Attainment Committee, and after long and careful consideration have decided to uphold the Committee's ruling. Your connection with River City University is severed as of today. Dean Wickoff will contact you about the details of your departure from the dormitory and other matters.

Such a decision is painful not just for you but for all of us. We appreciate your disappointment and frustration. I hope you'll find the resources to make a new start elsewhere. In any event, I wish you well in your

Dear Professor Westerly,

You won't remember me, but I was a student many years ago at River City University. Imagine my surprise on coming to this island to learn that you had retired here.

I just wanted to thank you for giving me the most important lesson of my life. You may not realize what positive results can come from harsh negative actions, or perhaps you do since you are the one who has to take such actions and people like me who have to learn the good that lurks within the iron glove.

In any case, I'm glad I found you, and I look forward to serving you at the Island National Bank.

> Yours truly,
> Sam Truro

Dear Mr. Truro: *(Copy)*

Thank you for your note. I'm delighted that something I did years ago should have had such a positive effect upon your life. I'm sure that it was well deserved on your part.

I look forward to seeing you at the Island National Bank.

> Sincerely yours,
> Thomas Westerly

Dear Mr. Truro: *(Copy)*

Thank you for speaking to me at the Bank. I'm flattered that you should have moved to the Island because of me.

I'm certainly glad that I was so helpful to you. My memory has grown vague in recent years but of course I remember you. I always knew you would turn out well.

> Sincerely yours,
> Thomas Westerly

Talk.

So he knew Truro.

What does he mean, most important lesson of his life?

It means Dad kicked him out on his ass.

Why this explains everything. Truro followed him and scared the shit out of him.

What do you mean, scared?

You heard him in the hospital. He wanted to make amends, amends to Sam Truro.

According to these letters Dad didn't remember him. He thought Truro was thanking him for a favor.

Eventually he knew. When he attached the old memo to the letters. Then he knew.

Does Mother remember him?

Mother, did you know Sam Truro moved to the Island out of admiration for Father?

Mother says she never heard of him until Thursday.

———————

THOMAS WESTERLY: As grasped by Philip

To: Thomas Westerly

From: Thomas Westerly

Re: Consciousness

According to Makrov, consciousness is mechanistic. No such thing as spirit, because that postulates energy without physical existence, violating thermodynamics. I-ness, identity, self, a mirage, result of multiple activity in the brain, giving an illusion of focus.

The argument is backed by wish. The author wants a mechanistic explanation, therefore he finds one. Let me propose Westerly's Theorem: human beings are driven by two opposing wishes. (1) To believe things are what they seem. (2) To believe they are not what they seem. One is to get along in the world, the other to escape it. Science and religion.

I too. Nature must be inviolable. That's why I deny God's intervention and reject heaven, hell, and life hereafter. In any physical way, I mean. That's why I need a materialistic explanation of consciousness.

But the other side too. I need more, something else, another view to bring me in out of the cold. If the whole universe, the physical world and everything, were an embodiment of sentience, would Makrov still find that a violation of thermodynamics? Subjective, objective. Neither without the other.

There must be a fallacy here and Makrov won't buy it. There's always a fallacy somewhere which Makrov won't buy.

PHILIP WESTERLY: *What to tell*

You could write the reading scene. The study, a corner room in back on the first floor, one window on the garden, the other to the garage. Books and papers, clips, pencils, a file cabinet, table for the printer. William in the leather chair with a manuscript in his lap. Philip in the swivel chair thumbing through file folders. Patty on the straight chair from the kitchen leaning over a file drawer. Others talk in the living room, the old squeak of Aunt Edna, Mother's soft low tone. Kids on the sunporch. Again Philip hears sobbing at a distance, not sure where nor who.

The study is alive, animated by him, pages of writing, letters, memos, in which his voice speaks through the type and you can smell him in the paper. You can group and perhaps date his writings by their look. In recent years the computer made austere pages, a heading or typed letterhead, clean text with few typos and no corrections needed. Older pages recall his electric typewriter, the small type, crowded and full, with inked insertions. Some papers bear the River City letterhead. At one time he used yellow paper. Still older writings go back to a manual typewriter with alignment problems and broken letters. Some cards, letters, and notes are handwritten. The writing varies, always small, sometimes neat and well-formed, a kind of elegant printing, and sometimes ugly and irregular and almost illegible. He had handwriting idiosyncracies: his *of* looked like *at*, his *ing* like *y*.

Philip is still not detached enough to write about the delicate shocks of his reading. Though most are small, they accumulate, they add up. A sickly feeling, like talking too long about a Relationship. The painfulness of imagining his dignified and capable father, humorous and wise, lying with his head in the lap of a flirtatious girl. Paralyzed by shyness, unable to kiss until she shows him how. Give the man his youth, Philip tells himself, allow him to have been a child once and to have changed and grown.

The queasy feeling has something to do with secrecy. His father's request, implying a secret to be destroyed. The notion of secrecy spreads and contaminates Thomas's otherwise innocent papers. The file cabinet is a fortress of secrecy, its cold steel front and smooth rolling drawers that seal shut with a click.

Yet everyone has secrets, Philip reminds himself, it's the human condition. Give Thomas his secrets too, allow him the privacy of his thoughts. The trouble is, he wrote them down. And writing implies an audience. Is that the issue: the hypocrisy in the idea of secret writing? But that's unfair too, for Philip knows (who better than he?) that not all writing is meant for the world. Sometimes you write for yourself, what no one else must read, so as to know what you think.

If it's not that he wrote secrets, Philip thinks next, is it that he didn't destroy them? He could have done so, or if that's too much to expect, he could have labeled what he wanted destroyed: *PLEASE BURN UNREAD. THANK YOU.* Why leave such a decision to his children? It was as if, by asking his children to find a secret worthy to be destroyed, he made sure that everything he wrote was a discovered secret and that every secret was discovered.

Why should Thomas do a thing like that?

A certain vanity. A writer's vanity that wants nothing that passed through his head to be lost. To underscore the difference between Thomas the citizen playing roles, professor and president, father and husband, mentor, guide, and model, and Thomas the writer whose words contain a world. Philip understands this. In fact, he knows it well. He thinks such vanity harmless as well as natural. Many writers have displayed bigger egos without being monsters.

So why is Philip still troubled? Is it that he doesn't, after all, want his father to be a writer? Doesn't want his mind spread out, doesn't want to know what has passed through his head. What Philip grieves for—is this what he is trying to write?—is the *role* Thomas learned to play so well, the character he created of himself: the gentle father, mentor, guide, and model.

THOMAS WESTERLY: *As read by Philip*

WYOMING 3

If you knew the truth about me, Penny Young said once, you'd be shocked. I knew this much. Sex in the forties came in levels, like classes in school or ranks in the army. A ladder of erogenous zones from nothing to all the way. Climbing the ladder was a ritual, my knowledge of which was hearsay. The only thing I knew directly was the lip to lip, which she taught. I had heard about the rest from talk and books. Open mouth and tongue, which I thought was a French refinement not standard in this country, followed by a graded sequence of bodily parts. These could be pauses on the way up or terminal points beyond which one chose not to rise.

The ladder was a device to regulate the horsing around of the young. Later generations abandoned it, reducing the whole thing (if the media are right) to two terms: Foreplay and Fulfillment. The levels previously discriminated were collapsed into Foreplay, whose merely preparatory function was defined by its name. It would be silly to set your standard, the limit beyond which you would not go, as a certain level of Foreplay. Therefore to these younger young there is no such thing as a ladder but only one question: Yes or No, On or Off. Sexual behavior has become, like the rest of the age, digital.

But in the forties there was a ladder, and my big question after the trip was where on the ladder she drew her lines, the question of her standards. She said I would be shocked. This seemed to imply that she was ahead of her time: digital-positive, though she was enough a child of her time to go lip to lip with me through four states without disgust. I did not want to believe it. Her various fiancés, what lines did she draw with them? Never having seen her draw a line, I couldn't guess. I hoped she had a limit of some kind. Almost any would do.

Rumors reached me through college friends, including one reported to have said she improved his batting average one hundred percent. The previous summer at the beach, batting average. Interpret the metaphor. It was hard to curb my own tendency to think digitally. Yes or No. Digitally speaking, there seemed to be no explanation for her but Yes. Which might be the true meaning not only of *engaged* but of *flirt*. None of this mattered until after the trip, for while it was going on I was under a spell. Later the digital conclusion seemed so obvious it started a memorable argument in my soul, a debate between me and an imagined Penny Young, whose replies I created for her. The debate went on until I gave up, because I always lost. As a result of that argument, I was forever after a more tolerant and liberal person.

The object of the argument was to persuade her not to screw Jule Foss, Harrison Glade, or anyone else. The first reason was that it was wrong innately. Good people don't do it. I cited ancient tradition derived from God and his Commandments, which unfortunately I regarded as either metaphor or superstition. So I abandoned that and argued on the basis of character, the looseness of character without standards, setting a low value upon itself. The trouble with that was that I thought her character fine, so I cited instead the Good of Society which regulates customs for the sake of children and social harmony. No use, every Society has its others, nonconformists and shamans and rebels, societies for people like Jule and Harrison as well as fast Mimi and your writers and artists and forward-looking souls who have different social imperatives and who say no if not in thunder then quietly. But what if you got pregnant? Or, what will your lovers do when they find out? What of the dangerous *habit* of wantonness, the fatal restlessness it will introduce into your marriage causing jealousy and fights and divorce and divided homes, distressed children, misery and despair? She had an answer for every argument, all right there in my head. All my arguments collapsed into one. I wanted her for myself. Be grateful for her free spirit, without which there would have been no kiss, perhaps no trip. I felt no rancor in her presence. It was only later, when her vivid presence was replaced by its vivid lack, that I was frustrated, angry, censorious.

A time came when instead of worrying about her lovers I wondered how far I could have gone myself. If I had been less bashful, moral, nice, or whatever I was. The signs she gave, how she held my hand, the offer to change my bandage in her room, which I ignored. What did I miss?

I imagined. If, after the sweet dry kisses, I put my hand on her breast. Would she have stopped me after her long struggle just to make me kiss? But if she permitted that and I then slipped the same hand up her leg, would she have drawn a line to say, I was only flirting? That's not what I meant, not what I meant at all.

The retrospective thought gave me a thrill. Could I have had her if I had dared? I imagined the room in the tourist home. She would fix my bandage. Kiss again. Find an excuse to lie on the bed. Help me out of shyness, teaching. A simple clearcut digital Yes.

The problem was the Thomas Factor. The distortion of an experiment caused by the nature of the experimenter, in this case the influence of my own peculiarities upon her. To the question of what she'd have done if I had responded more aggressively, the Thomas Factor replied: *I would never have had those opportunities if I had responded more aggressively.*

According to the Thomas Factor, if she had tried to seduce me, I would have been too shocked to respond. If I had been bolder, if I had been a fully confident male like Turley or Jule Foss, *she* would not have been interested. The older I got the more likely it seemed that my charm for her had been not my soul or my character, but only that perishable Thomas Factor itself, which was a challenge to her. Charming timid boy, what's left if you take the timidity away?

My speculations always took the same route: I could have had her, except that if I could have, she would not have had me, and therefore I could not have. Which confirmed this piece of philosophy: since it didn't happen, it couldn't have happened, which makes speculation pointless.

The story falsifies her anyway, makes her frivolous and empty-headed, a flirt, loose and wanton. An unfair distortion. And now she is seventy-one. On our last evening, when I took her to the play, in the New York restaurant recommended by a friend of my father's (a bachelor who knew the best places), we sat dressed up in an elegant room with green velvet hangings and a golden chandelier. The menu had a black velvet cover and gold tassel. I thought, I am here with Penny. But the inside of the menu was a shock. I was betrayed by my father's friend, who didn't know how limited my resources were. Perhaps she was shocked too, though she said nothing, but when the waiter came she ordered the sweetbreads. How kind of her that was. I didn't know what sweetbreads were, only that they were several dollars less expensive than anything else and were probably disgusting. Perhaps I should have urged her to get the salmon or the prime rib, but I did not. I ordered the sweetbreads too and relied on the sauce to conceal them.

———————

CHARLES WESTERLY: *To Greta Cordage*

Written by flashlight in my tent pitched in the backyard of Grandfather's house. Shared with David, whose back is turned, crowding. A lot of people here. Came by bus and ferry, Beatrice and kids also on the ferry. Greta. Sat around most of the afternoon. Missed Beatrice's walk with the kids and Greta. After dinner walk with Greta, harborside by the fishing docks. Dumb, though, stupidity growing through evening. Board games. I the big winner, Greta quit. Fat lot of good. Now Greta in the Inn with Lucy Realm. Blown it for good, sure this time. Unless a sweet-talking letter?

Dear Greta,

You'll be surprised to get a letter from me, I guess. I'm writing cramped in a tent by flashlight almost crowded out by my brother, who's sleeping with his back turned. I feel stupid. You must think I'm stupid too. When I took that walk with you this evening, I thought we could start talking naturally and sooner or later we'd get back to the last time we were together. I wasn't counting on my stupid shyness. I assume your shyness too, unless you really meant we shouldn't remember anything. But if you didn't want us to remember, then I guess you wouldn't have agreed to take a walk, and since you did agree I guess you must be disappointed that I was so stupid as if nothing had ever happened between us.

So I'm writing to let you know I haven't forgotten, and when we went for that walk I fully intended one or the other of us to bring it up, so we could decide what to do next. I didn't write before because it seemed more natural to talk but here I go writing after all, because I didn't have the guts to talk.

So I want you to know I have forgotten nothing. I remember not only the snow outside the car, and the light on the house down the street where we were parked, I remember also I mean especially your sweet gesture when you undid your blouse, and I remember your nipples in the street lamp, and I remember also your pants, and my fingers and yours too, yes, your magical fingers, and the panic when the time came and your laugh and the washrag. And I remember also how we talked about our mutual virginities, how sweet you were not to ridicule me (even though I'm already nineteen years old and you are seventeen) and how we decided not to go all the way because it was all too quick. Nor have I forgotten what you said about your boyfriend and how we must not get too serious talking about love or anything beyond the natural love of stepbrother for stepsister, and I agreed with you, which is why I haven't written you love letters in the interval.

On the other hand, as I said, I haven't forgotten what happened then, and there are one or two other things I also intended but didn't tell you on our walk this afternoon. For instance, I have rectified the virginity problem in my case. No emotional involvement, just a little girl in college, which has improved my confidence. (*Not* the one I called my fiancée by the way. No one knows what's become of her.) I presume by now you have probably done the same, for I remember you were going to start the pill, and a lot can happen with a boyfriend in five months. I suppose if you do happen to be emotionally involved with him in a heavy way you won't be interested in my present thought, but that's a chance I have to take, and I'm sure you won't mind my bringing it up. For what I really wanted to say this afternoon was that after long and careful consideration, I think it's time to complete what we started but did not finish last Christmas. It would be the most natural thing (unless you are too deeply tied to your boyfriend by now), especially after what we have already done, and it would so to speak correct our truncated and rather perverted memory of the other occasion.

It shouldn't be hard to manage. I can borrow the car tomorrow, and we can go down to North Point. It's warm enough, we could go out into the dunes and have all the privacy we need. I really hope you'll be willing. It's been growing on me all spring. I've been kicking myself for not arguing more strongly last Christmas—I didn't argue at all in fact and I've often wondered if you would have done it if I hadn't put you off with my serious talk about responsibility and all that crap. At any rate, I sure as hell am for it now, and not with just any girl (I got that from the little girl I mentioned at college) but particularly with you. And I can't help thinking, remembering how sweet you were, that you share the feeling at least a little, or at any rate are not totally averse. I won't ask you to decide in advance though. If you go for a drive with me tomorrow, we can talk it over.

I've given hard thought to the stepbrother question and have totally altered my position. The simple fact is that you and I are not related in any way, no more than any white Anglo-Saxon boy and girl are related. My father married your mother, but your father was not my father and my mother was not your mother. They call us brother and sister, but it is stepbrother and stepsister, which is different from half-brother and half-sister. There is no relationship between us.

Besides, I'm not suggesting a love affair. We'll see enough of each other for the rest of our lives because of our parents. You can have your lovers and I fully expect to have mine. Maybe we'll find that one little try on the beach tomorrow (tomorrow! My God, is it possible?) will be enough to last us a long time. Maybe on the other hand, we'll want a re-play now and then when we meet on vacations and other family occasions. Who knows how we'll feel? Only let's give ourselves the opportunity, let's not kill it off because of ti-midity, embarrassment, or superstition.

I'll need to get this letter to you without attracting atten-tion. At breakfast. I guess I'll simply tell you that I have a letter. That shouldn't surprise you too much.

THOMAS WESTERLY: As read by Philip

One last thing to read tonight, when everybody else had gone to bed, found accidentally by Philip in a file labeled UNIVERSITY FINANCES. It bore the title, "Things to re-member."

At that time obsessed with sex, though I'd never had any, which was why I was obsessed. Graduate school, Chicago after the war. Lucy Sycamore, little sister of my friend Fred who had once lived in Sherwood Forest. She was an under-graduate who seemed younger than she really was. She ate with us in the Commons and would look at me. With soft hair, bangs, oval face. She looked up from under her bangs with large eyes. Not a candidate for sex, off limits because of age and who she was.

Everybody was serious in 1946. I studied geology but had literary friends, Fred Sycamore's group. Slightly scorn-ful of my scientific narrowness, pressuring me to broaden myself humanistically. To be profound. Undergraduates in Chicago read Aristotle, Plato, Heroditus, Thucydides. The sublime and the tragic vision. Alcibiades and the Peloponnesian War. We ate in the Commons, carrying the cafeteria trays to the long tables under the gothic roof and vast English space.

She joined me with her tray one day at noon. Okay? We had a nice awkward little conversation. Repeated two days later. Our schedules created a routine. I played a role. My supposed years gave me an advantage with her which I did not have with my more sophisticated friends, enabling me to tutor, suggest readings, critique her responses, show off. She liked me. I didn't want to lose that, which hooked me before I knew it.

They invited me to family dinner in November, Brookfield near the famous zoo. Why me? Ostensibly because of Fred and the Sherwood Forest connection, but I suspected Fred of inviting me for her. We rode out in Fred's car with her between us that Sunday morning, bright and sunny and cold, the suburban house with leaded window panes, small rectangles. The professorial father, sherry before midday dinner, questions about geology and my career, with slightly condescending approval of people like me whose well-limited specialties combine for the general advancement of knowledge. She with the blue eyes, chaste sweater with collar tips folded over, listening more than speaking. After dinner she played the piano, Schumann and Bach. We walked in the woods with Fred in the bleak leafless late of autumn, talking of T. S. Eliot.

A new excitement henceforth in our lunch chats in the Commons. Imagined eyes on me, Fred's, parents', friends', her own. Was I now expected to ask for a date? Was it permitted? Think. Obsessed with sex, twenty-four and nothing to show for it, against her innocence, youth, connections (Fred's kid sister), and all my intellectual graduate friends scornful (probably) of my interest in one so young like a child. Who had no idea what lustful thoughts I tried not to have about her in secret.

The season rushed on, aiming at Christmas. Thanksgiving dinner in Brookfield, old school friends, tinder for jealousy I thought too proud to feel. Stamp out jealousy by forestalling its occasions. Touch football. This time I walked with her alone, leaving Fred and cousins, to the village center, railroad tracks, bridge. She asked, was Fred as smart as he thought he was? I replied generously. And justified my career in paleontology along with promises not to forget the humane and artistic values that separated me from ordinary paleontologists. She swallowed that, believing me superior to her brother's intellectual but scientifically ignorant friends. I took her to a movie, momentum and surge, dinner. Late evenings at the University Tavern. The word Love came up with two sides: what would her parents think, Fred, my parents? And what would she think? Pretty good notion of that by now. Walk to her dormitory late at night, first kiss, dared in perfume, cool air, heart near collapse, while she clung with surprising strength and said, God. Do you really? I think so. How long? Ever since I saw you with Fred in the Commons. Did you suspect? Is it okay? Love, love.

Does love necessarily lead to marriage? What people do in marriage, do you think we're compatible? If we get married. When we get married. Numbers of children, where and how to live. How people make children, do you think about that? I think about it all the time. Conversations in the dormitory, you should hear what they say. If we're going to get married, shouldn't I visit your family?

The long overnight ride on the train, head on shoulder asleep in the dark dawning Hudson Valley. The strangeness for her of returning to the town where she grew up, and for me of not having known her then. Five days before Christmas where Mother put her in the extra little bedroom next to Beth's, with the sights of New York and Westchester, an opera, a play, the Empire State Building.

The reason we were holding hands, yes, it means. In effect, Mother, we're engaged. In effect? The intent is there. Time, place, wherewithal, yet to be decided. She seems like a sweet girl, dear, I'm sure you'll be very happy.

Is there something we can do besides kiss? Late in the living room after the parents had gone to bed. Well, there are lots of things some people do. It depends, do you object?

Nobody'll come back downstairs will they? The hook's in the back. I was afraid you'd be disappointed. I always felt inferior, men make such a fuss about such things. Not me, I like them just the way they are.

That was a start. Are you curious? Just so long as we have limits and don't go too fast. You can't go backwards, you can't retreat. Should we stop here? I don't know. Not necessarily. What else would you like to do? Maybe tomorrow we can drive out into the countryside. What do you want to do there?

In the car in central Westchester, stopped on a stretch of country road next to woods. What? Nothing, I just gasped. Your fingers so cold. I approve of masculine restraint, I feel I can trust you. Now what happened? A little too much excitement. Are you all right? I'm just fine.

Another night, another country road, ending in a patch of woods near the skating pond in the night dark without moon. The secret species reality of this person I had picked or been picked by, linked to the corresponding secrecy of half the world's population assumed to be identical, therefore no secret yet secret for all that, endlessly repeated secret though known to me only in imagination and fantasy. Okay? Fine. How much further can we go? Let's go into the back seat.

What happened in the back seat. An experiment. We need to agree on a limit. Must we? Since we've come this far, be careful. It's hard not to, though. Oop. Did you intend this to happen? My lord, it's close, I never thought I'd be doing this so soon. I never thought, I never dreamed. Wow. As long as we're going to get married, maybe we ought to get married soon.

We can't go back, that's one thing. Therefore. Winter in Chicago, turning into spring. Difficulties for students living in dormitories. Cold winter nights. Dangerous campus bushes, the dangerous park. Radical adventure in the spring break in a hotel room over the lake, blowing a graduate

160

student's budget. Naked for the first time in the sunshine through the afternoon window, protected by the drugstore.

Obsessed by sex in charge of everything now that it was out. The importance of opportunity, the insatiable quest for opportunity. She moved into an apartment with a roommate in order to improve opportunity. Visits to families full of conspiracy in search of opportunity. Cape Cod and Maine, beaches, sand dunes, scrub woods.

Drugstore failure in August 1947. My mother said, Wouldn't it be more sensible to wait until next year and let her finish her education? No. At the wedding just before Thanksgiving in a chapel on the campus, she looked great in her slim white wedding gown with a flowery tiara over her bangs. When March ended in 1948, no one commented on the date.

PHILIP WESTERLY: *To Thomas*

Father, I read you unwillingly. I don't want to know about your coming of age. If what I love and mourn is the father you created, this story is irrelevant. It has nothing to do with him. It caught my attention and held me rapt, but only through the wantonness of my curiosity and the narrative qualities of your writing. I followed and bore it by separating the written you from the person I knew as you.

What your story ignores is that my father and mother founded an institution forty-seven years ago with engraved names, along with bonds, insurance, education, and history. The sexual goose laid her golden eggs in a back room out of sight and the sexual capital accumulated like compound interest. No one needs to know where you found the goose nor how you trained her, as long as she did her work, which she did.

From this institution eventually emerged five more establishments, similarly endowed with stock and insurance. They too shelter generative mysteries in the back rooms. The master company is now going out of business. That's a good and powerful reason to mourn, though inevitable. But the company was well established and its subsidiaries have a strong tradition to guide them.

———

LUCY WESTERLY

Dear Mother,

Tonight at dinner we used two tables. We used the wedding china, supplemented by Aunt Madie's, and your two lace tablecloths. We had a roast, and I was helped in the cooking and preparations by Mrs. Jordan as well as Patty, Melanie, and Beatrice.

We had seventeen people. At the main table, going around from me at the head were Philip, Beatrice, Henry, Melanie, Patty, William, David, Greta, Charlie, and Edna. At the second table were Tommy, Angela, Betty, Nancy, and Minnie. I must be forgetting somebody, but I can't think who.

Dear Thomas,

I thought it was you I forgot at dinner, but I know we had seventeen, and I can only add up sixteen names, so it must be somebody else. Because if I forgot you too that would make eighteen.

PART EIGHT

THURSDAY (2)

LUCY WESTERLY: Composed in bed

I thought I was traveling with Mother to Europe and you were waiting to hear from me. When I opened my eyes and saw the sunlight, thinking it was London, I thought everything I wanted is scheduled to come true. Then I heard the rain. The window had moved, which was why I had mistaken the sunshine, and I didn't know where I was. I woke up all the way and saw the sloping walls around the dormer window and the wallpaper of dogs and cats and I thought, what child's bedroom is this? I recognized the furniture, the bureau and table, the cover on the table, but couldn't remember what part of my life I was in—plus rain out the unfamiliar window and the foghorn which I did know was down at the point—all this before I remembered where they had moved me last night and what had happened to you.

HENRY WESTERLY: *Narrative*

No, the nakedness of Angel Vertebrate, I did not make that up. It was reported by the deputy Axel Gunner, as told to him by an occupant of the house across the street, looking into the lighted window from her own second story window—that Angel Vertebrate was sitting handcuffed in a chair in Sam Truro's living room and that he was naked. And what follows too, what she saw, into which the rest with the words spoken and the thoughts all fall into place.

Another day of the stalemate has passed, stalled because the hostage-taker has still not determined how to use his power. Fewer watchers out front now, and today in the rain only the pro forma deputy in the sheriff's car sitting with his rifle, trying to keep awake, his drooping eye on the silent blank house.

By now Sam Truro has surely considered the alternatives—all the political ones, at any rate—and has discovered the melancholy fact that there are, apparently, no alternatives at all. What to ask in exchange for the freedom of his hostages? A safe conduct? But safe conduct to where? And what would he have when he got it? In what way would his world be better than before, what could he be said to have gained? The conventional rewards for hijacking and hostage-taking—if not for a political cause then for a load of money, improve your standard of living under an assumed name in a foreign country? How strange the whole conception seems to Sam Truro, who knows that no one will give him money for his wife and son, nor even for Angel Vertebrate, and even if they did, it comes to the same question, what would he do with it, what difference would it make to the great pain, the great wound with which this all began? To cure the pain, heal the wound, that's the only outcome that could repay him, since it was the burn of that wound that first made him do it—but what could soothe or cool now, beyond what he has already done, the gesture he has already made? He can ask for an acknowledgement, that is all that remains, the most he can hope for, but who has the authority to acknowledge, whose acknowledgement would count, and what is it that must be acknowledged?

You know, don't you, in the silence of that house now, where still the siege goes on in its drilled routine, with its guards and checks and controls, the man in charge of it, this Sam Truro, has now faced up to the absolute perplexity of his wants, the absolute ignorance of what to ask or do next. He is caught in a gesture made permanent.

Yet today in the rain—I realized it this afternoon as I looked again at the house—one further gesture has occurred to him, what was only potential yesterday when he stripped Angel Vertebrate and made him join the family rituals with his privates exposed. Today it is clear, there in the afternoon as he watches them, his three prisoners drowsily looking at the afternoon soap operas. Once the idea occurs it grows big in his mind. He goes to the television set and switches it off. Hey, Georgette says. Aw Daddy, Roger says, although he had been almost asleep. Angel Vertebrate grunts.

Seems to me now, Truro says, if Angel here has to go around with his clothes off, it's only fair you do the same, Georgette.

Screw you, she says.

Off with that shirt.

Cut it out. This is going too far.

Already gone too far, Truro says. Just do what I say. Waves his gun at Vertebrate. Come on, Angel, he says. Tell her to get undressed.

He says to tell you to get undressed, Angel Vertebrate says.

When Georgette takes off her shirt she flings it at Truro. Same with the bra, the jeans, the pants. The pants land on the end of the gun. Good thing you didn't make me mad doing that, he says.

She is mad, sure enough, and she sits down in her chair, breasts and pubic hair in clear view of all three males in the room. She resists the feminine impulse to cover herself with her hands and arms. Sits instead boldly, thrusting her breasts out, as if there were nothing against her will that he could force her to do.

Now, he says. Grab his cock and give him a hard-on. She looks at him with hatred, then turns to Angel Vertebrate and looks only at him.

Why does she obey? In some twist of spite her anger against him and his against her now travel the same track, seeking expression in the same act. Defying him by her obedience she grabs Angel Vertebrate in the designated place and does exactly what she has been told to do. It takes only a moment, then the next command, barked as by a dog: Georgette, lie down on the cot. She leans back, taking care not to release her hold on Vertebrate, her other hand pulled back by the handcuff to the chain. Now, Angel, climb aboard and go to it.

I can't sir, you'll have to unlock me first.

He'll do that, taking care, watching with the gun as always while he undoes the shackle. He steps back and looks.

Watch this, son, he says. You'll need to know how to do this when you grow up.

He hears his wife's muffled voice, He'll never grow up.

Shut up and enjoy, he says.

We're enjoying, she says. We're having more fun than you ever had, jackass.

Enjoy it, enjoy it, you don't enjoy, I'll kill you. He is screaming. You're committing adultery, you damn well better enjoy it.

———

Austin Wright

PATRICIA WESTERLY: To Thomas

Dear dead Daddy, hey Daddy,

You suspected something. Talked it over with Mother. Wrote about it. No names named. If it was we you suspected you didn't say. Should I tell you, now you're dead?

Take one of those long vacation drives, all day on the Interstate, you and Mother in front, us crowded in back, on we go. The lakeside cabin ahead and motel with swimming pool tonight. The three of us in back—where were Philip and Ann? Summer jobs, college kids, I don't remember.

Moods change driving across country hour after hour in the haze of high summer. Air conditioning not good enough. In the back seat we slump, sick of games. Restless dog climbs from one lap to another. Why am I in the middle, though oldest of the three? Girl, right? Or to stop my brothers' slugging match, I don't remember. Nor which summer it was, though it could only have been when I was seventeen or eighteen and he fourteen or fifteen: 1970 or 1971. George ten or eleven.

You'll blame me for this, my age edge, supposed to know better. My discontents, all the things that pissed me off. I was in the middle with him on my right sulking about something, slouched down with the blanket in his lap. I was thinking about people who weren't there, things that weren't going to happen at the lake. It was either Ted Barney's summer or Studs Kuhler, can't remember which. With this new knowledge I had, which I figured nobody in this car knew, giving me an advantage, I thought. So maybe I was in a grouch too, my thoughts off out of the car, anywhere but the car, but I noticed. What I noticed was not just the blanket in his lap but his hands out of sight and a certain movement in the blanket which in my new knowledge (it must have been Studs Kuhler) I figured to yank the blanket off his lap and sure enough there it was. Long and red, which I would not have expected (only a kid with girlish eyelashes, chubby with a lot of growing yet to do), like Studs Kuhler in a state of gross demand. Cut it out, he yelped, grabbing the blanket back. Furious and silent because of the parents humming along quietly up front and George asleep on my other side.

So I played wise grownup, perfectly natural, nothing to be ashamed of, while he blubbered and half cried, saying, I can't help it. It's perfectly all right, I said, and, It's not all right, he said. He had all the shamed old ideas about everything.

I said, The only bad thing is the place. I mean, what are you going to do with it? I haven't thought that far ahead, he said. Well you better, I said.

I could tell him under the blanket trying to stuff it back. I wasn't going that far, he said snapping his lips as if I was the disgusting one. You'd better, I said. You'll be miserable if you don't. Give me your handkerchief. Is it clean? He was so confused I went my hands under the blanket with him. Let me, I said. I'll wash it out tonight.

You're crazy, he said. But he let me and it only took a minute, while he quivered and rolled his eyes, trying so hard to keep his convulsions invisible to you folks up front, I felt sorry for him.

Then he said, How disgusting.

It's not disgusting, I said. I rolled up the handkerchief.

He was crying. I can't help it, he said. I don't do it often.

It's better if you have somebody else to do it with.

That's perverse, he said.

Some girl, I mean.

I don't know any girls.

You don't?

None who'd do that. I'm too young.

You don't look too young to me, I said.

What do you know about it?

I told him about Studs Kuhler.

He looked shocked, even more than before. It's not that

big of a deal, I said.

Don't you believe in marriage?

Marriage is a different issue, I said.

I could see him thinking, looking at me as if he had only just realized.

What's the matter?

He repeated what he had said, like deliberately: I don't know any girls.

They're all around, I said. All you have to do is look.

I'm too shy.

You can overcome that.

I could see the idea in his head a long time before he said it. It came out finally quiet: You're a girl.

Don't be ridiculous.

I said it so quickly like bang before I had time to think like slamming the door to keep the rat out and only then, afterwards in the noise of the car, did I feel the silence and absence of thought. He was looking at me with white eyes in terror. I didn't mean it, he said, I'm sorry, I'm sorry, like he expected to be whipped.

Take it easy. I felt sorry for him. I was also thinking about Studs Kuhler and what I had had to overcome with him, that if I could overcome that I could overcome anything, and I was in the midst of my most violent disgust with the hypocrisy of the world, and I was afraid he was about to grow up into a right wing conventional prig, so I took a breath and said, Would you like me to?

Like you to *what*? he said, not taking any chances.

That soft still girlish somewhat plump face, he hadn't yet acquired the coarse stuffed look he would grow into in his maturity. I was thinking of that red growth sticking out of him like a parasite, and I thought I could educate him. I said, You know.

I don't know. Like he was going to cry again.

I could do it if you ask.

You could?

Once. To show you what it's like.

Really?

If you want.

When?

Tonight, my room.

Not tonight.

When we get to the lake. Tell me when you're ready.

The next two weeks he kept looking at me. I wished I hadn't suggested it and hoped he'd forget about it and after a while decided to deny it if he came after me, because the more I thought about doing it with him the more repulsive and unnecessary it seemed. He stopped looking at me and avoided my eyes and never did get to the point of mentioning it, so that after a while it was like nothing had happened and in the end nothing did happen except that we were always henceforth a little estranged.

This is in case you wanted to know, in case we were the ones you were thinking of.

DAVID WESTERLY: *To Olga his wife*

Rain all day is getting me down. Tonight we go to the Funeral Home. I'd rather not, I've never seen a dead body live. I'm immature for my twenty-three years.

I write at the dining room table. People reading everywhere, bored by the rain, discouraged by each other, too much time, too many of us. My Uncle Henry is depressed. My Aunt Pat and Uncle William are too polite. My Aunt Ann left for England and my Uncle George has not checked in and my grandmother is said to be furious though I think she's having the time of her life.

My immediate complaint is I'm banished from the tent by Charlie, whose tent it is. I was going out there after lunch when my brother grabs me. It's my tent, he says. Okay. Then he says to keep Tommy away, which makes me ask what's going on.

None your fuckin' business. So here I am keeping an eye out the window across the backyard near the hedge. The tent flap is on the other side, out of sight. I told Tommy what Charlie said. Oh, he says, that's so he can be with Greta. Greta, Jesus. So I'm not only banished from the tent but I'm aiding and abetting my brother in dirty work with his sister. I know what he'll say to that: she's not his sister. A technicality. A little later I catch Tommy going along the hedge. Where do you think you're going? If they're fucking I want to watch, he says. You'd better the hell not, I say. Aw David, it's a one-in-a-lifetime opportunity. So now I'm keeping Tommy like a dog on stay in the living room doing puzzles while I write.

My cousin Lucy Realm irks me. You remember her, Aunt Ann's daughter up Wildcat two years ago? The thick glasses and tumbling black curls. Graduate student in history. They sent me to meet the ferry today and she came with me. We met Uncle Carl and her brother Gerald (her other brother Larry and family are already here). The ferry was late. We're waiting in the car, the gloomy gray rain in the harbor and no ferry in sight, and she asks me if I noticed the black guy on the plane yesterday. Talking to Tommy and Angela, she says, with the pack. I remembered but I'd forgotten and she says, I guess you don't want to know who he is. Well sure, I says, I'd be interested to know if it's a case of your thinking I should. You ought to know, she says, because it's interesting family information. The interesting information turns out to be that Aunt Pat and Uncle William are getting divorced and the black guy on the plane is Pat's boyfriend. Came on the same plane and Pat met him. Only she had to pretend not to know him because of Aunt Edna. So says Lucy, and I say, Is that a fact? and it turns out it isn't a fact, it's a hypothesis, a reconstruction put together by Lucy on the basis of eager eyes or guilty looks or whatever she imagined she saw there in the airport terminal. Turns out she doesn't know a damn thing, not about Pat or William or the black stranger, it's all her imagination looking for sensation, but she's convinced because it hangs together and there's no use arguing.

Not only is she imaginative, she's snooty. She asks me what I think of Beatrice's kiddie books. Well not being a kiddie any more I had not formed an opinion, and it never occurred to me to have one, but she thought I should. Don't they embarrass you? she asks. Thumpy Puppy? Milkweed Pussycat? I wonder what's the harm, they're just kiddie books, and why should she go out of her way to knock my step-mother who is really a very nice lady (nicer than most in this family with the exception of you), but I can take it. The thing she's revealing in herself is her desire to put me down. She thinks I don't know that some people might find Thumpy Puppy and Milkweed Kittypuss nauseating. She thinks she is humiliating me by disclosing to me a world of sophistication I in my parochial family limitations am unaware of and therefore I must be abashed in her presence. That's a line of thinking I don't see any point trying to combat.

When finally the ferry appears around the point a big blunt gray shape fuzzy in the rain, she starts grumbling about her brother Gerald. I'll bet he's not on it, she says. He won't be there. You wait and see.

Well why shouldn't he be on it? I ask. Because he won't. Because he's a mess, she says. Because he's a bum. Why the animus? Don't ask, she says, just don't ask. Which arouses my curiosity but also accords with some feeling in me I'm ashamed of, like I never much liked this cousin Gerald, who used to seem spoiled or brattish in contrast to his brother Larry who's a real nice guy. It was Larry who taught me how to throw a curve, but Gerald was stuck up, center of the world. And he had that body odor problem, did I tell you about that? A kind of small whatchmacallit stink, you notice it when you've been around him a little while or when

172

he comes within a certain range. A certain whiff you wonder where it's coming and hope it's not yourself until you realize it correlates with him. He'd wear these big sweaters in Maine where we used to visit, and he'd come and sit down and I'd notice but not for sure until Charlie mentioned it. So he had that problem. But he also had a guitar and was pretty good singing old stuff, folk stuff, labor stuff, which we enjoyed, somewhat making up for the stink. Actually I'm not fair, for I didn't detect it today. But once a guy gives you a whiff and you notice it, it gets attached to him in your mind more or less forever so that whenever you think of him you remember it and maybe you'll smell it even when you don't, which is unfortunate.

Well he did arrive today in spite of his sister. She said he was ruining his life and going to hell, and she had given up on him, but when the boat docked there he was wearing a bright red plaid shirt and carrying a pack and looking just like always, a little truculent and mad in the eyes, and the way she greeted him you wouldn't know she had given up on him, so I don't know what the hell was going on.

Right behind him walked off the ferry the relative I admire most. That's my Uncle Carl, whom you've never met. My grandfather's younger brother, only five years younger but it looks like twenty. He strides off the ramp with his small bag, healthy and rosy-cheeked like a presidential candidate. Smiling over us, his powerful reality wipes out Lucy Realm and Gerald like a bright day. Wholesome and open, no ambiguity here, no hidden motives or dark compulsions. How there folks, he says to us, and though I don't know how well he remembers us, we're children in his shade.

My Uncle Carl is a great man. I never realized it until graduate school. He's the perfect scholar. You could call him an absentminded professor but I don't care, it's the devotion I admire, the ability to get entirely into his mind and shut out the world. The perfect civilized man. He's devoted his

173

entire professional life to the pursuit of a single man, the writer Fisk Purser. Do you know Fisk Purser? An American of the late nineteenth and early twentieth, who wrote poems and tales and articles, famous for a group of stories about the Civil War as well as a set of ghost stories. Uncle Carl edited his letters and his journals and has been working on a definitive biography for thirty years.

Back at the house Lucy Realm whispered, How could he spend his whole life studying somebody else? How servile can you be? Well, too bad. What I admire most in a person is concentration. A great athlete is a model of concentration. So is Uncle Carl in a different way. Some years ago I realized I would never make it to the major leagues. Then I discovered what Uncle Carl does and he became my model.

Tommy has escaped. If he's out by the tent, it will serve them right.

ANGELA KEY: *What to tell her mother*

I saw Tommy leave the house without an umbrella but I caught him. Asked where he was going. I twisted his arm and he said Pete Arena. I said he was crazy, and he said Pete Arena went by the house, strolling in the rain like he didn't realize what house this was.

I reminded him what you said, but he went anyway. What am I supposed to do, stop him by physical force? I went looking for you, but couldn't find you either. Are you seeing Pete Arena too? If you and Tommy meet, don't blame me. But if Tommy's late that's why. Just thought you ought to know, but someone else can tell you, not me. I don't tattle.

HENRY WESTERLY: *To God*

I may be depressed but I am not stupid. You know more than I do. This afternoon as I was coming back from my walk, entering the village, I saw my sister Patty standing in the door of the Harborside Bed and Breakfast. I recognized the maroon jacket. She saw me without realizing I had seen her, whereupon she disappeared inside. When I got to the Harborside I looked in. There was nobody around. The point is, I presume you know where she was going last night when I saw her go out of the house late in the evening just for a walk she said.

Second thing, a few minutes later: when I came up Main Street on the way home, I saw my nephew Tommy across the street heading toward the village center with a black man. My nephew was gesticulating and the other guy was walking fast with Tommy trying to keep up.

Third thing: as I approached the house, I noticed a movement in the bigger of the two tents out back, its green darkened by the rain. Walls bulging like something being rolled around inside. I happened to remember this morning kids in the kitchen giggling like Keep your eye on the tent hee hee. I'm sure you know more about this than I but I'm not totally dumb.

Fourth thing: old Aunt Edna sits in the living room. My sister Patty comes in out of the rain. Edna says, Ann (calling Patty Ann) there you are. Who was that Negro you were talking to at the airport?

African-American you mean? Why I don't know Aunt Edna. That was just some stranger who wanted to know the way.

Again, this afternoon, I heard the crying.

Here's a poem I thought of while walking in the rain, based on my middle name, which is James.

> I am known as Henry James, Henry James,
> I have claims on all the dames, all the dames,
> If you ask me what I do
> It is likely I will sue
> For I'm sick of all your games, all your games.

PHILIP WESTERLY: *Recalculation*

Necessitated by word that Professor McKarron Balsam will attend the funeral representing the University. Arrive late ferry tonight.

Mother complaint: Couldn't they have picked somebody a little livelier?

No room at the Inn.

Taxed to the limit, all these Westerlys.

Old Islander Hotel: single for M. Balsam. Why that'll cost a fortune. University's paying, Mother.

Meet the ferry? Conflict visitation. Call Mrs. Grummond. Backup, Jeffcoat.

PATRICIA WESTERLY: *To Pete Arena*

I'll write you instead. After lunch I went for a walk, this chilly desolate rain. Down to the Harborside expecting you. You weren't there. Where could you go on a day like this?

I went on walking. Past the hardware store and the school to the firehouse, then the fishing docks. I stopped at the ferry pier, the big three-decked boat easing in, the rain heavy now, feet wet, umbrella hard to control in the wind. All the way my mind was at work arguing fiercely as if even you were but a piece of imagination.

I went to look at the coast guard boat at the next dock. Mounted guns, brass fittings, clean pilot house windows. Radar going round on the roof, though the boat was tied up. I remembered my desire to be a sailor, how I imagined myself altered to make it possible. Then the heavy sea with me behind glass on the bridge, the charts and compasses and clean shiny instruments, knowing what to do.

I went to the jetty, where I walked out to the steel pyramid with its flashing red light, though the wind tried to push me into the sea and the umbrella was no good against the rain. I assured myself that wind is just wind, it has no body and my flat canvas shoes would hold me. It was pressure and I was scared, but even this was play and walking the stormy weather close to the sea was a game. I decided to tell Mother.

On the way back I considered whether it was cruel to do it at this hard moment in her life. Yet the decision has been made, the moving schedule is settled. The alternative would be to write her later, which would be cold and cruel in a different way.

I thought of asking William to join me but decided to tell her my own way. Back at the house, I saw my nephew David writing in the living room, and another game with the children on the sunporch floor. I peeked in the study where Philip was reading. He saw me and said, Grapevine.

Grapevine is rumor, he told me, circulating among the kids that you've got a lover on this island.

Wow. I acted surprised. Grapevine he met you at the airport. Ridiculous, I said, I didn't come by the airport. So you didn't, he said.

We had a good look at each other while deciding what to say. Not true? he said. I gave it a thought and said, Not wholly.

Partially? Partially then. How partially? he asks. Or don't I want to say?

I told him William and I were splitting (sorry to hear that, he said in his Philippy way, but not totally surprised) and there was somebody else. And true this somebody else came to the Island. I told him he came without my permission and I ordered him out of sight. I told him I wanted to tell Lucy in my own way.

He agreed.

I did not tell him your name, nor what you do, nor the thing you're worried about. I didn't tell because he didn't ask, and I believe in one thing at a time.

I found Mother in her room, which Aunt Edna was now

occupying. Aunt Edna was lying on the bed and Beatrice (Philip's wife) was in the other chair, so I had to stand. The little girl Nancy who is Beatrice and Philip's youngest daughter was leaning against Beatrice's front. Family scene. You said you'd tell me a story, Nancy said to Beatrice.

Yes I did. Is it time?

Telling time, Nancy said.

Ah so it is. And what time is it?

The little girl laughed. It's five o'clock.

Like an old mother-daughter joke between them. Let's go out and let the ladies talk while I tell you the story, Beatrice said.

I'm giving you a picture of my family. I heard a commotion in the living room and an angry male voice, Goddamn it brat can't you see I'm meditating? I don't know who that was, maybe my nephew Gerald who's been skulking. Aunt Edna said, If you don't discipline the young, who can you discipline?

Finally Mother excused herself and we went up to the bedroom to which she had been displaced. We shut the door and I told her the William part.

She was afraid of this, she said—which meant we haven't been good concealing. She felt it, so did Thomas, she said.

When I told her why, she did look surprised, a little shocked. She said, And is he willing to let that destroy his family and his home?

I told her it's not a question of choice. She said he seemed like such a decent person, and I said it's not decency, it's the set of his mind. She suggested we send him to a psychiatrist and I said you don't cure that kind of thing. I heard myself saying he was born with it.

Patricia, she said, you have two children. How did that happen? I told her it happened in the normal way.

Oh dear, she said, and she liked William so much.

I told her she could go on liking him. He loves her, more

than me actually.

She wondered if *she* could say something to him? I told her no. She said, You think I'm a dumb old lady, and I kissed her to show that wasn't so. I never did get around to telling her about you. One thing at a time.

TOMMY KEY: *What to tell Angela*

There was this guy at the playground talking to Mickey and Joe giving out free samples. When he left Mickey looked at the envelope and said, Hey I'm crazy, I don't want this stuff. So he gave it to me and I put it in my pocket, this small folded envelope, and went back to class, and then the problem. I didn't know what to do with it. I had this stuff which was probably good although not necessarily, and I didn't know. How you take it, I mean. I think you smoke it, but how, I don't think you wrap it in cigarette papers, and even if you do, I didn't have any and don't know where to get them. Probably the drug store, but I couldn't see myself facing the drugstore man asking what was wrong with regular cigarettes. And if it's not smoked in cigarette papers, which is what I've heard, how is it smoked? I needed to find out before I did anything.

The obvious solution was to ask one of those guys who hang around at the end of the playground. The trouble is they're not my friends, I don't want to get involved with them. If I told them what I wanted they'd probably help but they're not good company to be associated with. So I had this stuff in the envelope. I put it in the back of my drawer hoping Mother wouldn't snoop around. I kept it there while I was thinking who to ask. I only intended to use it once. No ruined life for me. I would use it once, if someone would show me how, so I'd know what it was like and stay clear of it forever after.

That was a long time ago. Last October and now it's

May and it's been sitting in the back of my drawer all that time because mainly I forgot about it. Until we came here. I got a notion. I thought here with all these cousins someone safe could show me. So I packed it and brought it along.

There was Pete Arena on the plane. I saw him and thought if anyone knew he would. At the same time, he'd be nice about it. He wouldn't let me get hooked, yet could understand the need to know what things are like. He'd keep me out of trouble and would appreciate having me on his side in his dealings with Mom.

But there was Mom's warning to ignore him and after the airport I didn't know where he went. And I forgot about it again. But today we have all this rain, which drove me crazy for something to do. I had another idea for this afternoon, but David squelched that. He made me sit on the floor and do puzzles half the afternoon while he wrote letters about the history of the world. But in the middle of the afternoon I happened to see Pete Arena going by in the rain. Right by our house. I guess he didn't know it was our house, he was just walking, but when I saw him I remembered what I wanted to talk to him about. So I slipped away from David and went looking for Pete.

He was on the next street and I caught up with him. We walked a lot. Drizzly rain, glum stuff, but okay, we talked about Mom and William and garage work and night school and he did his best to get in good with me. So I told him my problem. I told him how I never used it and only intended to see what it was like and only this much because it was free. He didn't interrupt and I thought he was listening to me. I said I had it with me and maybe he could show me how to use it. Why me? he said. I said because he'd be sympathetic and not tell anybody and not get me into trouble with bad company and such.

He says, What makes you figure I know?

Don't you? I say.

What makes you think so? he says.

I assumed you would, I say. Don't you?

He says, You sonofabitch.

Now why did he say that? All of a sudden he's giving me hell. Right there on the street by the docks. I can't remember all the things he says and it embarrasses me to repeat them. Just hell. Hell for asking him, like I asked him because he was black, like I thought all black guys—that kind of talk which I never thought of though he says I did. And hell for the stuff, for accepting it and for my dumb talk about trying it for educational reasons and hypocrisy and putting my life in jeopardy and the stupidity of hanging on to it and about being only fourteen and his responsibility to Mom and giving me a lesson, and in the end he's telling me to get rid of it.

He sort of convinced me.

I decided all right, I'll give it away. I wondered if we couldn't make a little something, its monetary value, but he says that's even stupider than what I've already said. Okay. It brings up the question how you throw stuff like that out. Valuable stuff which people would kill for, there must be a way of doing it, like getting rid of used motor oil, you don't just throw it down the drain. But he says this stuff you sure do throw down the drain, flush it down the toilet, get it into the sewer system. I wonder about the undesirable effect on rats or fish which would reach the seabirds eventually, and he says I'm stalling. He says we're going to throw it away and we're going to do it now. He'll supervise and if I don't do it, he'll do it for me. Meanwhile he's leading me out one of these long docks with the boats, the big oceanographical ship and diving equipment at the end, and stops in the middle and says, Here. Give him the envelope. Looking around now, making sure nobody's watching too close because this stuff could get you in trouble if it happens to be the law. So he opens it and kneels down. The gaps between the boards of the dock, the harbor water underneath. You do it, he tells me. I squat down and empty the envelope through the crack where I can more imagine than see it dispersing as it floats down into the water for the crabs and fishies and snails to get a kick if they can appreciate it. Last Pete tears up the envelope and drops the shreds through the crack.

We stood up and he put his hand on my shoulder and said some Boy Scout type thing like Good boy. I felt better though dumb. Rescued from dumbness, relief perhaps though I still think I ought to know what it's like if I'm going to be against it the rest of my life. I won't find out from Pete Arena though.

That's not the end unfortunately. When I came back to the house I ran into our cousin Gerald. He came in from the sunporch with the kids and invited me out to the kitchen. Started friendly. Who was that guy I was chasing down the street? You know what Mom told us, all I could say was, Just a guy. Just a guy. That made Gerald sarcastic, like why would I chase a black guy on this island where I don't know anybody if he's just a guy? I said I can't tell him, I'm sorry, I'm not allowed. That's all right, he tells me, he knows already. Knows what? Quit kidding around, he says, the guy's a dealer and I was going out to deal. Don't be an asshole, I say, denying, but the more I deny the more sure of himself and meaner he gets. He asks me what happened to the stuff I brought to the Island. How did he know about that? Jesus. There's only one possibility, which is that it leaked through Minnie Cordage because I swear she's the only person I told. That was another big mistake. She's so quiet and shy I thought she wouldn't tell, which shows how little I know, doesn't it? How supremely dumb I am. Because now this Gerald jerk, who really is a jerk as you are about to hear, thought I had some and was getting more from Pete the drug dealer on the Island, who identifies his business by being black. He wanted me to find Pete so he could get some for himself. He wouldn't believe anything I said. When I wouldn't help him with Pete he asked me to share some of my own stuff and I made the even worse mistake of telling him I threw it in the harbor.

I told him I scattered it through the cracks in the dock. If he wants to collect harbor water and filter it he's free to do so, only I didn't say that because he's bigger than me. When I asked why he wouldn't believe me he said it's too dumb to believe. He said my story was proof I was keeping it from him because any other reason I would have told him. If I'd used it already he'd believe me because that would make sense. But if I said I threw it away, it could only mean I still had some. He wasn't going to put up with that game so I'd better hand it over.

He twisted my arm. Literally. He grabbed my forearm where we were sitting at the kitchen table and pulled it back. He's stronger than me. I didn't want to fight and I was afraid if this got out I'd have to bring Pete Arena into it, which would doublecross Mom. So I sat there and you could call it passive resistance. He twisted my arm around back of my shoulder until I thought it would break. When I didn't do anything, he twisted the other arm. I thought they would both break. I said Ow. He laughed. Say Ow, he said. I said Ow again. Say Owowoo. I said Owowoo. Say my cousin Gerald is the Prophet Messiah and I am just a jerk. I said, My cousin Gerald is the Prophet Messiah and I am just a jerk. He put his big fist up in my face. He said, Are you going to give me some of your stuff or am I going to smash your face? He took my glasses off my nose and looked at them. Swap you, he said. You give me what you've got and I'll give you this pair of glasses. I said, I'm not above telling on you. He said, I'm not above telling on you either kiddo. I'm not above a little mayhem too. You know mayhem? What happens to brats who don't respect their elders in the month of May. Then I yelled. I said, Let go of me you fucking bastard and he let go. You probably heard me through the house. The only thing he said was, You tell anybody and there'll be a dead body on this island. I believe him. There already is a dead body on this island, so then there'll be two.

There's nobody I can tell but you and Pete Arena, and Pete isn't here.

ANGELA KEY: What to tell her mother

I told Tommy to tell you. Our cousin Gerald attacked him this afternoon and almost broke his arms. He thought Tommy had drugs and tried to take them from him and wouldn't believe when Tommy denied it. He's an addict and a bully. He threatened to kill Tommy and scared the shit out of him. He's not the nice little boy people used to think though I always knew better. Somebody should be told if only so he can be forced to get help.

I told Tommy if he didn't tell I would. He's afraid you'll give him hell. Because he had stuff which a man gave him last fall but he never used. Pete Arena made him throw it into the harbor. Tommy's afraid that if you don't give him hell for the stuff you'll give him hell for seeing Pete. So I told Tommy I wouldn't tell you, and I won't unless I have to.

But somebody should know. Tommy says there's nobody. He can't tell Dad because then he'd have to tell about Pete. Aunt Ann and Uncle Frank aren't here and probably wouldn't believe it about their son anyway. He doesn't want me to tell Beatrice, because she'll think it sordid. I want to tell Larry but Tommy's afraid he'll be in cahoots with Gerald.

I doubt it. Larry's like an older brother to me. But Tommy asked me please just forget it. So I won't tell you unless I have to. But somebody should. It's wrong not to tell somebody.

THOMAS WESTERLY: *As skimmed by Philip*

When I'm dead I won't know it. That's supposed to be a comfort. The world goes on without me, as unknown as before my time. Bees do it, birds do it, dog and cat, grandfather, great women of history. Only the invention of value is what makes death bad.

At seventy-one I thank you how good life has been   good luck, disgrace free, children, *Who's Who in America*   how bloody and cruel this job   the gory benevolence of this university in the name of The Good   standards discipline etcetera dripping blood

The culmination of civilization is on this island   what is civilization, name some attributes   living together   bonds and loyalties   cultivation of mind   consciousness   is mind good?   is it good to be human?

notorious terrible century   my privileged and peaceable life mostly lived under threat of Hitler, nuclear, end of the world   the cold war is over   will I know in time?

There was a folder tagged PENNY, *separate from the three-part Wyoming manuscript he had read.*

What should I do about Penny Young? Recently I saw a young woman in the bookstore who looked like her, but I knew Penny would no longer look like that, which made me wonder if I'd recognize her. And would she recognize me?

I drive out to the South Village several times a year. I do this to give guests a tour and refresh myself in the surrounding geography. I go through the little crossroads village with its grocery store and post office, aware of the possibility. I read names off mailboxes along the road. I notice the old women. I watch them wherever I go. I see them in our own grocery store and post office and library and on the ferry dock, some healthy, some weak, some with sad faces, depressed or grieving or bitter, some bright in their eyes, some with lipstick and rouge on their cheeks. The dazzling white hair flares, and I go on wondering which one could be she? I try to project the likely changes from my snapshots of her at twenty-one. I watch the short ones especially. Noses and chins never stop growing, and I enlarge hers until she looks like Aunt Edna, which is probably wrong since her chin as I remember it was small. She'll have put on weight, is she now fat? Is it hard for her to get about?

Things have happened to her, the probable and the possible. She had children, or she did not. She takes care of a jolly large family in her living room reading letters from five kids around the country, while three small grandchildren play on the floor. A stable hearty marriage. A difficult stormy one. Fidelity and loyalty. Philandering and adultery. She's a widow, she keeps a shrine to him in a corner of the bedroom and his name still in the telephone book. She was ill and watches her diet now with a regime of pills. She has spent the last ten years of her life doing volunteer work. Her bones ache, arthritis. She goes about the house gaunt and skinny leaning on a cane, angry with her fate, waiting bitterly for death. She's dotty with obsessions. Her memory has failed, she sits in her room served by her sacrificial daughter, not remembering Wyoming or the summer of 1941.

If she is in good health, sound mind and good nature at seventy-three, she won't mind telling me about the life she's led. I can respond. Dear Penny, I know what a child I was. I grew up. I fathered five children. I was admired by students and colleagues including women much older than she was then. I became President of a University. I was big and powerful.

For years I scorned her memory. I made her symbol of my ignorance and the shallowness of the age. Yet when I think of her at seventy-one, what I remember is sweetness, generosity, her good and honest heart.

What would happen if I called her up?

May I speak to Mrs. Glade please? Are you the former Penny Young? Did you go to Wyoming to study field geology in the summer of 1941?

Consider this letter.

Dear Mrs. Glade,

This is to ask if by any chance you are the former Penny Young. I once knew a girl by that name who later married a Harrison Glade. I've not heard from her for many years.

If you are not she, please forgive the intrusion, though if you're related or know what became of her, I would appreciate hearing from you. If you are Penny, I wonder if you remember me. Thomas Westerly. I studied field geology with you in Wyoming in the summer of 1941, and after the session was over, you came back East with others in my car. You even spent a night in my family's house before I took you to Greenwich.

We seem to be neighbors. I found the name of Harrison Glade by accident in the telephone book. I have lived on the Island with my wife since my retirement in 1988. We live on Peach Street.

I do hope that you are Penny and that you don't mind my writing to you. Also that you are in good health and that the years have been kind to you. I would love meeting you again to say hello, if you don't object to that.

Yours sincerely,
Thomas

Was this letter sent? The draft begins on the same page with its introduction, so that if it was sent it would need to have been copied. Philip wonders. If it was sent, was there an answer? Did they eventually meet? Or did Thomas delay again until finally it was too late altogether? There's nothing in this folder to give Philip a clue.

LUCY WESTERLY: *To Snowball, Fred and others*

Dear Snowball and Fred,

Thanks for calling, Snowball, your good kind voice and Fred too. *You never thought my brother would outlive you, did you?* Of course I understand why you can't come, I'm just so glad Fred continues to progress. How sad everything is now.

We had the biggest dinner ever. It took Thomas's death to bring such a dinner to this house. Then we went to the visitation in the funeral home. The big false gothic room with the rugs, vases, Victorian chairs, Thomas like a nineteenth century head of state in state. He looked as if he were about to speak, a piece of vagrant life in the midst of the freeze. I saw two things: my husband lying there dead, who was not my husband, and my husband lying there alive, who was not there. It dispelled fancies. *Like what adventures you had been through since we saw you last. Drained and pumped, stretched and put into clothes. Your face powdered and rouge, all wrong. When you died your mouth was open so Mr. Gregory must have wired it shut. That must be why you look as if you're about to speak. It's your mouth trying to pop through the wires saying, Let me out.* Thank you for your love. We must stand together.

MELANIE CAIRO: *To Dr. (not Parch) Saunders*

Probably I don't like William Key though it's hard to know. Whether his kindness is ironic or straight, his gentleness an island volcano in a southern sea. Last Saturday he looked at me. His upper lids cover half the irises making his eyes peek out as if they didn't want to be seen. I saw my dislike of him in his look, which you'll tell me (you psychiatrists) is nothing but his dislike of me.

There will be no repeat of what happened last summer. The sad occasion, he can see the inappropriateness. I told him so this morning. The day is gray, the rain steady. He and Patricia came over from the Inn after breakfast. When I came up from the cellar with the laundry basket, he was in the kitchen. A moment just the two of us. I just wanted him to understand. We hadn't spoken to each other in five days, and I thought it should be made clear. So I took the opportunity and said—this is what I said: William I just want you to know that as far as I'm concerned nothing happened last summer. He stared at me like a movie star. It irked me, Dr. Parch—no, Saunders (yes). That he should pretend to forget. He said, May I ask what didn't happen last summer? That made me mad, and I grabbed the laundry basket and went on up, but you can see for yourself why I don't like William Key.

This evening we went to Gregory's in the rain for the viewing. Somebody decided there should be a viewing and nobody had guts enough to say no, so there was a viewing. I walked with my umbrella and found myself with Patricia. Henry's sister, William's wife. I didn't intend it. I have nothing against her, but I wouldn't have picked her to walk with, and I thought it was accidental. Halfway there, however, we had pulled ahead of Philip and Beatrice and she said, I want you to know William and I are getting a divorce.

I wasn't surprised. I suppose what happened last summer was a symptom if not a cause. Yet I was upset. It makes me sad to see the old statues fall, no matter what they're statues of.

Thought you should know, she said.

No time to reply with the visitation then, old Thomas reduced to a corpse. We looked at it and sipped tea and introduced ourselves to strangers, and I was in the parlor looking down at Thomas trying to remember what he looked like when I felt William standing next to me. I thought he was going to speak but he didn't. Just looking too while the rest of the room chattered with people. I thought of him getting the divorce and the two of us as outsiders in this family and now he'll be cut off, leaving me feeling precarious like flapping in the wind with the cords snapping. His standing there was a gesture. It was full of meaning. The problem is, I don't know what the meaning was.

The question arose, why did Patricia make such a point of telling me? With everything falling apart enough for paranoia I found myself with Patricia again on our way home. I protested their divorce. Isn't there some less drastic solution to your problems? I said. I said how much I appreciated my own attachment to this family, what wonderful people and all the good times in Maine and Vermont, Michigan and River City. The importance of holding things together not to capsize when the wind gusts but stay the course, keep the boat steady, steer close to the wind.

She was rude to me. You've got your problems and I've got mine. Mind your own, okay?

Once years ago Henry told me an unbelievable thing about his sister Patricia when they were teenagers. It exemplified Henry's libelous imagination. Since he never mentioned it again, I concluded he made it up, which I still think mostly. Nevertheless I remembered it when Patricia was rude. I thought I could check it out by asking her.

But I didn't. I didn't want to betray his twisted imagination to her. That was right of me, don't you agree?

Dr. Parch, I appreciate this family more than its members do. The good parents, the bonds, the memory. Henry has no sense of it and neither does Patricia. But I do.

I wish I knew who's crying. It drives me bats.

CHARLES WESTERLY: Diary

Thursday, May 26. By flashlight in the tent while David groans. Saw my grandfather tonight at Gregory Taxidermy. Hardly recognized him stuffed, like a portrait, the identifying signs but no whole. As a result now I can't remember what he really looked like, leaving me with nothing.

The other thing was this damn Greta. Who came to the tent this afternoon like she intended to create a catastrophe from the start. Began by criticizing my letter, ridiculous, naive, what a fool she was not to kick me out on my ass for writing so asinine. Why did she come to the tent if that's how she felt? To straighten me out, she said. I thought she was just taking the long way around and tried to make friendly talk about like her boyfriend and who had she fucked since I saw her last or was she still a virgin, but she gave me such hell I wondered what I was doing here with the rain coming down all over.

Suddenly she gave a screech and lurched toward me, and I thought she was coming over to me at last, but it was only Freud out of the rain rubbing his wet fur on her leg. This made her laugh so hard and crazy, picking him up and hugging and drying, the poor kitty kitty, with all that love and laughing, that I figured she was okay, so I reached over and grabbed her. She gave me a shove (while the cat ran out into the rain again), which I mistook for horseplay, grabbing her again. She was wearing this green dress with bare legs, which I misinterpreted like everything else. She socked me pretty hard and tried to stand up but bumped into the tent so she had to bow down while yelling at me.

All the time I thought she didn't mean it because why would she come out to the tent if she did in that loose dress with those bare legs hugging that cat and laughing with all those gooey noises, and I thought yelling at me was just something a girl has to go through, a gesture of atonement before sinning so she wouldn't have to say she didn't resist. But it was pretty fierce and violent if it was just for show.

I mean it was rough. I didn't see anything but to quit. The insults. She said she was going to show my letter to her mother. What a dirty trick that would be. I said, You don't dare. Another mistake. I'm going to show it to Mother and your father too, she said. I said, If you do that, I'll tell everything I know. She said, Your letter speaks for itself. I'm going to show it to Philip and Mother and David and Minnie, and you won't be able to show your face around here again. Well maybe it was weak of me, but I'm not a macho type, I can't simply ignore that much resistance. I'm too sensitive for that. Okay, okay, I said, forget it. Forget I ever said anything. Forget it happened. You know, forget it!

Finally she calmed down. All right, she said, look. I'm going back to the house now. I'm going to pretend none of this took place. But if you ever annoy me again about anything, I swear I'll show your letter and tell my mother and your father and my grandmother everything. Okay?

I tried to patch it up. No hard feelings? I said. But all she did was call me an asshole, the bitch.

So I'm an asshole. Must be.

———————

PHILIP WESTERLY: *Question and answer*

Mr. Gregory at the door, flower in lapel, black suit smiling, gums and dentistry, shakes your hand and suggests you through the door on the left.

Victorian mountains and surf, a small boat with sailors drenched in slickers, gold twined mirrors. A piece of nose sticks up in the coffin. A smile flickers across his face, and there's a joke stuck on the verge of his mouth.

I have some questions for you.

Go ahead.

I've been reading your papers and would like to know.

Unfortunately I've forgotten my papers.

If you could identify certain people whose names I don't recognize.

By now I don't remember them, which makes them unimportant.

Should I talk at the funeral tomorrow, because I'd rather not?

I don't care.

Did you ever get in touch with Penny Glade?

I don't remember.

Would you like me to notify her?

I have no opinion.

I wish you'd tell me the joke which Mr. Gregory wired into your face.

I'm taking it with me, need it for Saint Peter.

Should I continue to read? Have I found everything you want me to find?

I have no idea.

Who's been sobbing in the house all afternoon?

I don't know.

WILLIAM KEY: *Family discussion*

In the study after the visitation Patty came in. Do you want to read? Philip said.

I've got a question for Mother, she said. I want to know what was going on when they left Chicago. Why did he ask if she would come with him to River City?

You don't want to ask that, Philip said.

All right, I don't.

You can read Thomas's account of their courtship, Philip said. It raises the question of when I was conceived in relation to when they got married.

Hey good, I'll read that.

Henry came in. What's this? More wallowing in Father's remains?

Patty said, We're trying to decide what to ask Mother about these revelations in Daddy's papers.

No we're not, Philip said. We're not going to ask her anything.

I want to ask about Father's suicide note, Henry said.

No you don't, Philip said.

Melanie came in. All you folks reading poor Thomas's papers.

We're all in on it now, Philip said.

I have a theory, Patty said. Mother had an affair in Chicago before we moved to River City, and when we moved she had to choose between her romantic lover and her family.

I don't believe that, Melanie said.

Neither can I, Henry said. What do you think, William?

I wouldn't know, I said. It's your family.

Philip looked uncomfortable, as if he had lost control. I've got to pick up McKarron Balsam at the ferry, he said.

Who's he? Patty said.

A shrunken head. A man of absolutely no interest.

Oh.

If you find anything pertinent let me know.

What would be pertinent? Patty said. He didn't answer.

After Philip was gone, Melanie said, Who is McKarron Balsam?

He's the university where Thomas labored for twenty years.

———

THOMAS WESTERLY: As read by Philip Westerly

Late in the night after he had taken McKarron Balsam to the Harborside. Philip went back to his father's files. The rest of the house was dark, everyone was asleep. For a long time he shuffled through pages in the narrow light of his father's desk lamp. He found a typescript in a folder labeled OLD BILLS, THROW OUT. The concealment aroused his interest. There was no title, no date, no page numbers.

Five years ago. An evening in the Christmas season, I can still name the date. I'm driving home through suburban tracts north of town, an area of estates and country homes going fast for a reason that doesn't need to be named. From a place that doesn't need to be named. Worried, hurrying to find out what was wrong at home. I was taking a direct route, a dark road through the invisible affluence with large houses back behind lawns and shrubbery, marked off by walls, high hedges, fences. Mailboxes along the road, no sidewalks, perhaps a ditch.

No streetlights, only the space which the headlights opened up ahead difficult to interpret since this road had no center line and only an occasional reflector to hint where pavement ended and countryside began.

Going too fast, listening to the radio playing something I've forgotten. There was a dog in the road. Rewrite that: there was a spot of light in the middle of the road, which might have been a roadside reflector out of place before it turned into two bright spots like animal eyes, around which emerged in the light the gray and white furred shape of not a fox but a German shepherd dog.

The dog stood broadside wondering what to do, body right, head left, looking at me, and I could not tell whether the dog was on the right of a road that curved left, the left of a road that curved right, or the middle of a road that went straight. The headlights of an oncoming car straightened the road, putting the dog between, a confused silhouette in the middle.

I used to examine this scene often, reviewing its details, trying to produce a more coherent account. If I am to write this finally after five years, it's no good if not true. If I can't tell it without lies and excuses, I shouldn't tell it at all. I should stop. It was impossible not to hit the dog. There was no time. The dog appeared, the car appeared, the dog was in the middle. The most coherent account is this: seeing my car coming, the dog trotted left into the path of the other car. I either remember definitely or assume I felt a natural pang for an animal in front of a speeding car, but it was the other car that would be the murderer. Then the dog saw the other car and whirled back into my path. Unable to stop, I veered right, taking a chance on the shoulder, which I *could not see*, a risk of skidding, overturning, crashing into something, but I hit the dog anyway, heard the thump, saw a flash of something fly as if the car had flung it into the air. The car bumped and jolted on the ditchy shoulder and regained the road full of shock and sorrow, still going fast. The dark place of the accident fell behind, and the ignorant taillight of the other car in the rear view mirror, and the question whether a civilized man would stop and drive back to see the dog he had killed, all of this perplexed by what seemed like a memory inserted into my mind after the fact of the thump not on the left but on the right, accompanied by an image of a skier jumping with ski poles through the light into the grass or the ditch.

The memory had no origin, it was simply there in the restored silence of the road while the taillights of the other car vanished from the mirror. The memory resisted explanation, or I resisted it, until the persistence of that image forced me to ask: Why was the thump on the right not the left, and why did the sight of the flying dog print on my mind a skier jumping through the light of the car on this flat road without snow? While the car continuing to advance left the dog behind, questions blotted themselves out, hiding the answers: what did I see? did the dog escape? what did I hit?

Now read this: under no circumstances should this be written without providing a full explanation of the circumstances. Question and answer: Why didn't you stop?

Imperative reasons of utmost force, forgotten now since it was five years ago, but they were urgent, both before and after the dog appeared. Against this preoccupation, the dog was an irritating distraction. Besides, I did stop. I would have stopped.

I drove on but it was so quiet and so dark I felt as if I had stopped. Looking into the mirror utterly dark, nothing to see, and no sound, thinking it was all my imagination, asking what evidence there was. I did slow down.

Don't make false excuses. What was I thinking as I drove on? I was trying to determine what had happened. I had faced the possibility of hitting the dog or the other car, but I had seen nothing. I assumed the blow I felt was the impact of the dog, and the confusion as to right and left was the shock of the car bumping in and out of the ditch. The only evidence was the momentary flash of a ski-suited body flying through the lights. It was only through questioning that image, that mirage, asking how such an image could have entered my head. I had to review the memory of what I remembered, and there was no way to check it against the truth since the only source of truth was the memory that needed to be checked. Whether it really was a flying figure I had seen and not a pedestrian standing by the road, the possibility that it was simply my inflamed imagination reacting to the urgent compulsion to go on. I had to work through and eliminate the hallucinatory and wishful possibilities before I could face clearly the question of what happened. By the time this had settled in my mind, the car had traveled several hundred yards.

So I was slow to react. When I realized what I had done, why didn't I go back? Don't say I realized what I had done. I considered the possibility, which was only a possibility then. Don't say I didn't go back, for I did. I decided to go back almost as soon as I understood the possibility. I did not stop and turn around, which would have been dangerous on this dark road. It would also have been an admission of guilt before a question of guilt had been raised. I looked for a turn off, expecting to go around the block and return to the spot. Only it wasn't a block. It was a distance to the first turn off. I took that road to the right with the intention of turning right at each successive intersection until I was back where I started. It took longer than I expected, winding roads by private estates and wooded country and horse farm fences and stone walls.

But I did get back in a few minutes. Why didn't I stop then? You must understand how short the moment of choice actually was during which I could have changed the course of events. I came back to the site driven by humane feelings, expecting to see the dog I had killed, hoping it was dead and not in an agony I could not relieve. I came back to the original road and drove slowly watching the wash of light from my headlights on the right shoulder. I did not know exactly where the spot was, for I had noticed no distinguishing landmarks (as I discovered in the daytime a few days later when I returned to the site and could not find it). I thought I had passed it, which would mean there had been no accident, and it was only then I saw the dog again. The dog standing at the side of the road, on his feet, tail up, sniffing at something. As I approached the dog looked at me, again the two points of reflected light, and turned back to whatever it was sniffing in the grass.

My great relief to see the dog unhurt.

It was more complicated than that. I knew what I was afraid of had happened. Don't say that. I knew no such thing. I considered it a possibility. I slowed down but did not stop.

You must understand: I saw nothing but the dog. I did not see what the dog was sniffing. To this day I can only assume what was lying in the ditch out of the range of my sight or lights. I assume that, but the truth as I remember it is that I saw nothing but the dog. So I drove on. I thought I was free. Relieved thinking the dog had escaped and the skier was imaginary. I drove on.

If that's what I thought, why did I go around that so-called block yet another time? There was a moment of freedom when I could have stopped and chose not to. When I drew abreast of the dog and had the opportunity to look, get out of the car if need be and see what was there. But I was too preoccupied with relief over the dog's escape, and the opportunity vanished after I passed the spot and the car recovered its will. But I was troubled by what my imagination had invented. I realized I could simply not have seen what was in the ditch or out of range of the headlights. At the same time I was thinking what was happening now might be as important as that other important thing which had interfered with my attention. So I decided to turn around and go back but that another set of headlights appeared in the rear mirror, which made stopping awkward. I came to the road where I had turned off, and I turned again and found myself making the square through the countryside a second time.

It brought me back to the site a third time. Driving fast this time, hurrying, thinking as I drove with what seemed now like a cleared head. I was asking why anyone should expect me to return, and I saw one good reason: to render assistance. Save a life. The reason to return was to give help. I drove back with the clear intention of stopping where the dog was, where I would do what I could. I could even make a trip to the hospital if necessary. Or if that was medically undesirable, to hail other cars. And take the consequences.

When I got back to the straight section of road on which the accident had occurred, I saw lights where the dog had been. Headlights on the left, which were stopped, and taillights on the right. At least two sets of taillights. Someone else had found the accident and stopped, and other cars had stopped. I (admit) was afraid.

Why was I afraid? I thought the people in the cars would know when they saw me because of returning to the spot, a clear indication of guilt.

How would they know I had been there before? They couldn't. It was this realization that enabled me to suppress the impulse to flee. I returned to my plan: to stop and offer help, which would be a good thing to do and easier with all these other people helping too.

If that was my plan why again didn't I stop?

I slowed down, expecting to stop, but the man waved a flashlight at me. I thought I was being arrested, but the man was only waving me by. Impatiently, imperiously, refusing to let me stop. Go by, it's not your business, we have enough already, don't block the road.

So I went on. I decided to obey authority. I could have stopped even so, but with all those people gathered there, my addition would have been superfluous, that's what the flashlight told. I thought, she's being taken care of now, removing the only rational excuse to stop. To stop merely to confess something would not be rational, it would benefit no one. So I obeyed the man with the flashlight and went on home, where I had to face the other problem, whatever it was, that was obstructing my vision that night.

I have never told this to anyone. What good would it do? I found a small item in the paper, naming her: Maud Merlin, a jogger, found by a passing motorist. No mention of a dog. I never told, thinking of the unnecessary distress it would cause to people who knew me. What good would it do? How selfish to comfort my conscience by an act that would help no one but me and might even do harm.

I was already sixty-two years old. Fully formed, not much room for growth. I'd like to think I have changed and would do differently now. That five years added to the original sixty-two could separate me from the man who panicked on a road at night, leaving a victim to die. I suppose that's too much to ask.

Throw this out. Think before you do, but throw it out.

Puzzled and disturbed, Philip put the manuscript away. He went back to his room, where Beatrice had turned out the light. He groped his way to bed and waited for the noise in his head to subside, allowing him to hear Beatrice asleep. From the town came a flash of music and a short laugh, then a bell struck the time followed by the bare clink of a buoy. In the rectangle of the window he saw trees shaped like laughing horseheads in the sky and a giraffe and a shape he could not decipher until he recognized the executioner's two-bladed axe. He wanted sleep to kill his thoughts but sleep was laggard tonight. The corpse of his father dropped off its stand. It fell spinning through the planetary night and shrunk by distance and rot it disappeared. That left only the dog sniffing in the ditch. As he fell asleep Philip's dreams stuck on the question of what the dog had found and during the night he concocted a thousand theories, none of which he remembered later.

PART NINE
FRIDAY

LUCY WESTERLY: *To Thomas*

Today it ends. I'll meet you at two. They'll bury you and we'll not see each other again. I missed you at the showing and it was no fun. This is the fourth day. Soon it will be a year and I'll say, Thomas has been dead a year.

I'll write you less often. I'll think more about our early days and less about what you became, which is too bad because I liked you better nearer the end. I'll remember my disappointment in you when I grew up and discovered you weren't as special as I thought. Your famous virtues, but you weren't adventurous. In spite of which I chose you a second time. Remember that. It wasn't just his refusal to make the same sacrifice he asked of me. I chose because I could trust you which is what mattered in the end. When you turned into a success with everybody looking up to you and criticizing you behind your back, I killed my resentment and took your side. I'm glad how it came out. I'm reconciled, Thomas, if you are. I just want you to know.

Tomorrow night I'll be alone. My children will invite me for visits. Fussy Philip and cool sweet Beatrice. Gloomy Henry and anxious Melanie. Wild but cautious Patty without her William (I'll miss him looking at me behind her back). No George, nor your favorite Ann gone to London. I'll be all right. I'll check out the Island widows and have widows for company. You've been good. You have a right to die and I won't complain.

———————

PHILIP WESTERLY: *Anticipating a memoir*

This morning with time free before the funeral, I took old McKarron Balsam and Aunt Edna around the Island along with Betty and Nancy stuffed in the corners. Aunt Edna half blind in the front confusing what island or cape this is, mangling proverbs, a worm in time spoils the broth. Balsam stiff in back looking straight ahead, children peeking at his liver spots.

With old McKarron and old Edna hearing nothing out we go past the notorious Truro house with the deputy on guard sleeping in the car parked in front. Past the junior high school and road above the outer harbor looking down on moored fishing boats in the coves and across to the jetty where Patty went yesterday in the rain. Today the sun's like English moors, the golf course with motorized carts and flags on the greens, before the road swings to the ocean side. There's rich light blue with tints of rose into the horizon, some fog out there, and a ship trying to bring itself into view unless it's my eye trying to create a ship into view. Shingled cottages, dunes, surf, birds yelling around the point.

Sick of reading.

The Island belongs to him. Everything on it, the low hill with the water tower, the dunes and plateau to the south, the inland lake, the reeds and scrubby woods and rockpile, was created for me when he took me out to see the countryside on our first visit, only six years ago. Which I didn't appreciate until this stunned knowledge that he was dead.

Can he survive this?

Edna said, Never could understand why Thomas wanted to come back to this godforsaken place. McKarron Balsam said nothing the whole trip. Maybe he was dead.

Island is father, an equation. I'll need to decide what difference that makes to this, or this to that.

When I was a child I was in love with Debora Mason, but I forgot why, so I reconstructed her out of images, trying to recreate the feeling I had lost. When I told my father, he laughed, but not unsympathetically. Don't try to vomit memory, he said.

Let it bubble, you remember a person best when you don't look straight at her.

I need to decide. Is it possible to separate the father from the man in the writing? Would censoring work? Or is he already destroyed?

Keep this out of the memoir.

———

THOMAS WESTERLY (handwritten): As read by Philip

An unlabeled file he had noticed before without understanding. Some few inconspicuous sheets crumpled and smoothed again, no beginning or end. Each paragraph crossed out by a line down the page.

the flashing lights ahead, cars stopped, the police already there. As I approached, I intended to stop, but they waved me by, my presence only an interference. I could not see the results of the accident as I passed. But it should be obvious to you from this that I came upon it only after it had happened and could not have

To Lucy: Something I need to tell you in case it comes up. But maybe you can advise me on whether I should do anything about it. This happened when I was coming home (*illegible*). I was on a road in the northern suburbs, I'm not sure exactly where, I had given a lift to someone at the party and was on my way home, a dark road on which I may have had this accident, although I'm not sure if there really was an accident. It was a dog ahead in the middle of the road and another car in the opposite direction   I may have hit the dog   I wasn't sure   as I was passing the other car and the glare of headlights. I went on, but I was distressed about the dog, distressed enough to go back and found my way by country roads to the site, at which point flashing lights and a police car   as if there had been an accident. I thought the police car had stopped because of the dog, but then   No, the dog was   No, then I saw the dog, if it was the same dog, standing by the side of the road   So I hadn't hit the dog with other cars stopped where the police lights   The point is, the police, the flashing lights implied   They waved me by, wouldn't let me stop, and I couldn't see what had happened, but since then, this is it, yes, I have been racked by concerns as to what happened along the road and whether I had anything to do with it when I thought I hit the dog

To Lucy: Something in the paper this morning, which I have just seen, requires I tell you this which I   This morning in the paper I've just seen   There's an item in this morning's paper which   Last night when   Night before last when I was coming home from the office party I need to tell you, on the road in

I truly thought I had hit a dog. There was every reason to believe it was a dog I had hit, only a dog

To Gene: May I confide in you a certain trouble which I don't think I can confide in Lucy? I was at a Christmas staff party, after which I took Elaine home, she without her car that night and because it was a kindness, nothing other than that, not after all these years. Well, the point is this: I received word that there had been an accident at home. Nothing specific, only that Lucy had called to say there had been an accident and would I please be informed so I could go home as quickly as   Well, the point is this: this message went directly to Elaine's house, that is, she called the party but after we had left and then she called Elaine who answered the phone and received the message—even though no one at the party knew I had taken Elaine it was Lucy's guess Lucy's assumption, that is, a The point is this: when Elaine took the call she failed to tell Lucy I was there. There was no reason for her to do this, I mean what reason could she   feeling uncertain about Lucy, I guess she decided it would be more discreet to deny of course I only happened to be there for a moment, I was not staying, I had just delivered her to her house when the phone rang, and she answered it and thought mistakenly that it would be discreet to say she didn't know where I was, and then Lucy told her there was an accident at   The point is, this is how I got the news about an accident at home. Well naturally, I was alarmed and hastened to my car and drove home fast as I could. Now when I got home, I was of course, desperate to know what the accident   there was Lucy calmly reading in the living room. I contained myself just barely, that is, prevented myself from asking what the accident   realized fortunately in the nick of time that if I asked she would know where I had been, which would have seemed extremely suspicious to Lucy considering Elaine's denial   acted as if I had not heard anything while Lucy calmly went on reading and I hung up my coat and went to the refrigerator and settled down in my chair, still with no word about either accident, and in fact there's been no word since. From which I conclude there was no accident (at home) and this was a ruse on Lucy's part to make sure this was no repetition of last year's   relieved I guess that I did not react   That's beside the point   The point is while I was hurrying home, riven by anxiety about (we're living alone here now with only Darwin for company, the kids have all long since gone), I myself had a kind of accident It's this I need your very wise and totally confidential advice

To the Board: Ladies and gentlemen, I need to inform you of an unfortunate accident which may have some impact upon your deliberations concerning my candidacy for I hope of course that No You will I trust recognize that what happened has little connection No no no Simply! I need to inform you that as soon as I have finished this letter I will be turning No I need to explain to you why I have turned myself over to the No I need to explain to you the content of a meeting I shall shortly be having with the   concerning an accident to which I was a possible witness. It appears that a certain pedestrian or jogger was accidentally killed by a hit and run driver three nights ago on a lonely road in the northern It so happened that on that same evening at approximately the same time I was driving near there and happened to see No

---

LUCY WESTERLY: *To Thomas*

We made this date forty-seven years ago. The only unknown was who would be in the coffin. It looks like you won.

Between Philip and Henry while the organist plays. We tried to make it nice for you. See how many people came, some from far away. The flowers, the music, the old-fashioned minister. This is the moment to celebrate ends. You and me. Patty and William. Henry and Melanie, on the way. George, Ann, who did not come. With tents in the yard, grandchildren. I saw Greta going into the tent with Charlie in the rain. Beatrice said they are not related, being only stepbrother and stepsister. Times have changed and I kept my feelings to myself.

Remember our worry about that sort of thing? How remote and forgotten it was, how foolish it now seems, if I didn't make it up myself. I'll never worry again as long as I live.

Will we talk again? Your muteness is an obstacle if it persists, which I've been led to believe it will. Your old aunt is senile. Philip cries. But he's not the crying I've heard in the house every day. I can't figure who. I've eliminated everybody and still hear it.

I'm not concentrating. People talk, the words pass through me. Abel Jeffcoat. Patty stands up to say something. Philip does not speak, nor Henry, nor I. McKarron Balsam gives a sleepy tribute. Jerome Dawson, the usual. William makes an odd philosophical speech, I'm not following. I hear the distractions. People sniffling. Coughing. I've noticed police sirens for the last fifteen minutes, outside in the wilderness where we live.

PHILIP WESTERLY: *Anticipating a memoir*

The funeral at two. The bright day, the wooden church, white in the sun. Cars on the grass, the hair of women, people in the doors. Down the aisle with my mother to sit in front. The coffin now closed waits in front of the middle aisle. Inside unchanged, the hands folded, the expression on the verge of a joke.

All of us contributed to the ceremony. Music my father liked as remembered by my mother, now played by an organist named Juliana Flower: funereal Chopin and Beethoven, mournful Tchaikovsky, transcriptions of Debussy and Samuel Barber's Kennedy strings. The music has a strong flower smell. Non-religious except for the local minister Jerome Dawson who sits beside the pulpit in his robes.

The ceremony began with Dawson reading a short prayer. Next Abel Jeffcoat on Thomas as Ordinary Joe. Original poem, "To My Grandfather," by Larry Realm. Original poem, "Verses on My Neighbor's Passing," by Ezra George. Memories by Patty and Melanie. Official tribute by Dr. McKarron Balsam, aged colleague, with suspense as to whether he will live long enough to complete his speech. Dawson gave a sermon not to my taste and William gave a speech which people considered cynical and inappropriate.

While the hymns sang the words ran on. Threatened by things I would rather not think, I tried to control them. Neat and skeptical sentences. I read: If the present is no more definite than it is, how can the past be more so? The usual way to deform the past is to make things coherent. Everything falsifies in the gloss of coherence. See how the past lies as it recedes, whittled and revised by your coherence-mad mind. A mere automobile accident... Ellipsis there, a lump of distraction which will require me to look back how this paper ended.

I wanted to speak, unbearably, but to him, not them. Just one question, that's all I ask. Can't I have one question? What would it be?

Save him, save him. This is his moment, then he'll be gone, how unbearably sad that is. Slowly slowly but always perceptibly he will be destroyed by the chemistry of dripping time. And the slow erosive action of my own killing mind. That which I alone know, that I wish I didn't. Ask him if it's true. Ask him tonight, or tomorrow, when he returns to visit in your dreams, ask him then.

New era. Ways to put it.

Panama Suez Cape Horn Straits of Gibraltar

In the straits though the land on either side is not close (haze fields and pastures on one side, pale bluffs on the other), the water is full of eddies as the wind fights the tide, but soon the first undulations of the new sea penetrate and lift you on a different rhythm seasick and as you look back and see the dark clouds over the old sea, already it's impossible to distinguish from the agitated straits themselves.

We are now in the act of creating history, as distinct from being created by history, which is our usual condition, and after this moment has passed, will be the condition to which we shall return, controlled by whatever we have created in this moment.

At the signal from Dawson, sons and grandsons of the deceased stepped from the first two rows to the coffin where we lined up grasping the bars to divide the weight. On the right myself, then Henry, William, David. On the left Charles, Larry and Gerald Realm, Tommy Key. Down the aisle and out to the hearse. Then the ceremony at the cemetery. The old woman in the wheelchair in back, I never did get a look at her.

What I am I owe to him. He said the eye would be a good specialty if you don't think it tedious. The eye draws light into a single point so as to build a replica of the world in your head. It projects you into the world sending messages to other eyes, telling them who you are with flashes from your intelligent brain. It dilates your anger, smiles your pleasure, weeps your grief. Just one caution. Take care you are not blinded by looking so long at the eye instead of through it.

CARL WESTERLY: *Not to be written down under any circumstances*

All these people talking about how great my brother was, I can't believe it.

That old bumblehead, forget his name, can't read, correcting himself, losing his place. *Thomas Westerly more than a dedicated scientist. Vocation avocation, all one to him. Fruit of civilization* (Jesus) *entrepreneur of Mind* (gag) *negotiating Mind managing Mind* (blah) *cultivating Mind of us all.*

What will they say about me?

Carl Westerly, Human Being. What is a balanced human being? Mind and body as in all created armadillos lions hares because without body where's mind? So though Carl Westerly was a humane scholar (as distinct from a mere scientist, most of whom are as ignorant and uncultivated as any philistine outside their fields) he was prouder of the healthful balance in his life. Golf, fishing, tennis into his sixties. Lover of good things, cars, wines, women (appreciative, I mean, of their virtues and beauty while faithful of course to his wife). Worked when he worked, played when he played.

Bumblehead has an overbite, his teeth tangle his mustache. *Thomas no narrow specialist bridged not only science and the humanities but intellect and action recognizing his responsibility to lead the academy as dean provost president giving broadly of himself.*

Carl Westerly no flashy showboat gave his life to the biography of Fisk Purser (the great American writer, equal to Ambrose Bierce, in a class with Hamlin Garland) which when complete will be a model for biographers to share the shelf with Ellmann on Joyce, Edel on James. Devotion to the life of one man. A true surrender of the self. What a profound dissolution of ego in altruism that is.

Overbite's generalizations need concrete examples if they are to convince. *Thomas's abilities, how easily he worked, how naturally everything came to him.*

Carl Westerly's scholarly patience, his hours in the library (on a regular schedule never too long to be unhealthy), scrupulous in detail. Not the facile superficiality that passes for study today.

Stumbling along losing his place: *Thomas the writer, the grace of his language, writing as writing beyond the necessities of its message.*

All his life Carl Westerly valued substance over style. His inborn hatred of public relations replacing thought, fools posing as intellectuals.

Now he's citing students. *What a bright enthusiastic teacher when he had the chance* (There's the rub. How much teaching did Thomas do from his presidential chair?) *interest in students as people, keeping in touch, letters he wrote.*

Carl Westerly taught by example, building his project a little at a time. No flashy lectures. Stuck to business.

A grandson speaks, what's his name, who cares? *Thomas's good sense. His contempt for bullshit.* Bullshit? This guy thinks he knows bullshit?

Tortoise and hare, Carl Westerly knows the difference between quickness and intelligence developed by steady work. Kept in place by proper attention to body needs.

Now the daughter-in-law, simpering and full of goo. *His shy dry wit. His tact, making it impossible to quarrel. His perception, surprising even family members who have known him all their lives.* Not long enough, kids. Only a brother knows the brutality, thick-headed stupidity and gross arrogance of a brother.

Qualities are relative. Carl Westerly came from a family of sensitive, intelligent people. Credit for wit and humor belongs to their father, and for empathy and tact to their mother who taught them to see themselves in every baby animal. They did not develop these qualities on their own.

A blustery neighbor, blowhard at a glance. *The scrupulous honesty of Thomas Westerly, almost disgusting* (meant to be a joke? Some joke.) *with anecdotes. Couldn't last in the presidency because of his disdain for begging.*

Carl Westerly was unfailingly decent and honest. This was a family virtue, not the private property of one individual.

The daughter, smart-ass since she was a toddling brat. *Thomas's scorn for cheap belief, creationism astrology cultism. Contempt for fads, his deep regard for reason and the advance of truth.*

Unlike most academics, Carl Westerly kept up with pop culture and the younger generation. Don't forget, Fisk Purser was a popular writer in his day, who attacked elitism, and

212

Carl Westerly attacked the same through him. This elegant well-researched scholarly edition of Purser with notes will be another gesture against academic showboats and snobs everywhere.

Thomas the loving father, gentle uncle, loyal and devoted husband, grandfather, impossible not to love.

Carl Westerly's wife and children will vouch for him.

If I had to speak here, what would I say? All my life he got the honors, the attention, the privileges, the respect.

MELANIE CAIRO: To Dr. Parch

If you could discover why this Truro wakes him from apathy like an electric shock. At the funeral he sat like a dummy following the others, looking where they looked without eyes, sitting through the music and the prayers and the poems and the speeches with his face dead. He wouldn't make a speech himself, so I willed myself to overcome shyness and speak in his place. I owed it to Thomas, or someone did, and if he wouldn't, someone representing him would have to, which could only be me.

However, when the sound of the police siren broke into the silence behind Mr. Dawson's voice, that siren speaking of event and crisis going on as they always do outside this quiet space where for a moment we were facing the question of questions, at that moment his head turned like a dog catching a scent, his body shifted, his face alive and irritated as if we were idiots for not running out to see. If you could make sense of that.

Again at the burial on the hill overlooking the dunes the siren sounded, a police car or ambulance or fire engine full speed along the shore road. He heard it and looked around trying to see and even wandered off while the minister was speaking just before the coffin was lowered, itchy like a boy wanting to pee.

RUPERT NEWTON: *As read by Henry*

The Island's celebrated Sam Truro case ended at 2:53 today in a bloody tragedy. Four people were killed, including Truro and both members of his family, whom he had been holding prisoner in his house. This was the ninth day since he had barricaded himself in and announced that he was holding them hostage.

The first break in the long stalemated situation came shortly before two. The house was being watched by Arnold Starbell, a deputy stationed since noon in a parked car across the street. "I heard a shout from the window like 'I'm coming out,'" Starbell said. The shout was repeated four times before Starbell realized what it was, proof according to Starbell of Truro's desire to be noticed. Thereupon the front door was flung open and there emerged in succession, blinking in the sunlight, Truro's eight year old son Roger, his wife, Mr. Angel Vertebrate, who had been brought into the case on Tuesday as "negotiator" but was captured by Truro, and, holding a rifle and a pistol trained on the others, Truro himself.

Marching single file, the trio of prisoners went around the side of the house to the garage, where they got into Truro's car, while Truro shouted at Deputy Starbell, "No tricks now." At the car, it was Vertebrate in the driver's seat, Truro beside him in front and the woman and child in the back. A moment later the car backed out of the garage and sped off down the North Point Road.

The police were notified by Starbell's radio when the group first came out of the house. One police car was dispatched to pursue them, and another went across Harrison Lane to the Shore Road to cut them off if they went that far. The first car came within sight of them just beyond North Lighthouse. When it came into view, the Truro car increased its speed and a chase down the Shore Road ensued at 100 m.p.h.

214

The car that had crossed on Harrison Lane was notified by radio and a roadblock was set up on Shore Road. This was in the middle of the long straightaway by the house of Mr. Danner Fritz, between a stretch of dunes along the beach and the marshy lagoon inland. After coming into the straightaway the speeding Truro car screeched to a stop just short of the roadblock. While Truro stuck his head out the window and shouted something unintelligible, the car, driven by Vertebrate, turned around to face the direction from which it had come. Meanwhile the pursuing police car appeared on the straightaway. As Truro's car started up again, it looked as if the two cars must either pass at high speed or collide head-on.

The Truro car had hardly started, however, before it veered and plunged into a ditch by the marshes. Officer McHale at the roadblock thinks he heard a shot in the car before it went off the road and believes that Truro shot the driver, Vertebrate. Whatever the case, when the car stopped in the ditch, the woman and child emerged from the back seat. As the police ran along the road above, Truro crawled out of the front. He appeared to be injured, unable to get to his feet. It was discovered in autopsy afterward that he had suffered a broken leg. When he saw the police officers running with their guns drawn, he raised his rifle and fired at them. The shot went astray, but it provoked a volley of police fire in return, in which not only Truro but his wife and son, who were standing near him at the time, were struck with bullets.

After a short interval, the officers descended the slope. All three members of the Truro family had been killed by the gunfire, probably instantly, and Angel Vertebrate, still in the driver's seat, was also dead of at least one bullet wound through his head.

Sheriff Haines responded to questions about the police action. When asked what Truro was trying to gain by emerging from the house, Haines said no one knew. No message had been sent, no demand had been made. When asked what Truro had asked in exchange for releasing his prisoners, Haines replied as he had daily for the last five or six days: nothing since the arrival of Angel Vertebrate, and no one knew what he wanted.

When asked why the police decided to pursue Truro, Haines expressed surprise at the question and said they just wanted to keep an eye on them, since he was holding those people hostage. "Strictly speaking, it's a kidnapping case," Haines said. "It's our duty not to let them get away." When asked where they could go since they were confined to the Island, Haines said, "They might have had a boat in a cove."

According to Haines, Truro probably shot Vertebrate while the latter was driving and this was what made the car go off the road. He said they could determine in a day or so whether the bullet in Vertebrate's head came from Truro's gun or a police gun. He had no theory as to why Truro shot him.

When asked why the police killed Truro, Haines replied, "Because he was shooting at our guys." When asked why Truro's wife and son were also killed, he said, "That's the too bad part of it, the tragedy. The innocent bystanders caught in a hail of bullets." Haines denies that the marksmanship of the police officers left anything to be desired. He insisted the innocent victims were simply in the way, between Truro and the police officers with whom he was exchanging fire. When asked about a report that the victims had already run around to the other side of the car and appeared to be seeking rescue by the police, Haines warned against rumors and insisted the police never shoot anybody unless they have to.

Reminded that it was for the sake of the woman and child that Truro had been guarded and pursued, Haines repeated, "That's the tragedy part of it."

Austin Wright

MELANIE CAIRO: *To Dr. Saunders*

As I'll also tell Dr. Parch, I'm afraid most that he'll commit suicide. When he gets home, or a week later, or a month. I expect it all the time. Dr. Parch will ask why I think it, and I'll say it's only what I feel when I try to imagine what it must be like inside that face of his. And now that Truro has blown up himself and his hostages together, I should think he'd kill himself at the first opportunity, for what else is left to him in life?

That's how Dr. Parch and I will talk, but you'll ask why I care. My reasons. I'll say what reasons had Sam Truro to blow everybody up? What can you expect, a man who reduced the world to Sam Truro, if Truro goes and does a thing like that? Studying Truro for his own attitude and behavior, look at the answer he gets. You'll ask how do I know what Truro means to him, and I'll say you don't have to know to know, he's stuck in it like his life depended. What can you expect when what your life depends on blows up like that?

Again you'll ask why I should care, wouldn't I rather be free of him? Not by suicide, I'll say. Why not? you'll say. Let him kill himself. It's not your fault, think how convenient it would be. It will be shock for the rest of my life, I'll say. Shock? Shame, make it. Shame? Guilt, then. *Guilt!* Your eyes will open, your mustache will tremble, your cheeks flicker, I can see the contempt now. You'll make a speech, I can imagine it well: did you make life for him? Did you decree the conditions under which he was born and grew up? Did you put him under the spell of the seasons, give him the rhythm of autumn fall winter and spring, put him on the life track through infancy youth old age, did you establish the dichotomy of mind and body and the further dichotomy of mind and self, did you invent the sexes and plague your invention with disorders, did you create the institutions in which he is prisoned, did you build the cities, found the colleges,

217

establish the churches, did you invent the language, the vocabulary, the grammar, did you distill the corruption and inject it into human veins? Who (you'll ask) do you think you are?

Nevertheless I'll defend my distress. It's the repudiation, I'll say, the total rejection. Rejection of you? you'll say. Rejection of life, I'll say, which includes me of course. This will start you up again, and I'll have to hear it all a second time, since when are you responsible for life?

So. If what you're saying is, if he commits suicide I should shrug my shoulders and say trala, that's how it goes, trala trallala, if that's what you're saying—

Not me, Dr. Saunders.

HENRY WESTERLY: *To his father*

Since this was what you were thinking about last, you'll want to know how it came out. When asked for the reasons, Sheriff Haines said, As far as we know it was motiveless. No one knows what he was trying to do.

Motivation, probability. Let's project what we know into the events, so as to infer likely motivations. Nine days they endured the isolation and austerity of their regime, with only two externally observed breaks in the routine: first the illness and release of the daughter Dinah, and second the capture of the negotiator Angel Vertebrate. The latter chained among them always naked and required to perform intercourse with the wife at Truro's gunpoint and for his pleasure from time to time. As time passed and Truro thought what to ask in exchange for his prisoners' release, evidently the answer eluded him and days passed with no further messages coming out. He must have grown still more desperate from the blockage of his own mind that refused to give up its secret. Inarticulate that he was, stupid with words, the idea of hostage-taking derived from the newspapers, he could not

218

say even to himself that what he wanted was for someone to prove to him the importance of being father and husband, of protecting his family and his career as the world expected him to—if indeed that was what he wanted. Nor that he wanted to be honored and praised for it, his fatherhood and husbandhood—if that's what it was. Nor could he say that he wanted to be shown reasons why he should continue to live as a civilized being and not some wild thing, conventional in his box house among everyone else's box houses, protected from the real world by the drowning element—if that was a part of it. Nor that he wanted proof by irrefutable argument of the value of life or of having a name title and file of numbers. Inarticulate, with such great wordless pain, dissatisfaction, restlessness, it must be that after a certain length of time, of what seemed like timeless waiting, while he huddled in the shelter of his absolute power, barricaded in his perfect privacy, sovereign in his fortified home, at last and perhaps quite suddenly this longing and dissatisfaction revolted like an overdose: nausea, so that instead of protection he craved freedom; instead of enclosure, space; instead of power to contain a world, power to break out and spill.

Get dressed. No doubt he gave the command to the naked Vertebrate and his wife. We're going out.

You want to know how he described it to himself. Going for a ride, he says. Taking a trip. Is it a vacation, a holiday afternoon drive around the Island, taking the air for refreshment before returning to the labor of the cell, or is it a major change, a bid to solve the problem or bring it into a new stage? Is he expecting, wordless as he is, to find the solution by driving about, does he think he has a goal, some place he'll recognize from which he can launch his effort in a new way, or does he merely mean to shake out the creases of his confinement by a stretch? Are these ends distinguishable to him without words?

They got dressed and he unlocked them and pointed his

gun at them as they marched out to the car, and he made Angel Vertebrate do the driving to keep them under control. All the things we don't know which he probably didn't know either. Was he expecting the police to pursue? Was it a surprise or one of those facts of life you must live with if you want to live life? At any rate, there they were, the police tearing after them a hundred miles an hour, he could see them across the dunes in the slow winding of the road out by the North Point Light. And ordered Angel Vertebrate to step on it, don't let them catch up. Like the exhilaration on a roller coaster, go faster around the curves, give it all it's got, you son of a bitch.

Why were they pursuing, have you thought of that? You drive on the Shore Road around the Island and you come back to the town where you started. Where did the police think he could escape to? Why should they care, a private family outing? Only that he himself had defined it nine days before, not a family outing but a kidnapping. The police were taking him at his word, wordless though he was. Because of his word, they chased him. Once the chase began they could charge him with speeding if they couldn't get him on anything else.

Looks like he was inviting the police to pursue, don't you think? Guess it how you like. They come finally to this straightaway, a mile along the duny beach and the marsh on the other side, opening out to a hundred again but for the roadblock they now see at the other end. Wordless, his brain cooks up the plan for escape, not to crash through the roadblock but to turn around, pass the other car as it tears down the road, for surely no sane cop even on a crazy chase will risk a head-on collision. Turn around you son of a bitch—to Angel Vertebrate—who doesn't like that gun at his ear and does what he's told. Turns around and here comes that pursuing car bearing down where they're starting up in the opposite direction, too fast to stop, so you'd think the trick

220

would work, he would get by them and be on a clear road again—back to the North Point (and eventually of course, in either direction, the town).

So you would think, but for whatever went wrong. The car, turned around, facing in the direction from which it had come, the roadblock behind it and the other speeding police car unable to stop—it starts to go, but only for a moment. Suddenly it veers off the road.

Afterwards the police discover the bullet hole in Angel Vertebrate's head and though the tests have not yet been completed, everyone knows what they will show—the bullet that killed Vertebrate came from Sam Truro's pistol. Close range at the temple. The question is not whether he shot him but why. You could look for some desperate motive. Something subtle enough to justify the whole adventure. His opportunity for suicide at last, making sure he takes his most particular enemy with him. A pretty good explanation. Or maybe this was the moment that Angel Vertebrate decided to be a hero. Maybe he was trying to put the car in front of the screeching police car, deliberately seeking a collision, upon which, seeing his intent, Truro shot him. Maybe he was pleading, arguing, and Truro lost patience. All these are good explanations. The one I prefer has less motivation. It was the nerve and panic of that moment of crisis trying to slither out of the trap. He was holding the gun at Vertebrate's head, squeezing hard and holding tight, while he urged with his body the effort to get turned around and moving again— urging with the twist of his shoulder, the push of his hips, every shift of gear, turn of the wheel that Vertebrate made— until he squeezed the gun too hard. Bang! Off it went—loud— as much a shock to Truro as to the others, who screamed at the explosion and the body of the victim leaping all reflex and falling dead on the steering wheel while the car skewed and toppled into the ditch, throwing everyone upside down. Seeing the man he had killed, and the car stopped in the sandy grass, hearing the screams of his wife and child, maybe now the wordless man recognized the moment he had been preparing for, whether to avert or to meet head on—and saw nothing left to his life but gunfire. The final gesture whose aim was to prove that whatever other vague things he wanted, one thing at least was true: he was serious, he meant it. With his leg broken from the twist of the crash, he didn't wait for them but pushed the door open himself and dragging this new and unfamiliar pain beneath him got out onto the grass and fired into the air the shot whose echo he had been longing to hear.

WILLIAM KEY: *What to tell Philip*

The old woman in the wheelchair spoke to Melanie as she came out of the church. She was with a blond young man. I asked Melanie who she was.

Penny Glade, Melanie said, I think that's the name.

I recognized the name but couldn't remember where.

I asked her, Melanie said, did she want to speak to someone but she said she didn't know anybody so no thank you.

Then I remembered Wyoming. The blond young man was helping her into her car, which was on the grass at the end of the row beyond the church. I remembered everything, the long trip across the country, the lip-to-lip, the two fiancés, the geology of the West. She was already in the car and about to go when I caught up. I wanted to see her. I wanted to see what she looked like and how she would talk. Penny Glade, I said.

She didn't look like much. She sat small, frail, shoulders hunched. Her face was puffy and pale. Close up I could see the residue of old intelligence printed around her eyes, but it was slack now. She was tired and gazed up at me with mild patience. She was not interested in me.

I tried to find the right thing to say, thinking what a dramatic reunion this would be if the right people were here. Is there anyone left with an urgent need to meet Penny Glade? Maybe Philip. I said, I remember your name. You were a friend of Thomas's.

Are you his son?

Ex-son-in-law. (I don't know why I had to be so precise.)

He was a friend of my husband who's now dead, she said.

According to the narrative Thomas never met Harrison Glade, so why did she say that? I wanted to make the connection, get something going, so I said, You went to Wyoming with Thomas. Then instantly I was afraid she'd ask how I knew, and I'd have to reveal Thomas's obsession with her. But she ignored it almost as if she had forgotten there ever was a Wyoming.

She said, I knew he was on the Island but we never got in touch.

That's too bad, I said. He would have liked to see you.

She introduced the blond young man, her son Harrison. I saw in the paper where Thomas got shot by Sam Truro, she said. That was heroic of him.

I decided not to correct her. I wanted to hear her mention Wyoming. I'm sure his son Philip would like to meet you, I said.

Philip was at the church door shaking hands with guests. If you can wait a few minutes.

I have to go, she said. She wasn't interested in Philip. Why should she be?

She wouldn't stay. The son, who had said nothing, drove her off and I watched the car down the road. If the original Harrison Glade is dead, it must be the son who's in the phonebook.

———

LARRY REALM: *What to tell Dolores*

I'm sorry in a limited way. I'm sorry on account of you and the baby and Grandmother. Not on account of him.

He's had it coming for the last year and half. I'm sorry it had to be just now, but this was my only opportunity. I've been holding it back since Angela told me this morning, or I've been postponing it for a year and a half. But I didn't realize what I was postponing until Angela told me. That electrified me. I had to wait though. I couldn't do it dressed up for lunch with all the people. Balsam and Carl and Edna and all the relatives. Then the funeral, where all through I was distracted thinking about this jerk brother next to me. I gave him a hint then, I said I need to talk to you and he mumbled something hostile which I didn't get. Then the hand-shaking and everybody back to the house for outdoor re-freshments and I had to put up with that too, when suddenly he started off down the street, and I knew if I didn't act now I never would.

He was leaving. Back to the Inn to change his clothes to take the late afternoon ferry and hitchhike home. I don't know if he said goodbye to Grandmother but he didn't to me. I saw him down the street and knew he was gone.

I ran after him. I apologize for running off, but I couldn't take time to explain, or to change my clothes, which was not so nice for my suit. I ran after him, leaving you with the baby and all the people on the lawn with their plates, and I could hear the party behind me as I went down the street. When he saw me he went faster which just stirred me up, so I ran hard and finally he stopped.

Not exactly friendly. What the fuck's the matter with you? he said.

I was too mad to tell him. We were at the corner and there was an open lot. All I could do was call him a sonofabitch. He had a smart reply: Don't say that about your mother.

224

The reason I didn't tell him the matter was that he ought to know without being told. If he didn't, too bad for him. I hit him. Not hard yet, more push than hit. I shoved him. He tried to talk, What's the matter with you? and I shoved him harder. Once I started shoving I wanted to shove more. I shoved him off the sidewalk into the lot and toward the bushes, and he tried to ward me off and asked what the fuck was wrong with me like it was all he could say. Finally he said, Cut it out, and hit me, which is when I got really mad and slugged him in the face.

That knocked him down, but he jumped up, and we slugged it out. Haven't had that kind of fight with my brother since we were twelve. When we started I didn't know if I could still dominate (I was taking a chance), because he's put on weight and I'm lean, but his weight's not strong whereas I've been running every day. The only thing he had going for him was desperation. But when he tried to fight, that just provoked me. It was his attitude, by which I mean not what he said but his manner of fighting which implied I was imposing on him and it was my fault and he was just enduring. It made me even madder. I slugged and pounded, and everytime he hit back it made me mad and when he hunched and protected his head it made me mad, and when he grunted and moaned it made me mad, and every word he said, like Cut it out, or What's the matter or Please Larry or God damn you or Fuck, it made me mad. The fact of his existence made me mad, so that anything he did which reminded me of his existence made me mad. The madder I got the harder I smashed and the harder I smashed the madder I got.

I got him on the ground and sat on him. I pushed his face into the dirt and banged it. He curled like a hedgehog in his Sunday funeral suit where I sat on him slicing my hand across his back chop chop.

I heard a warning voice in my head: Don't kill him. It

was like your sweet voice. It wasn't for his sake though. It was the trouble for me and you and the baby if I killed him. I saw a big stone near where I was pounding him, and I seriously thought of smashing him with it, which would have finished him, but I heard your sweet voice, so I didn't.

Uncle William stopped me. I didn't know he was there until he grabbed my arm. That's all right, when I saw him I realized I was done. He was saying something like Stop Larry and somebody was talking about the police. It's all right, I told him. You don't need to call the police.

There were others, townspeople, I don't know who. William asked me what it was about. I pointed to Gerald on the ground and said, Ask him. When he said, Damned if I know, I wanted to hit him again, but I was tired enough to resist the impulse.

He looked bloody. His suit was a mess. So's mine.

Gerald was crying. Sitting on the ground looking up at us and crying. Unexpectedly I felt sorry for him. I didn't want to but I did. I remembered some brotherly things which at that moment I didn't want to remember. He said, I'd like you to tell me what I did.

I said, If you don't know you're dumber than I thought.

He was sitting there thinking and I thought it was finally dawning on him, until he said, The only thing I can figure is that you hate my guts for being born.

So what's the use, if that's all he can get out of it, a lesson gone to waste.

He needed information, but damned if I'd spell it out in front of these people. It was demeaning to lecture him after what we had been through, which was like a furnace with its meaning in a flame contained entirely within. I settled for a hint. I said, Ask Tommy if you don't know. Then I realized I had betrayed Tommy and all I could do was make threats, like, If you touch him again, I'll come back and finish the job.

I watched him plod toward the Inn. He'll have fun hitchhiking with all those cuts and bruises. I wonder if we'll ever speak to each other again. When William and I came back to the house, we went behind so people wouldn't see us. I'm sorry I'm a mess, but I had to do it. I couldn't stand myself if I didn't.

LUCY WESTERLY: *To Thomas*

I'm in a bad mood. We had refreshments on the lawn after the funeral, prepared by Beatrice and Melanie and Patty, and there was a fight. It just sickened me and falsified everything.

I didn't see the fight, which took place down the street. I saw my grandson Gerald leave the party but not his brother Larry, who went after him. I was talking on the lawn receiving condolences, thanking people. I saw news run through the party like a flash of wind, one group to another, but I noticed they were keeping it from me. I had to ask and Melanie told me.

At first I thought it unimportant. Everybody has problems and things will erupt. You wonder but it doesn't have anything to do with you. But this gave me a bad feeling like spoilage. Grandchildren fighting at their grandfather's funeral, leaving a festival dedicated to family so as to fight. I tried to think it natural, boys as boys, but I heard a deeper feeling waking up that called it desecration. Denial of you and me. Repudiation, that's the word I'm looking for. Blood against blood.

I didn't want this thought. I wanted to think it a squabble. Brothers have squabbles. But desecration grew like fungus. Like rot, like a smell, a whiff of ruination. I was smelling it when the guests left and we got ready for our last supper together.

There's a difference between sadness, which I felt all day,

and a bad mood. Sadness is good, but a bad mood kills. I forced myself to be cheerful, which I don't usually have to do.

This Larry appeared at supper. Though he had cleaned himself up, he had a bruise on his cheek and a black eye swollen like a pig's snout. No one talked about it, which wasn't natural. I brought it up, but all I got was the polite equivalent of Shut up Grandma, none of your business. None of my business the family splitting apart like atomic energy, and my private thought dangerously close to Go to hell, all of you.

I got through by thinking this is the last time we'll be together, dwelling on the present joy and underlying sadness. Wholesome feelings. After supper I took Dr. Balsam to the ferry while David, who admires Carl, took the old people to the airport. When I got back Philip and Company were in your study again. They've been doing that all week. Your papers. I allowed it, thinking I was obliged to, having no say in the matter.

But the word desecration is like a bat, it flew around and attached itself to things. When I heard my grown children in your study shuffling papers along with the particular squeak your file drawer makes, it attached to them. Desecration, the beginning of a new era more chaotic than the last.

I took a look. It was lax of me not to have challenged them before. I went to the study door and saw the four of them (William included) with your file drawers open and your papers all over the place. Belatedly, days late, I was shocked. They looked guilty like rabbits in the rabbit act. Which proves desecration was the right word.

Theft. Burglary. What are you *doing*? I said. Going through Thomas's papers, they said. I knew that. Why? I said.

They stammered around. Do you have permission? I said.

Father asked me to, Philip said.

You don't have my permission, I said.

Philip said *you* asked him on your deathbed to go through and weed them out. Weed out what? Whatever might hurt somebody's reputation, he said. They thought they had a right to go through your papers looking for scandal. What an appalling idea. And to do this even on our last family night when we could have been all together in the living room.

I thought of the personal things that must be in your papers, the secrets of students and colleagues not to speak of you and me and I couldn't believe you would knowingly turn your children loose on them. They even brought William into it, whose very connection to the family is shortly to be severed. If you really did make such a request, you were not in your right mind, deathbed or no.

I told them that. I was firm. You can't go through those papers without my permission, I said, and you don't have my permission. I had no intention of giving it.

Philip mumbled that you wanted to save me the agony and shock (something like that), but I said if you meant that, you would have talked it over with me. It was deathbed panic for you, a last reflex of unfinished business.

They asked what I would do with the papers and I said send them to the library. I'll make sure there's nothing inappropriate and I'll send them. They fussed about the burden on me. Nonsense. The activity will be good for me. Only I can understand these papers. Only I know the names mentioned, the circumstances, the significance of things.

With plenty of time to find scandals if there are any I wondered what their raids had already found. Truth is, they wouldn't know a scandal if they saw one. Forget it, I told them. Thank you and forget it. Don't bother to put them back, I'll do it. It will be the first occupation of my new solitude.

Did I fail you in failing to catch them at the start? It's your fault, but I hope they haven't found anything to embarrass you. If they had they would have told everybody so I guess they haven't. But how much junk have you left rotting in your files for me? You who would never throw anything away. Maybe I should burn everything.

In the end it won't matter. Their merciless eyes will strip our bones like the sun, but until then, I'll hold my parasol high. They looked chagrined. I'm glad I stopped them. But I feel rotten with the nastiness of a new age and for the first time not sure I want to survive.

———————

WILLIAM KEY: Narrative

Funny how they looked when she stopped them. She came into the room like a seismic wave, guilty guilty children, what are you doing?

We slunk away, the belief we were doing good corrected in a moment to shame. Instead of protecting good people we were scandal mongering. Scrabbling for shocks.

We talked about it in low voices on the sunporch, out of Lucy's hearing. Philip, Patty, Henry and I.

So much for that, Henry said.

I'm ashamed, Patty said.

What's there to be ashamed of?

We were hunting for gossip.

I wasn't.

We got carried away, I said.

He didn't ask any of you, Philip said. He only asked me.

I'm glad she stopped us, Patty said. It was getting creepy.

What?

It made me realize how dead he is.

If Lucy reads those papers, Henry said, she'll read the suicide note.

She'll read the Wyoming story, Philip said. She'll read about their courtship.

It won't hurt her. You can't change the past.

Sure you can, I said.

Nobody's changing the past, Henry said.

Yes we are, I said. We're trying to control the past.

Trying to control someone's *perception* of the past, Henry said.

Same thing, I said.

She'll read his most shameful secrets, Philip said.

What shameful secrets? I didn't see any shameful secrets.

Well, Patty said, she married Thomas and she got Thomas. If she didn't know him after forty-seven years, that's not our problem.

There are certain papers that should be destroyed, Philip said.

I didn't see anything like that.

I did, he said.

Scornfully: What do you want to do, steal them?

He looked around anxiously. No one seemed to care as he did. I never saw until this visit how much he depends on the past, as if he could not exist without its encouragement.

Henry is different. For Henry the past is a ball and chain, like the dead hand of Aristotle he keeps talking about. His only hope—but how do I know what his hope might be? Patty would like to kick loose, rebel girl, too bad for me, but it don't come easy. Can I put the other two into this framework, the ones who have really kicked loose? No problem for them. George doesn't care. Ann cares, but she's too busy picking up sticks.

––––––––––

PHILIP WESTERLY: *What to tell the Judge*

Unless he told someone—the unknown Elaine, some deep friend, Lucy herself—what happened that night is known only to me. The knowledge is my property which I may dispose of as I wish.

It's a question of remembering him in his role, my good

and loving father. Of what they would say if they read it, even the closest, Henry and Patty, Ann, William, Frank, Melanie. Love or not, they'll criticize him. Their blame will sting me like arrow poison.

It will be said that he committed a crime. Technically, legally. Morally too. They'll use the word *cowardice* to which some will add the word *vile*. That while he might not have been able to avoid killing the jogger, he failed to help her. That he panicked and scurried around the countryside thinking how to save himself while making hypocritical excuses. That panic or not, ultimately he had time to think and correct his mistake. But never came forward, which undermined his hope of having changed since then. That his attempt to alleviate guilt by writing was belied by concealing what he had written, as if he had not written.

I'd like to defend him but I've lost the ability to judge. A crime that seems big from a distance, unspeakable, unforgivable, looks different close up with my father's figure superimposed. It fills the sky and disappears as if it were no crime at all. I ask you to judge it for me, because what I fear most is not the damage his reputation may suffer with others, but the damage the judgments of others will do to his reputation with me. What words like crime and cowardice and rat can do to my love, my grief. That such words will make me doubt my memory. That I missed the truth of the life I lived. That loving my father's memory will make me a hit and run driver too.

You must help me imagine it, how it could happen and he still the Thomas we knew. A man who always tried to live by the rules but had no rule for finding himself in a case like this. Because he knew (as we all know) that he was not the kind of person to be involved in a hit and run. Reason enough to drive on except for the integrity that refused to release him without more evidence, leading to the decision to go back and see. When on his first return to the scene he saw only a dog and on his second policemen who waved him by, it's easy enough to read the rulebook as letting him off. He was not that kind of person. It was only the next day's papers that suggested indeed he was, he fit exactly the rulebook definition of a hit and run. From that point it's easy to imagine the struggle, how to reconcile the person he thought he was with an ignorant act in the night. A man of integrity, pride, a president, who might have left behind some overlooked clue that would lead back to him. Looking in the rulebook to see what a university president would do and finding only that a university president would not be in this predicament because he would not have been on that road or if he had, he would have stopped at the accident and taken the consequences—though he could not think of any university president who had ever done such a thing.

If after long thought he concluded that the rulebook wanted him to give himself up there would now be the question why it took so long for a would-be university president to recognize a moral obligation a child would see in an instant, and is such a man fit to head our university? Perhaps he squared himself with the rulebook by observing that running away had hurt no one, for he couldn't have helped, even if he didn't know it at the time. To stop would only have added to the world's misery, by increasing the misery of Lucy, Elaine, the university community and himself, without alleviating the victim's, so it was better that he did not stop. You must credit him with suffering, having to bear the secret knowledge (while the rest of his life went on with its innocent ups and downs) that at sixty-two he was a hit-and-run driver and the designation would not go away. You must give him credit for writing it down, to show that he knew the rules, his confession to a future reader policing the past.

Could it be said, on some other hand, that what he did was rational, logical and intelligent, in which case his hidden confession was an excess of virtue? He hit the stranger by accident while avoiding the dog. When he found the police at the scene, it was logical to go on. There was no need to turn himself in since nothing led to his trail. It would not help the victim or anyone else. Logic said to let the incident die. It was the principle of high politics, justice, and law. Judges passing sentence, politicians waging war. University presidents. Things had priority, things are ranked, things are always ranked. One thing is always more important than something else.

And perhaps it never happened at all. A literary fiction, an exercise in writing, how Thomas loved a polished narrative. The style, the writing, organization, chronology, suspense. Once proposed, the possibility cannot be dismissed.

I did not want to take the chance. When Mother came and stopped everything, I saw a crisis. She would read the papers or send them unexamined to the library for anyone to riffle through, indefinitely into the future. I saw my task like Hamlet's ghost. I could say, Mother, I found something in Father's papers which nobody should read, but I couldn't say that.

Theft (the word) is romantic. Stealth and care. I would lie awake until everybody was in bed. Mother upstairs because of Aunt Edna in the master bedroom, I would sneak by Edna's door in the middle of the night. Too deaf to hear me.

Middle of the night, adventure and heroism for any memoir. Protecting my mother and father. I didn't want to do it in the middle of the night but that's the only way I could think of. Meanwhile she went to the bathroom. Because I was thinking of midnight heroism, it took me a moment to realize that if I didn't take opportunities when they came I would never take opportunities when they came. The others were in the living room and sunporch, a lot of loud talk. I didn't know how long Mother would be in the bathroom, and I had already used up time thinking about it. Excuse me, I said. I went upstairs for my briefcase. When I came down, Mother was still in the bathroom.

I went into the study where I had been forbidden, dark since she kicked us out, with papers still on the table and floor. I went to the drawer where I had concealed it from my siblings. I heard the toilet flush and for a moment couldn't find it. Then I found it, just as she came out. I shoved it into my briefcase and she saw me. She saw plainly, exactly what I was doing.

Philip, she said.

It's all right, I said. I forgot something.

She couldn't challenge me because that would deny the trust we take for granted in this family. I let that trust swallow my shame. The danger of a heart attack subsided gradually, not pain, just a tightness, shortness of breath, heavy beats.

THOMAS WESTERLY: *As read by Philip*

Up in his room when it's bedtime and Beatrice in the bathroom, Philip opens his briefcase to check the stolen manuscript. He flips through the hit-run narrative to make sure it's complete and discovers he has also grabbed a loose page from a letter. He reads it as best he can through the fires in his brain.

Tender feelings aren't the only feelings as you know, as you know   Nor are they helped by mean talk and threats yes threats, Threats can blot the light tender feelings need to survive

It's not all your fault but on this point you are *irrational* not saying I don't love you   yes the curve of your   the curve of your buttock the unbearable glow the hairy push of your the sweet warm opening to   the urgency of my   the joy of my illegal cock sliding   sliding in into

As for who seduced whom, don't try to change the facts.

Check your memory, for *I wrote it down*   so please don't talk betrayal to me

———————

PHILIP WESTERLY

Damn it Father you should have burned them yourself.

How can I destroy my father's writing?

To put them in my own files and deliberately forget. The moral equivalent to destroying them.

Not quite. Eventually I will die. Then David or Charlie or Nancy or Betty, by then grown, will go through them, and I will have passed the problem on to them.

Maybe when I am older I will know what to do. I will put them in my files to postpone a decision, while I await the growth of wisdom.

Perhaps I am waiting for Thomas to die. Is he not dead yet? Eventually he'll be a mere historical figure. Then I can open the book on his weaknesses and put his lapses in perspective.

Or return it to Lucy. Give it to her outright with an excuse, how I thought it was too sensitive but on second thought etcetera. This would multiply the shock we were trying to save her from. Or slip surreptitiously back into the study and restore it to the file cabinet.

Destroy the adultery letter anyway. Take it home, burn it, tell no one, not even Beatrice. Never mind curiosity. Who was she? Was she Elaine? Or was she another without even a name to be remembered by?

There may be other letters I never found. He "wrote it down," he says, but I didn't find it.

Tear out this page? No, wait a day or two.

236

PART TEN

SATURDAY (2)

LUCY WESTERLY: *To Thomas*

We were in the kitchen this morning, putting the dishes away.

Mother, Henry said. Did you ever hear of Pete Arena?

Is that a rock star?

No ma'am. You never met him?

Should I? I don't recall the name.

Not even from Patty?

Is he a friend of Patty's?

You could say that. Or more.

Oh my. She didn't tell me about that. Is it serious?

Ask her.

I asked Henry what sort of person Pete Arena was. He said that was an interesting question, involving the meaning of terms. One point of interest, he said, was that Pete Arena had been here all week and sat in the back at your funeral.

Well for heavens sakes, I said. Why didn't Patty tell me?

Ask her, he said. My hands are clean.

Later I asked Patty. I said, Why didn't you tell me about Pete Arena?

She was plainly embarrassed, though she pretended not to be, asking me how I heard about him. When I said Henry told me, she wondered how Henry knew and I mentioned the rumor trail of children. She said, What is the rumor, exactly?

What, exactly? Can a rumor be exact? Two things, I said. He's close to you (boyfriend or whatever the word is now). And he's on the Island.

Is that all?

Whatever more there is, I'll have to learn from you, I said.

She said he was just an ordinary guy, simple, working class. That's her language. Little education but nice. Sweet. Kind. Religious.

Good adjectives. She expected me to object, but I fooled her. I scolded her for bringing him to the Island without meeting me. Hospitality, I said. I'm ashamed he had to hide, that you required this of him.

She said he came against her wish. He came on his own without warning her and that's why she made him stay out of sight.

In other words, who has the power, that sort of thing. I said I'd like to meet him before he goes.

He's leaving on the ferry, she said.

Take a later ferry. Call him where he's staying and make him come.

Not with all the people who are still here, she said.

I said if he's going to be associated with the family he should meet the family.

She said she was not ready for that yet, and then added in a secret way, It's a delicacy about William.

Oh.

I guess that means William doesn't know about Pete

Arena. But it's hard not to suspect Patty's concealing something from me. If you have any theories let me know. You must know everything by now.

PATRICIA KEY: *To Pete Arena*

This little plane with the propeller roar, I'm watching a loose screw jiggling in the engine cowling, so get me out of here. Sitting in single file behind Melanie with Henry across the aisle, Lucy Realm and David somewhere behind, dreaming of a letter to you, though with such a view of the islands I'm supposed to be more interested in the scenery or my imminent death.

Funeral's over, burial, last family dinner, pack your stuff. This morning goodbye goodbye. Goodbye Mother through the porthole probably crying while she waves. Here we go to Boston and our connecting flights. Where are you at this moment? If you've left already or are lingering still. Thank you for how you stayed out of the way. In spite of which there was a leak. Mother heard and wanted me to invite you over. I'm not ready if you don't mind. I need to prepare her first, and I put her off.

I saw you at the funeral, looking us over. I apologize for the lack of ritual and the simplicity of our Reverend Mr. Dawson who makes the noblest ideas ridiculous. And William. I saw you staring at him, trying to figure him out. Don't let him scare you, my friend, he's no smarter than the rest of us.

My crazy brother Henry sits by the window staring at the sea, the slow islands, the coming land. Trembling, looks like giggling, is it giggling? His wife across the aisle fidgets, embarrassed. As always. To be embarrassed by Henry, it's Melanie's distinctive feature.

Once Henry and I were close in a treacherous way. I was the third child, he the fourth. I gave him incantations. Together we tortured the baby George, while Philip and Ann stayed aloof. Henry was fat, which is either important or it's not. He was fat, which embarrassed him so he tried to turn fat into muscle. Athlete. Henry the athlete, defying the world. Defying us, all these snobby children with our arty pretensions—Philip's writing, Ann's dancing, I and my cello, even George, who was going to be a movie star. The athlete would play football, basketball, baseball, all the high and visible sports. Went out for the high school teams. Exercising, stretching, grunting and gasping, around the block, sweaty and running like he would cry, damn he was determined. Nothing's impossible if you try hard enough. Yeah. Climb every dream impossible mountain sort of crap. He just wasn't very good. They made him manager of the football team, who carries the water bucket. Dropped from some squad, I forget, and what a time we had in the family then. We consoled him by telling him it wasn't important, which was the worst dumb thing we could say, proving exactly what he wanted proved, how little we knew. Worried about his loneliness, Mother would invite his teammates to the house, ice cream, dinner, the ones you like best, whom you consider your friends. She would ask him and he'd name the stars, who thought we were a bunch of groupies (including Henry) as they swept like horses through the kitchen.

He dropped sports with a crash, cut cold like an addict, with more scornful anti-athleticism than any of us, and dropped himself at the same time with an equal crash. Looked for the most self-ignoring alternative he could find and ended up a social worker in permanent depression. The crater left where his Henryness had been.

He persuaded Melanie Cairo to take on the tender job of caring for his depression. Don't let her tell you she didn't know what she was getting in for. Her hope and his hopelessness lived off each other, each requiring the other. He's been fighting hope all his life. His career in sports was a

240

demonstration against hope, since he knew it was hopeless from the start and needed only to prove it so he could be depressed and hopeless and fat and taken care of by Melanie forever.

For ten years he's lived in a smelly apartment in Stony Hill. That's a seedy old section of River City, a changing neighborhood full of transients and drugs, where he stays without noticing the changes. Twenty minutes from my parents' house at the University, except that they left in 1988. He and Melanie remained. No one knows what kind of social worker he was, for he never said. I suspect his unselfishness was too selfish for him to be any good. I used to wonder, before I gave up the practice of wonder, if he was afraid of his work. It's impossible to imagine him giving advice to anyone.

His wife's an elementary school teacher. No children. Ten years and still no children. It's quite noticeable. Without actually mentioning it, they keep the awareness alive. When you listen to Henry and Melanie, you'll find yourself soon noticing that they never mention their lack of children and you'll wonder how you happened to notice it.

The doctors and hospitals and Melanie all call Henry's depression an illness, but I wonder because I can't imagine a Henry not depressed. What will be left if they get rid of it? They talk of the progress of his disease, but how do they know it's not the natural growth of who he is? A year ago he quit going to work. Now he sits around. Melanie speaks of recovery: When he goes back to work, she says. She also talks of his forthcoming suicide like a scheduled event. And she interprets: unfortunately he was not good enough at what he really wanted to do, she says, but he's too smart to become a bully or deceive himself about the modest available alternatives to glory. A bully? Instead he chose to become dull, abandoning the marks of identity one by one, as if identities were skins that itch and sting and press upon the heart, too painful to wear. So he cast them off and now there are none.

Nobody in the family noticed. Except Melanie, who lives on it. For the rest, Henry is Henry, which is exactly how I feel. It should be terrible. We should all be full of woe and charity, what to do about this poor brother who's slipping away? Nobody wants to be bothered. Which is how I feel too. I don't care what happens to Henry. I've come to the conclusion it's his own fault. Since I'm not a mean or nasty person, it can only be that. Something he does, like the smell emitted by a skunk, which keeps the people who would help if they could from approaching.

Now the giggles. Henry, Melanie whispers across the aisle so we can all be sure to hear. People are looking at you.

In the ferry down below, far behind, is William with what used to be our car. He's taking the kids to the mountains. If you're on the same boat stay away from them. William and I had an argument about eternal life, and I'm surprised he thought he could beat me. What you say is impossible to refute, he said. He seemed to think that rendered it invalid, which is dumb since its irrefutability was exactly my point.

Philip with his families is also on that boat. He told me he stole some of my father's papers which he thinks would ruin Father's reputation. I doubt it. Father's dead, so who's to care outside the family? I told him to go ahead, burn and forget them, but he won't. Not without writing an opera about it.

Left behind is my poor mother, last seen as a figurine in blue by the airport fence shrinking into a speck while the land dropped into a detailed model of itself.

––––––––

MELANIE CAIRO: What to tell Dr. Parch

He didn't want to leave the Island. Wild enthusiasm as I packed him up, a complete change of mood. Now I know everything, he said. You go home, I'll stay behind. Fearing suicide, I said, Henry what are you talking about? and he made up a reason, Mother needs me. I wondered what help her depressed son could give, but he said he wasn't depressed anymore.

He went out and came back and said, I just told Mother about Pete Arena, but I didn't tell her who he is.

This is an allusion to my sister-in-law's new fiancé, who happens to be African-American. We only found out about him on the last day of our stay. By not telling who he is, Henry meant he did not tell her he was African-American.

I said, Why did you tell her?

Because she ought to know.

I thought it was up to Patricia to decide what and when Mother ought to know.

Well I left it to Patricia to tell the rest.

His giggling made me suspicious. What is it you find funny?

Mother. I can't wait to see her face when she finds out.

Finds out what?

Who he really is.

I told him he was a bigot.

What do you think, Dr. Parch? Is it bigotry or is it Henry? If it isn't bigotry, how do you distinguish? I admit I was a little shocked when I first heard about Mr. Arena. It made me wonder why Patricia was not drawn to someone of her own kind. To me it's too big a difference to throw my life into. But evidently not for Patricia, and if that's what she wants, more power to her. I think it's a courageous social gesture, except that for Patty it's not a gesture, it's how she wants to live. I admire that, don't you? But Dr. Parch, I guess you being what you are you don't either judge or admire anybody.

I'm not a bigot, Henry said. I'm a writer who sees clearly what other people don't.

A writer, ho? The distinction between writing and bigotry, that's another one I wonder what you think about.

He said, I'm going to write a book about Sam Truro. This made me realize he had been thinking about Sam Truro the whole time and Pete Arena was merely overflow.

I pass it on for you to consider. A book, after a while he was calling it a novel. I said what do you know about writing books? I argued how every ignoramus thinks he's an author, but he didn't hear me. Just babbled on, a book, Sam Truro, a book about Sam Truro, babble babble. Why Truro? I asked. Why Truro and not your brother Philip? Or your dead father? Or your sister dropping William for the black mechanic? What's Truro got that makes you so wonderful? He goggled his eyes at me. Ha, he said. Little do you know. Little do you know what really happened between my father and Truro.

So he explained or should I say "explained" in quotes, and let me pass the explanation on to you and let you judge how crazy or uncrazy this man of mine really is. Why Truro? Henry said. Because the real killer of his father was Truro. Not as in the discredited newspaper rumor by the reporter who said Thomas had been literally shot but killed by some symbolic Truro and all he represents. Moving us into the realm of fantastic interpretation. A long explanation of what Henry called *everything*. The Story of Life. Guilt, he said. In Henry's view it started long ago when Thomas kicked Truro out of the University and thought nothing of it. Just part of the academic carnage which he was well used to until something in old age sensitized him to the blood and gore of all human venture. And made him take the blame. Now why would he do that? Henry asked rhetorically, as if his father were the unreasonable one. The trouble began when Thomas discovered why Truro had followed him to this island. The man whom he had kicked out of the University. According to Henry, Thomas took that as a sign, like nemesis, you know, life's conscience catching up to you. So says Henry. I don't dispute when he's in moods like this, he's always so fixedly right.

For a long time, Henry says, Thomas didn't remember Truro, with Truro working peaceably in the bank. Even after he realized who Truro was he didn't notice the irony in Truro's admiration until the very last moment. That is, he thought Truro really did admire him. Until the moment when Truro broke. Broke, turned the gun on his wife and child to make an example of himself. Which suddenly, according to Henry, made Thomas see his mistake, what he should have seen from the beginning, the nemesis and all, the shock of which—well. Please follow this if you can, Dr. Parch, Henry's interpretation of Thomas's interpretation of Truro's psychotic break. Truro's break, which could only be interpreted as a twisted ironic gesture of some sort, the self-appointed symbolic victim, a gesture which Thomas in his guilt, the accumulated guilt of his whole professional career, instantly assumed was directed at him. President of the University who had fired him. Demonstrative revenge through a Significant Gesture.

You have here three madmen making interpretations, or at least it's three if you believe Henry. In any case, when Thomas first learned that Truro had hostaged his wife and children, says Henry, he instantly interpreted what Truro meant, which he also assumed Truro himself didn't know. Therefore, having faith in his ability to speak, the rhetoric upon which his career had been based, those powers of persuasion by which he had once (to some extent) induced rich men to give their wealth to educating the young, Thomas made it his duty to talk Truro into a state of reason. Supposing he was the only one who could do this because only he knew what was wrong with Truro, only he understood the irony as well as the real cause of Truro's distress. He went over to Truro's barricaded house, past the cops and up the walk fully intending to explain Truro to himself and thereby restore civilization. Are you with me still?

The trouble was, according to Henry, Truro was not interested in disguised meanings. If he had seen his disguised meaning he wouldn't have bothered to disguise it. All he could do was shoot and his bullets could only miss since if they hit there would be no point in taking hostages, who were only tokens anyway. But says Henry the missing bullets were as good as a hit for the senior citizen on the walk because of the shock of revelation they produced. This man is shooting at me, Thomas thought though in fact this man was not shooting at him. The shock would be final confirmation of his career-guilt, enough to precipitate bang the stroke which had been building up in his brain vessels for days or weeks looking for an excuse to finish off the dirty work in his gut for the last half year.

Into the hospital goes the stricken Thomas (as Henry sees it), his hypothesis confirmed by the bullet that came so close, his personal dedicated bullet, the bullet meant for him. As he lay in the hospital evidently Thomas decided that civilization still depended on him, that his responsibility as a leader in the world (university president) required him to make one more approach to the man with the grievance and make the amends that needed to be made. It was Thomas's disease and Thomas's mind working hand in hand, each with its goal (both goals the same in the end, if you ask me) and each learning how to assist the other to make Thomas when the time came get up, elude the nurses and security and make one more approach to Truro. Now get this Dr. Parch and add it to your Henry bank. What Thomas planned to say to Truro would not be another futile attempt to persuade him to give up. No, Henry said, Thomas was too imaginative for that, so he must have had a more radical idea (only a more radical one could have dragged him out of his stroke bed in the middle of the night). What he intended, says Henry, was to offer himself as hostage. To join the little group under the sleepless carbine. Or better still if Truro would allow it (Henry's eyes agleam with romance) to replace the other hostages, take over the hostage role. Which Truro ought to welcome since not only would it liberate the wife and child from their bondage as symbols but it would identify for him and put into his hands the true object of his revenge. I think it's ridiculous myself.

However, it's true that Thomas did get out of bed and escaped from the hospital and went to Truro's house before the stroke cooperated with the police to stop him. I say there's no way to know what he intended, but Henry's sure it was to make the sacrifice Truro needed to bring him out of his siege. A great heroic final act. I think it says more about Henry than Thomas or Truro, but don't let me influence you, I'm sure your interpretation is different from mine.

Whenever I raised a reasonable doubt, Henry would say how little you know, how do you know so little, and I ask, does Henry know his way out of clichés? What makes him think he's a better writer than anyone else? Meanwhile I packed him his things. No resistance, just babble. I led him to the car, to the airport, said him his goodbye to his mother, took him aboard the plane. Shivering. Hee hee. Some joke. Misunderstood genius. I tried to hush him, but he said, Don't you like me better? At least I'm not depressed. Dr. Parch, am I really supposed to like him better?

Like Henry James, he said. Henry James Westerly. Good name for a writer. Let me calm down a bit and you'll see.

It's like he's denying all I've done him for him over the years and my whole life is thrown away.

DAVID WESTERLY: To Charlie

On the night bus. Good seeing you again and I enjoyed tenting with you in spite of my complaints. My objection to

Lucy Realm is her negative attitude. I sat next to her at the funeral and she whispered all through. She complained about everybody's long faces. I say people have a right to long faces at a funeral, and I didn't see all that many anyway. Most people looked pretty happy to me. She complained about people tiptoeing but everybody I saw had their heels on the ground.

It made me mad for her to be so sure of everything. When she dies, Lucy said, she wants someone to take her back into the fields (what fields? Do you know any fields in Greenwich Village?) and burn her. Bonfire. No ceremony, just a few words, her poet friends could write a poem and her artist friends could toss some of their more valuable paintings on the fire with her corpse as a symbol of loss. (I don't suppose it would do to sacrifice their poorer paintings, right?)

On the plane we argued about the funeral speeches. She said Dawson's was an insult to the intelligence and William's didn't have anything to do with Grandfather. I said it didn't matter what anybody said. Dawson was there. Think of him and you'll automatically remember Grandfather, which is the purpose of a funeral. It could all be gibberish or the owl and the pussycat, and it would serve the purpose. By the time I thought of this it was too late because the plane had landed.

So she went off thinking she had won. I wish I had made my point. But even if I made it she would think she'd won because she wouldn't agree. Making my point won't make her agree if she doesn't agree. Actually I won the argument because her points didn't take into consideration my perception of their limitations, only unfortunately she'll never see that and will just continue thinking she won. Not only that, she probably thinks *I* think I won, which she takes as a sign of my stupidity because she's so convinced her arguments are right and mine are obtuse. What she doesn't see is how obtuse it is of her to think that. So really there's no way to make her see that she lost, and even if she knows I think so, she'll go on thinking she won because she thinks it's only my stupidity refusing to admit. If you follow me.

In spite of all this I feel sorry for her. I asked about her brothers fighting, and she said, The family's finished. Done. Nice while it lasted, a good growing-up environment, but now it's over. She's going to Seattle as soon as she's free and live for the future not the past.

As for you and Greta, my advice is forget it. Don't tell Lucy Realm. Don't ask Aunt Edna. Certainly not Father or Beatrice. Keep Grandmother in the dark. Don't confide in Melanie because she's distraught nor Henry because he's depressed. In fact, I don't think you should tell anybody because you must find it hard to keep explaining that she isn't really your sister.

WILLIAM KEY: *What to tell Patricia*

I finally met your man. I see now why you kept him away, plain as the color of his face. I wonder which of a variety of possible fears it was that prevented you from telling me.

You Westerlys are all the same. You take your inspiration from your father, though it's a different inspiration in each case, and you go crazy because there's always a catch. Like Philip, who thinks of Thomas as organization and control, except for those intimate papers full of groping youth. Or Henry whose father was a model for sweet feeling, crushed by the authoritarian order and control. And you my love the skeptical rebel a little short of courage for your beliefs.

Well. I was on the upper front deck with Philip and I saw Angela and Tommy talking to a black man in the bow below. A big man with a back pack and a baseball cap. Then suddenly the three of them appeared beside me on the deck.

This big man holding out his hand at me, thick-chested, tough with a beard and dark skin, his heavy pack and well-made jacket and baseball hat with NY on it.

Saying, Mr. Key? I'm Pete Arena.

So that's who Pete Arena is. We talked like civilized modern man. He asked about my work and the ACLU.

I'm deliberately, intensely, energetically refusing to resist your plans. Go your own way. I stay as calm as my heart permits and act as if I wanted it as much as you. I use my professional training to bear everything intelligently.

I wasn't prepared for the helplessness I felt when I saw your Pete Arena as a live person. How real and big as well as dark and how powerless I am to stick even a toe outside the liberated circle within which I live.

PHILIP WESTERLY: *To Ann*

Here's the news. There was a fight between your boys, someone else can explain it to you. In town, Sam Truro broke out at last and got his family killed. Himself too. Henry thinks Father was going to offer himself as hostage to Truro when he had his stroke. Wow. Patty and William are splitting. I met her new boyfriend on the boat. He's black. Why must I specify that? If I didn't mention it, would you think I had failed to tell you something important?

Father's papers are innocuous. I left them intact, and Mother can decide where to bestow them. Coda to Wyoming. Penny Glade the kissing teacher showed up at the funeral. A little old lady in a wheelchair. I missed her, unfortunately. She talked to Melanie and William. Father postponed calling her until he was dead, just the way he postponed kissing her, only this time it was too late.

Henry thinks Father was full of guilt but that's because Henry is full of guilt. What am I full of?

Raw material for a poem.

About looking down before the boat sailed at the fence

beside the cargo shed where she scanned the ship for a last glimpse. About how she took care of me under the blanket, her girl face when I cried what a terrible world, her soft woman voice lullabying me. Crying now on the receding dock, the crumpled ex-girl face folded into the crowd. The deep chord of the ship's whistle blast, lullaby to the bereaved mother as dark opens between ship and dock, water rushing in.

About going west into the sky cleaned by last night's cold front. Brisk afternoon sea, the ship vibrating faintly, tightening breeze, North Point Light behind, the dunes and road where Truro died. The high bow with its flag staff and black wind vane blowing. Faint blue of line of mainland west.

When they look, no one will know that it's missing. Not knowing there's a gap, no one will see a gap.

Poem about what?

He was the model of a good man. Proof the good man can exist through cynicism, nihilism, and irony. Despite Patty, Henry, William Key, and skeptics. To make sure of this, keep out what the world can't understand. Drop it into the unrecorded past until it never happened, like everything else that never happened.

He returned to the idyll island finally to escape sociology. Also anthropology, psychology, and politics. The old heritage-carrier who had done his work, to donate what he had and forget the rest.

Make it that he wanted to be good whether he was or not, and persuaded at least one of his children to emulate. That's the point if the poem can take it, not that he succeeded or failed, only that he thought it important to want to be. Make the poem connect this with the concrete moment on the forward deck under the pilot house where the poet lets the wind blow his face. Life in the contemporary world all around, a wife below, children of all ages exploring the decks, a man with him by the rail soon to be dropped and another, black, a stranger introduced by children, to take the first man's place. In the poem only the son tries to re-member how the father looked, the sound of his voice, the pitch of his vocabulary in the wind screech where the sky is now blazing over the continent, our mainland country and home, turning it into a band of black under fire.

Use the gulls screaming on the wind to drown out distrac-tions such as stolen papers in a briefcase. Let the wind con-fuse the sensations of his face in an imitation of blindness so that he need not name colors or specify tears but use only what the poem requires.

Turn away from the wind to look past the davits and lifeboats at the receding island. It fades into omnivorous blue before sinking in the sea beneath the advancing night. Bury the mourning mother with the dead father in the descending blue of the devouring poem.

Dedicate the poem to the slave-binding past and bring it finally to the hospital room where you lie in the tiled walls, the empty light, back raised, ribs heavy, mouth an expand-ing hole in the room sucking up the walls, sea and sky and everything until the whole day has passed through inside out, and the whole world has reversed direction on the way back to the big bang.

There's no poem though. Too much bias. The night kills the words and soon you will forget everything.

LUCY WESTERLY: *To Ann and George*

Don't tell the others but you were our favorites, you two. Maybe the mails will find George. Enclosed are copies of Dr. Dawson's and William's funeral talks, which I won't venture to judge.

I sat through the ceremony like a substitute funeral, not the real one. This is not a criticism, I was moved and grate-ful, so I don't know why it felt like a substitute. We had a last family dinner which I hope is not a last family dinner. Expect both Balsam and Edna to die soon, which is too bad though it does seem temporarily unfair that they're living and Thomas not. Their going will rectify that but leave a colder world behind, so I mustn't rush anything. I'll probably live a long time. Then I'll be like Edna.

JEROME DAWSON: *Funeral talk*

What is there to say about the Old Prof, as he was known in this town? Six years ago he came to the Island to retire with Lucy. They stayed in the Inn and called Foersly's real estate and came to me. In my office Lucy admitted that Thomas was not a believer but they thought the minister could give them advice, telling me how he had retired at sixty-six and wanted this place which he loved from the summers of childhood. So we gathered to help, and Joe Foersly found a house and Janet Prism introduced her friends. Also the doctors and our hospital. Neighbors took them to the Library and the Historical Society and the Island Museum and my wife acquainted them with a carpenter, plumber, handyman. We took them into the community. And though I seldom saw him in church, I saw him often around the village with his white hair, and though I regret his not being religious, I know he was a good intelligent man.

Others will speak of who he was, praise his nature, record his works. Let me address the grief you feel and the monumental question on all our minds as we participate in this rite.

The monumental question is this: how can a body so full of life turn into that inert and decaying copy of a man we call a corpse? What has become of the spirit we knew, with the vitality to plant a portion of itself in each of our souls?

I'm told that Thomas did not believe in the heavenly solace in which this community believes. This may grieve us.

How can you endure the foreverness of his going if there is no return in the end?

Fortunately, Thomas was wrong. This is fact not fancy. I say it not in a spirit of argument but joyfully, for now that he has discovered the fact he is joyful too. Nor do I say it to condemn the genial skepticism which was the rule of his life. You will note that all my life I have marked and insisted upon the limits of skepticism, but I nevertheless do respect its uses. Skepticism was the natural habit of Thomas's intellectual life. It's an exploratory tool, helpful when you are trying to learn, if you don't take it too seriously. It's temporary, eventually you won't need it. Thomas's exploration is over now, the hunt is done, quest finished. He's face to face with the ultimate and has discovered what we already knew. He has discovered God's reason for death, which transforms all woe into joy. Do not grieve for Thomas, he lives in heaven. Since he thought he did not believe, I reckon he's surprised to find himself there and maybe a little chagrined that the solution he so skeptically declined to accept was waiting for him so patiently.

He's there. We've had that assurance for two thousand years. Our souls do not die. The body cannot move without spirit, and the spirit being independent cannot be constrained by body. Proof is the Resurrection and with proof like that nothing more is needed. Take comfort, you will meet him again. He's merely gone on a little ahead. Rejoice in his happiness now and yours in the time to come.

I too look forward to meeting him in heaven. When that time comes I will congratulate him and tell him I spoke at his funeral and was glad to do so regardless of his beliefs. I'll shake his hand and say, Thomas Westerly, you were a good man.

———

Austin Wright

WILLIAM KEY: *Funeral talk*

I have one objection to what we just heard. The notion the soul is not confined by the body. Ask the lady in the wheelchair about that.

When we visited in River City he used to take me to the faculty lunch. He liked to tease the chaplain, questions like what will our immortal souls do when the sun blows up and the earth is a cinder? Will we continue to dance around in the cold dead universe? What will be *in* our immortal souls? Will we retain our split personalities, our senility, and our chemical mood changes? There was a lot of talk in the faculty club and some of it was about things like that.

Thomas at lunch. He talked about human skulls, which we all have. Like little fortresses, barriers of lead to keep the radiation in, or the turmoil of thought like boiling soup. What's in your head, he says, you couldn't tell me if you wanted to, but I'll bet it's full of wickedness along with the good. Flux and flow, Thomas says, which at any given moment you can never name because there are so many thoughts at the same time, right?

So what you do, according to Thomas, you turn your thoughts into words, which is like picking up liquid with a leaking cup. Cupping a little of the liquid to turn into something solid. It's not that hard, you may tell me, thinking how the words rush through your own garrulous lips, what could be easier than talk? But think how the words disappear when you speak, fast as they come, and all the residue of the unspoken too, besides which, who can remember anything anyone ever said? So you write or think your speech like writing, which makes you feel like one of these stencil boards, a piece of metal with holes for letters cut into it, the holes being your words. People know you by the words but never see the board. And you remain hidden in your skull, mysterious, immense, no shape or body, and what you say or write is not you but a replica of you.

Think of that: the person you know through words is not the person but a replica. You live life creating replicas of yourself. What does it mean, friends? It means the replica is incomplete, like an image on a screen, but it draws attention from what isn't visible, what you can't show and can't see except in reflection and oblique glances. No one knows you, least of all yourself.

Which brings me to this. The secret of life, which in my view is secrecy itself. Our handicap and motivation, root of evil, root of joy. How did I come up with such a preposterous idea? It's Thomas's idea, the unavoidable result of the fact that we live like hermit crabs inside our skulls. We deal with secrecy all our lives: we pursue the secrets of others, we protect our own, keep some even from ourselves as we struggle to learn them, as Thomas would say by talking to ourselves or writing.

The universe has its secrets too. We live like moles in the tunnels of ignorance, with language chipping like picks at the massive earth. The future, life emerging from darkness into light as time is unveiled, but even as it's unveiled new darkness appears. The past, where what was known or partly known dissolves back into secrecy through the slippery hands of memory. Death. My colleague proposes that Thomas now dead knows all there is to know and is a little surprised by that knowledge. Try another view. Think with me about a place where there are no secrets and all there is to know is known. A consciousness transcending death. If there are no secrets you must dissolve the barrier skull which contains your consciousness. You must spill your eddying you-ness into the great all-ness. To partake of universal knowledge without secret you must be at one with no margin of ignorance, no process of learning or coming together. You must abandon your self, including your personal soul immortal or otherwise, to merge amalgamate into one.

So how should we think of Thomas now he's gone? Should

we think him merged in the universal knowledge, melted in the transcendental stew? Or remember him as we knew him, who'll never return to us except in our own circling thought? Take your pick. I believe Thomas would say that the Thomas we remember and miss is the replica. He would want us to remember the replica rather than the original. No one can know the whole Thomas, for he was infinite as the universe, whereas the replica was Thomas's deliberate creation, manufactured with hardship and trial and not too bad a job in the end despite the inevitable flaws, patched spots, and loose connections.

We're here to filter the memory of the Thomas replica through the cacophony of his departure. It's fragile, for the replica lives only in our minds. The job of creating the replica has passed from Thomas to us, distributed through all of us, a multiplicity of Thomas-replicas like an army of kites in the wind, your kite, my kite, frail and disintegrating, our kite versions of Thomas. Poor Thomas. They're blowing away. Hang onto them while you can.

LUCY WESTERLY: *To Thomas or somebody*

I went back to the house. I parked in the garage and walked to the front, opened the door and went in. I saw the living room, our furniture, books, pictures, and through the doorway the dining room with the late afternoon sun. I heard the machine humming and identified it as the refrigerator. The afternoon paper was on the rug by your chair and I remembered William Key had sat there last. I took the ashtrays into the kitchen. There were glasses, cups and saucers, and Freud looked up at me by his dish. In the dining room I wondered when I would remove the extension leaves from the table. In the study, I wondered when I would pick up the files of your papers which the children last night had not put back. Your dictionary was open with the magnifying glass on the open page. I looked to see what words showed through the glass, but I knocked it: it jumped from *diplex* to *diplopia* to *dinosaur*. I felt a superstition against moving the glass or the dictionary.

I switched on the radio without thinking and suddenly was hearing a familiar song in the old dead voice of Marlene Dietrich. It distracted me. It was a sad little song, though the words don't sound sad, only rueful, dealing with a problem I'll never have to face again:

Falling in love again,
What am I to do?

That's all the words I remember. I listened and when the song was over I switched it off so as to hear it again in my head. I wondered why a song by Marlene Dietrich should haunt me now. I was never interested in Marlene Dietrich, who was my mother's contemporary not mine. I couldn't remember her movies and knew only a few of her songs. For years she was in the papers with pictures on the decks of ocean liners and getting off airplanes. She wore army uniforms and entertained the troops in World War Two. She was a friend of Ernest Hemingway, who praised her for exotic qualities and knowledge. With her arched eyebrows and long cigarette lighter and deep bass voice full of irony, she stood for sophisticated celebrity in the outside world, the world of movies and magazines and America. She was a communicable symbol, which meant that everybody in my lifetime knew who she was, I could say her name and know the image in your mind. Through most of my life she was famous also for resisting age— famous legs still beautiful at fifty and sixty, her masklike face. Then suddenly she was too old and refused furiously thereafter to show her face. I saw her shortly before that, a farewell concert on television in which her face was veiled by a blurry lens, and she sang the song over and over like a theme, the one I had just heard:

Falling in love again,
What am I to do?

The song seemed mysteriously and even unbearably sad. As I let it repeat, something happened to me. I thought, I am alone in the house. No one's watching, no one can hear. Not even you, Thomas. There was some thought which I have forgotten and there was the melancholy music, and there was a distant scream like someone scalded or shocked. But the scream was not distant, it was close, it was in my ear, and after a moment I realized it had come out of me. Involuntary. I listened with amazement. It came up like a geyser. When I realized who was screaming I screamed louder. When I realized how still much louder was possible I pursued that loudness. I opened my throat, brought up the power of my lungs, stretched my back and howled and wailed and roared and sobbed. I was a hurricane.

No one heard me, or so I assumed. Not my neighbors across yards and through walls, nor you. My letters to you this week have no destination, the words stay in my head. You will not hear from me, because according to William in church yesterday (at the ceremony intended to honor you and comfort us) you do not exist and what I mistook for you is a replica in my imagination. Only Freud in this household hears me, and when I screamed he ran away. Up into the attic, I think, and he's not come down yet.

I can't talk to empty space. I can only scream there. You are dead, you are dead, you are dead. The song repeats, the old husky voice once so smart, now dead, falling in love again, what am I to do? I stopped screaming so as to hear the song again, repeating the two lines of words I knew all through.

Falling in love again
What am I to do?
What am I to do?
What am I to do?

It brought back the complete history of my life. I remembered everything, but what I remembered most were picnics. The history of my life concentrated in picnics. I remembered picnics in the Michigan woods with my father and mother and brother, a blanket spread on a piney floor, deviled egg sandwiches, wax paper, ants. Picnics on college weekends, my brother Fred and his glamorous shy friend Thomas on the point off Chicago sticking into Lake Michigan, peanut butter and jelly, beer cans. Pregnant on a picnic in the Forest Preserve with two babies in the sandbox and my friend Leila Jones now dead and her baby twins, hot dogs and mustard. Picnic on a scraggy mountain top in Maine with a lazy view, five children ranging two to fourteen and a family of friends (the Goldsteins later divorced whose address I have lost), Ruby Goldstein's magic tricks, more deviled eggs and ripe plums and lemonade in a cooler. River City where picnics ceased, but we had catered luncheons under a tent for alumni and new graduates and century donors to the Fund, large noodle casseroles and barbecued chicken wings. Here on the Island lunch outdoors in the backyard with a card table, you and me and Abel Jeffcoat and the Grummonds with soup in a crock and ham sandwiches.

Marlene's hoarse old song turned all the picnics into feasts of love, which I hadn't realized at the time, with death following like a vacuum sweeper cleaning up the mess. And I without realizing was an executioner assisting in the process. I saw my life in stages, one stage after another, each one killing off the one before. Spaced among the picnics were the griefs, mostly forgotten, a funeral here, a memorial there. When I realized the cleaner had finally reached you and was hot after me, and that my protests would not be heard and even the singer who had expressed this woe without understanding it was dead, it seemed like such a crime I just howled again with the misery of it, and howled and howled, I don't know how long.

When I felt the touch on my shoulder, I thought I was in another world. The voice said, It's all right, Mother, I'm here.

It scared me, who had invaded my house as if it were an open field, and brought me back to myself embarrassed to be caught so wild, and then I saw him and wondered if I was wrong not to believe in ghosts.

His mild voice, I finally got here, he said.

I could forgive anything.

I was crying, I said.

I noticed.

I wanted to explain why but when I tried the waves came up, for the hurricane was still on, and I couldn't. He put his arm around me, and his sympathy renewed it all, and I said, Why isn't everybody howling and screaming?

He said, You're right. I'll scream with you.

So he did. I watched. First a small tentative shout in a rough male voice, then a curse and then a lion roar splitting his vocal cords, at which point I joined in, accustomed to screaming now, and we roared together side by side. It was competitive, each trying to be louder and more desperately angry and hopeless than the other. I noticed his eyes glinting at me as we roared, and suddenly realized his had turned into laughter and mine too had imperceptibly changed from sorrow to show to laughter with little change in sound, and finally we laughed and laughed together until we were exhausted.

I said, Where did you come from?

Snuck in on the last ferry, missed everyone.

What an unexpected joy, deferring the shade a moment longer.

I asked why we hadn't heard from him, and we had a long sweet conversation. I'd tell you if I thought you could hear me, but I don't, and besides, it's a secret.

PART ELEVEN

SEPTEMBER

MELANIE CAIRO: To Patricia

We took your suggestion and went to see her. She does not look like a forlorn widow.

She knows all about P and wonders when you are going to tell her. She's distressed you thought she should be shielded. What is there to be shielded from? She regards herself as open-minded and is waiting to hear from you.

The rumor is true. W is staying in the house. He had the back guest room, we the front. He's doing a project. He writes all day, which makes me wonder what happened to the ACLU? With all the encroachments in the world today, it seems to me there are more important uses for his talents than sitting upstairs writing, but I suppose that depends on what he's writing about. She said he wanted a retreat, so she let him stay. He ate with us but otherwise out of sight. He and she have been reading Thomas's papers together.

Sorry, Patty, I didn't know how to ask. She said she still regarded him as a son and it wasn't she who divorced him. I didn't hear any stealthy movements at night. Where did you get the idea? I don't know what the neighbors are thinking. She doesn't seem to realize that neighbors think.

I wasn't going to tell you this but a young woman last spring—I won't say who—told me he made a pass at her after the funeral. She was shocked, though flattered. Don't know what she means by a pass, a remark or a touch or an outright proposition? She wondered what she had done to incite him and decided it was because she's so young and pretty and exotic. I'm quoting the lady herself. She was surprised because she thought his reputation ruled him out, but apparently either the reputation is wrong or she's so overpoweringly young and pretty and exotic she mows down all reputations. Or he's simply omnivorous. Is that the word I mean? What do I mean? Voracious? Ambidextrous? Heterogeneous? Multinatural? You know him better than I. He always seemed normal to me in the vulgar sense of the word, so I can't imagine where the reputation came from. All I really know is, if anything's going on, they're behaving respectably for us, and I guess the neighbors don't matter.

She's worried about George again. Hasn't heard since he left with no idea where he went. We advised her to forget him, remember the child he used to be, ignore the rest.

HARRISON GLADE, JR.: To Lucy Westerly

Thank you for the letter to my mother. Unfortunately it came too late. After a long illness she died last month.

It is interesting that your husband wrote a memoir about her. I didn't know they knew each other that well, for she never mentioned him until we saw the death notice in the paper. I must pass up the opportunity to read his paper since I am busy taking care of the estate, though I might have enjoyed it in other circumstances. As for disposing of it, I presume it depends upon whether yours is a family that keeps old papers. Since we do not, I'm afraid I can't advise you.